THE NEW OWNER

She looked at him now with hurt, puzzled eyes. He
did not seem unduly perturbed that the hotel which
his father had built up with such industry and
enthusiasm should be passing out of his hands.
His family had owned this place ever since it was
built, first as a family residence, then, as death
duties and taxation grew, it was added to and
turned into an hotel. But still the Marbury family
had felt that it was their home, had maintained their
pride in it. John's father had loved every brick of
the place, and Stella had grown to love it, too. Now
John, the last of the family, had sold it without a
qualm, and without saying a word to anybody.
As she looked at his handsome face, with the
chiselled features of his father, and the same
intense blue eyes, she wondered for the first time
whether she really did know this man as well as
she thought. or whether she loved a man she only
half knew. His fair hair glinted in the sun. It was
beautiful hair, wavy and silky, which any girl would
have envied. A thoroughbred, one would have said,
for in spite of his absurdly good looks and his
grace, he never gave an impression of effeminacy.
He excelled at most sports, although his chief
enthusiasm was for cars and he took part in as many
car rallies as he had time for.

The New Owner

Iris Bromige

CORONET BOOKS
Hodder Paperbacks Ltd., London

Copyright © 1956 by Iris Bromige
First published 1956 by Hodder and Stoughton Limited
Coronet edition 1975

Printed and bound in Great Britain for
Coronet Books, Hodder Paperbacks Ltd.,
St. Paul's House, Warwick Lane,
London, EC4P 4AH
by Hunt Barnard Printing Ltd.,
Aylesbury, Bucks.

ISBN 0 340 19675 0

Chapter One

WHEN Stella Verney left home soon after nine o'clock on that sunny September morning to go to the Cormorant Hotel, where she worked as secretary from nine-thirty until five-thirty each day, she had no reason to think that this day would be of any particular significance to her.

The early morning mist had lifted, leaving jewelled spiders' webs glittering on the garden hedges and the grass verge. Church Lane stretched ahead, peaceful and mellow between its rows of trees. She could remember when those trees were planted: hawthorn, wild cherry, mountain ash. In her school-days, the walk home from school down Church Lane had been the hottest walk she had ever known, for the lane was long and uphill; now the trees had grown and provided blobs of shade all down the lane, a chequered pattern which never ceased to charm her eye.

It was a particularly calm and peaceful morning and her heart and mind were untroubled as she strolled along, for she had plenty of time. She glanced at Brierley, the large red brick house on the corner, but there was no sign of life. Some-times she ran into one of the boys, late, dashing off to the town, but today, apparently, the various members of the Elmore family had dispatched themselves punctually.

At the end of the lane was the grey stone church with its square turret, and behind it the cricket green and the mill pond. The church, the cottages round the green and the mill pond represented the old Ashcombe, before Ashcombe, the seaside resort, had come into being. Now it had become an old little suburb of the flourishing town built round a sheltered south-coast bay which attracted winter visitors as well as summer holiday-makers.

Stella took a short cut across the green, through some

pleasantly laid-out gardens blazing with geraniums, and lingered by the harbour wall where the assorted craft and the hungry gulls were a never-ending source of interest. Then, more resolutely, she climbed up the long, winding cliff path to the top road, along which were the biggest hotels, some of them rather vulgar in their splendour, she considered. She passed all these monsters and turned off the road through some wide gates over which hung a painted sign indicating that this was the Cormorant Hotel. The drive wound through a belt of shrubs and trees which completely screened the hotel from the road, so that visitors coming to it for the first time felt that they had strayed into another world when they saw the creeper-covered walls of what had once been an old mansion set on a promontory at the end of the bay. The cliff face fell away steeply from it so that on three sides it looked out to sea. It stood there in splendid isolation, a representative of the past, built before the town and the hotels had been thought of.

A few people were strolling out on to the lawns after break-fast. Bob, the porter, gave her a cheery grin.

'Morning, Miss Verney. Holiday weather at last.'

'Yes. Grand, isn't it?'

'Mr. Marbury's in conference in your office. Said would you mind using the outer office this morning.'

Stella looked surprised.

'Oh. That's odd. Righto, Bob.'

She ran up the wide staircase and went into the little room which was no more than an annexe to her office. It held a desk and a typewriter, and was used by Bryant when he was acting as office boy, but since he had multitudinous duties in other departments of the hotel, for he was there to learn the business, Stella was seldom able to have more than a couple of hours a day from him. This morning he was absent. The post had been left on the desk. From behind the closed door of her office, she could hear the murmur of men's voices.

She put her hat and gloves on the window-sill, and began to open the post, wondering who on earth John was closeted with and why. He had said nothing to her yesterday about expect-ing a visitor. Could it be a sudden visit from an Inland Revenue official? But in that case, it would have come within

6

her province. She kept the wages book and made the P.A.Y.E. deductions, and John's income tax affairs were handled by his accountants. She gave up guessing, and was still opening the post when John Marbury's head came round the door.

'Can't find last year's accounts, Stella. Would you come in and fish them out for me?'

Seated at her desk, a mass of papers in front of him, sat a dark, clean-shaven man. He appeared to be lost in thought, and was doodling with a fountain pen as his eyes studied some figures. He didn't look up as Stella crossed the room to the filing cabinet and drew out a file.

'They're all in there for the past five years.'

'Thanks.' John hesitated, then said:

'Right. That will be all just now, Stella, thanks.'

The stranger still did not lift his eyes. Stella had an impression of grim concentration. She found it a little disconcerting to be so completely ignored by a pair of eyes. If anybody came into a room, one usually looked at them. She slipped out quietly. Somehow, he didn't look like an Inland Revenue official, but why should John be showing him the accounts?

They did not emerge for another hour.

'That's settled, then,' said the stranger as he came through the door. 'You'll hear from my solicitors in a day or two.'

'Right. Won't you stay for lunch here?'

'Thank you, but I've got to be back in London early this evening, so I'd best be on my way.'

John had stopped and turned to Stella.

'Perhaps this is a suitable moment to introduce my secretary. She sees to all the office work involved in running this place. And does it very well, I may add. Miss Verney, Mr. Darrington.'

He was as tall as John, but more strongly built. John was very slender, and beside his elegant charm, Mr. Darrington seemed a somewhat grim character. He had oddly pale grey eyes beneath heavy black brows. Then he smiled, a crooked smile which brought warmth to his face, as they exchanged the usual polite acknowledgments. This time, his eyes did take her in as a person. In fact, she felt rather as though she were being X-rayed. Then John, a shade hurriedly, she thought, ushered his visitor out. A few minutes later she watched from her office window a long black car drive off. It had a G.B. plate on the back, and looked pretty powerful. She turned quickly as John came in, her eyes questioning.

'Sorry I had to commandeer your office, Stella. How's my girl this morning?'

He put an arm round her shoulder, smiling, but his eyes slid away from hers.

'Consumed with curiosity. Who was that, and why was he so interested in our accounts?'

John moved away and began to stack up the papers and files on the desk.

'Afraid I've got a bit of a shock for you, Stella. That man is the future owner of the Cormorant Hotel.'

'What! You're joking, John.'

'Sorry, dear. It's true. I realised months ago that I'd have to sell the place. You know what bad seasons the last two have been. I just haven't the cash to keep the place going any longer.'

'But you've never even hinted that such a thing was in your mind.'

'I knew you'd be upset about it, and I didn't want it known until everything was settled.'

'How long have you been trying to sell?'

'I advertised in *The Times* last June. Darrington was one of three people who were interested, but the others backed out. He's driven a pretty stiff bargain, but I've accepted his terms. I can't ride out another winter here.'

'When did he arrive? Last night, I suppose.'

'Yes. Just before dinner. I took him over the place last night.'

'And you never even mentioned to me that he was coming.'

'My dear, it was something that had to be done. Darrington might not have liked the place. It might have fallen through, and I didn't want to upset you before it was necessary.'

'But I'm not a child. I worked here for your father, and you and I have been close friends for five or six years now. Since your father died, I've done everything I could to help here, and I love this old place. It's not as though I'm just an

8

employee, concerned only with my monthly salary. We're old friends, and this place means as much to me as to you. Surely I was entitled to your confidence.'

'I knew you would hate the idea of selling, pet, and I could see no point in arguing over the inevitable. I can't afford to keep the Cormorant, and there it is.'

Stella was on the point of asking him where the money which his father had left him had gone, for old Mr. Marbury had left the hotel in a flourishing condition financially, and he had died only three years ago. But John was unlikely to welcome such an enquiry, and she supposed that she had no right to make it. Although she and John had been friends for so long, and most people took it for granted that they would eventually marry, John had never raised any suggestion of an engagement, merely monopolising her with a cheery affection which sometimes developed into something warmer, but which never appeared to suggest any contract to him. This had not worried her. She was young, she enjoyed his companionship, they had fun together, and she knew that John was not the type to welcome responsibilities. She was content to wait until he was ready to settle down, for she had no doubts about his devotion. Their friendship had lasted too long for that. But this morning's events struck a blow at her confidence. Surely, if they were as close as she had imagined, she should have been told of this sale which seriously affected the structure of both their lives.

She looked at him now with hurt, puzzled eyes. He did not seem unduly perturbed that the hotel which his father had built up with such industry and enthusiasm should be passing out of his hands. His family had owned this place ever since it was built, first as a family residence, then, as death duties and taxation grew, it was added to and turned into an hotel. But still the Marbury family had felt that it was their home, had maintained their pride in it. John's father had loved every brick of the place, and Stella had grown to love it, too. Now John, the last of the family, had sold it without a qualm, and without saying a word to anybody. As she looked at his handsome face, with the chiselled features of his father, and the same intense blue eyes, she wondered for the first time whether she really did know this man as well as she thought, or whether she loved a man she only half knew. His fair hair glinted in the sun. It was beautiful hair, wavy and silky, which any girl would have envied. A thoroughbred, one would have said, for in spite of his absurdly good looks and his grace, he never gave an impression of effeminacy. He excelled at most sports, although his chief enthusiasm was for cars and he took part in as many car rallies as he had time for.

'Cheer up, sweetheart, it's not as bad as all that. I'm to be manager, and things will go on as usual, only our friend Darrington will have the worry of the losses and I shall have a decent salary. I'm jolly glad to be rid of the responsibility and you won't be affected at all.'

'Do you mean Mr. Darrington will take no part in running the business he's bought?'

'Oh, he'll be in the background, but I don't think he'll interfere much. A rum chap. He's just come back from an exploring expedition in the Andes. He's a geologist and he's going to write a book about the expedition. Thinks he'll get peace and quiet down here to do it. Don't think he'll bother us much, ducky. These scientific types live in a world of their own, you know. He'll probably be off to the Himalayas or the Andes again soon.'

'But why on earth should he buy an hotel, and one that's not paying its way, if he's an explorer?'

'Well, I don't know that it's a bad idea. If you want a business which will provide you with an interest, run itself while you're away exploring, and give you a comfortable home when you need it, an hotel's the answer.'

'One that loses money?'

'Don't be so analytical, darling. Anyway, I told him that a few years ago the place was paying handsomely but that death duties and a spot of bad luck on the Stock Exchange pegged me back. I've convinced him that with a bit of capital, this place can pay as well again as it ever did.'

'And he has got a bit of capital?'

'Seems to have. His father's recently died. Probably inherited a bit. I flatter myself at having found just the right kind of buyer – to put up the capital and leave the managing to me.'

'I hope you're right. I thought Darrington looked far from stooge-like.'

'Oh, he's no fool, but his interests lie elsewhere. In exploring the earth's crust in remote places. Suits me. The remoter, the better.'

'When does he take over?'

'On the first of October. He'll be moving in that weekend. Proposes to make the lodge his private residence.'

'He'll have to spend a lot on it, then, to make it comfortable. Or perhaps explorers don't mind leaky roofs and stone floors.'

'We shall see. Now stop being practical, sweetheart, and give me a kiss. People with a smile like yours should never be serious.'

'You shouldn't spring such devastating news on me. Selling your heritage isn't like selling a car.'

He tilted her chin.

'I've never been all that keen on my heritage – too many responsibilities. A dull subject. Let's drop it. Just now, I'm much more interested in a certain young woman's face. Rather an intriguing one.'

'Bryant will be in at any moment now. And he won't knock.'

He made no attempt to release her.

'Yes, an intriguing face. Hair neither red nor brown. I suppose it would be called chestnut. Brown eyes with gold in them. A good straight nose, but those flared nostrils hint at a mettlesome temperament in need of soothing now and again. A mouth that curls delightfully at the corners and is so tender and inviting that it can't possibly be concerned with practical matters. Below the face there are points equally intriguing, but I won't go into those now.'

He kissed her.

'Like me, heritage or no?'

She smiled.

'I do, rather. Can't think why. You're far too handsome and sadly lacking in ambition.'

'My ambition is to enjoy life. And I do, on the whole. Ah well, duty calls now. Anything that matters in the post?'

After he had dictated a couple of letters and left her to deal with the others, Stella leaned back in her chair, unable for the moment to bring her mind to bear on correspondence. She still found it hard to realise that the hotel was about to pass into the hands of a stranger; that she and John would be employees of that stranger. Still felt a little hurt at John's secrecy. Moreover, she had an uneasy feeling that Mr. Darrington was nothing like so easy a proposition as John thought.

She voiced these fears to her father after dinner that evening. Nan had brought their coffee out to the garden where the oblique rays of the setting sun still kept the chill of the autumn night at bay.

'He may be an explorer, he may be more interested in rock structure than anything else, but I wager a pound to a gooseberry that he's not the type of man to take a back seat in any enterprise. Things will never be the same.'

'If he wants to make the place pay, I expect he hopes they won't,' said her father equally as he sipped his coffee.

'I hate to think of the Cormorant belonging to anybody but a Marbury.'

'A very feudal outlook, my dear.'

'Well, don't you think it's a shame, after being in the family all these years? After all old Mr. Marbury's work and enthusiasm, too.'

'But if the young Marbury doesn't want it, that's all there is to it.'

'I can't understand John. I thought he loved the place, but he seems relieved at having got rid of it.'

Her father looked at her pensively.

'Have you and that young man of yours any plans for a joint future, or shouldn't I ask?'

'Well, it's a joint present,' said Stella, smiling at him, 'but I haven't asked if his intentions are strictly honourable. Perhaps you'd better do that.'

'Heaven forbid. Our generation has to wait until it's told.'

'Do I ever keep things from you? Things that matter, I mean.'

'Bless you, no. I was only thinking that you and young Marbury have been running round together a long time now, and wondered whether you'd thought of making it a permanent team.'

12

'That, I've always thought, was the idea, but nothing has been committed to paper, if you know what I mean.'

'Well, at twenty-four, you've plenty of time. Does John intend to stay on permanently as manager of the hotel?'

'As far as I know. I had no idea that the financial situation was so bad. It's all been rather a shock, I must say.'

'I shouldn't worry about it, my dear. John knows what he's doing, and it's only sensible to cut one's losses. If he's doing it cheerfully, so much the more credit to him. Sentiment has no place in business, I'm afraid.'

'And you the most unworldly man in the world!'

'That's why I chose the teaching profession, dear, knowing that the business jungle would be too much for me. It's getting chilly, and I've some essays to correct. Those chrysanthemums are late this year. Doesn't look to me as though they're going to beat the frosts.'

Stella stayed out until the moon rose behind the beech tree, her thoughts unable to leave the events of the day. If she had been John, she would have fought to the last pound to keep the Cormorant. He could have raised a mortgage, perhaps, and reorganised the hotel. She sighed. Perhaps it was unfair to let her love for the place condemn his action. But she wished he had talked it over with her first.

Her father had finished his correcting when she went in, and was glancing at the *Radio Times*.

'Did you say that the name of the man buying the hotel was Darrington?'

'Yes.'

'Recently back from the Andes?'

'Yes.'

'Then if you tune into the Third Programme in five minutes' time, you'll have the pleasure of hearing him talk about the expedition.'

For the next twenty minutes they listened to Darrington's account of the expedition, given mainly from a geologist's angle but with interesting sidelights on the flora and fauna of those regions. He had a good broadcasting voice, resonant and well modulated, and he managed to convey in a calm, unhurried manner a deep enthusiasm for his subject. He concluded with a brief, faintly humorous description of the practical difficulties the expedition came up against and the way they were solved, and left them wishing for more.

'H'm. An interesting man, that. I should like to meet him.'

'I shall *have* to meet him, and quite a lot,' said Stella a little grimly.

Her father looked at her quickly.

'Well, don't blame him because John had to sell the hotel.

'Of course not. But do you think he sounds the kind of person to keep in the background and let other people manage his business?'

'I refuse to commit myself. He may be so immersed in his book that he won't be aware of the hotel. A lot depends on John, of course. If he runs the place efficiently, Darrington will have no reason to interfere.'

'Of course John runs the place efficiently. He knows the job from A to Z.'

'Then there's no need to worry.'

'You haven't seen Nicholas Darrington,' said Stella darkly.

Chapter Two

THERE were only seven holiday-makers left at the Cormorant Hotel when the new owner moved in. Besides these, there were three old gentlemen and two sisters, both retired school-teachers, who were residents all the year round. With the staff reduced, this was the time for taking stock and putting in hand any decorations, repairs or improvements that were needed. Now, waiting for the new owner to take the reins, there was an uneasy hiatus while the staff marked time and wondered how the change-over would affect them. Only John Marbury remained outwardly unperturbed, and as cheerful as ever.

The first weeks under new ownership passed off remarkably smoothly. Darrington called the staff together on his first day

14

and delivered a pleasant little speech about co-operation. He followed this with an interview with Marbury, during which he agreed to Marbury's suggestions concerning the maintenance needed for the hotel and left him to put them into effect. He himself had in mind increasing the garage accommodation, which was pitifully inadequate in view of the fact that nine out of ten visitors to the Cormorant Hotel came in cars, and he intended to discuss this with his architect, who was coming down from London to inspect the lodge with a view to making something of it for Darrington's private use. He would make an appointment for the architect to meet both Marbury and himself on the spot at the earliest opportunity. Meanwhile, until the lodge was re-built, he was taking over two rooms on the first floor of the hotel for his own use. All this Marbury reported to Stella in due course.

Stella had little contact with Darrington for the first month. She occasionally had to obtain his signature on cheques, but he seldom showed himself in the office and was content to accept John's methods there. She often saw him strolling round the grounds, studying the house, apparently lost in thought but in reality, she guessed, summing up his acquisition.

'Nothing to worry about there, pet,' John said after a conference with Darrington at the end of the month. 'Here is your salary cheque. You might distribute the wages, as usual. Our rugged explorer compliments me on the staff and is purring like a contented cat. He likes this place. Thinks it has great charm, and sees no reason why, if we advertise its scenery and play up its attractive situation a bit more, we shouldn't be crowded out with visitors each year.'

'I hope he's right. It always did do well, and I see no reason why it shouldn't again.'

'He's spending a packet on the lodge and the garages. At least, by the look of the plans the architect has submitted. Still, if he's got money to burn, so much the better. By the way, Stella, I've arranged to take three weeks' holiday from next weekend. He's not keen on both of us being away together, which is reasonable enough as he's so new to it, so what do you propose to do? I told him you had a week in April and had another due now.'

It was one of the drawbacks to her job that she and John had never been able to take their holidays together since John's father had died, but she had hoped that the advent of a new owner would, at least, have removed that disadvantage, and she and John had discussed spending one week in Ashcombe together, going out in the car for picnics, riding, and playing tennis, before John went off to the Continent to take part in a car rally.

'But surely a man who can organise expeditions to the Andes can cope here for a week without us. There are only the five old regulars left now, and Mrs. Dacres is very capable on the domestic side.'

'You can see if your charm will persuade him, pet, but he didn't seem keen when I mentioned it.'

'I will. I'll go now. It's too absurd,' said Stella, her disappointment feeding her annoyance.

'You'll find him in his study, surrounded by plans. Try the famous Stella Verney smile. I always find it irresistible myself.'

'I don't think he's susceptible. Anyway, I'll see what I can do.'

Stella knocked at the study door and went in with what she hoped was a pleasing smile masking her determination to salvage her holiday. Darrington looked up from the plan he was studying.

'Could you spare me a few minutes, Mr. Darrington?'

'Certainly.' He knocked out his pipe on the ash tray, and nodded to a chair. 'What can I do for you?'

'It's about my holiday. I have a week due to me, and wanted to have it at the same time as Mr. Marbury's first week.'

'Yes, so I heard. I'm afraid that won't be possible. I'm sorry. I must have one of you here.'

'But surely that's not essential now that the summer season's over.'

'People are writing in for Christmas bookings, I understand. Decorators and plumbers are about to invade us and will be here for the next month. I must have one responsible person on the management side, since I expect to be fully occupied with these plans for the garages and the lodge, and with a book

16

I'm writing. I don't want to have to run the office as well, even if this is a slack time. I'm sorry if this spoils your plans, but I believe you and Mr. Marbury have never both been absent at the same time before.'

'Not since Mr. Marbury died, but circumstances are different now. Nobody is indispensable, after all.'

'It's not a question of being indispensable. It's a question of inconvenience to me. You are a very capable person, Miss Verney, and the obvious substitute for Marbury. I've only been here a few weeks and I've a great deal to see to at the moment. Perhaps in future we can arrange for help in the office for you, as I understand that you are overworked in the summer and that Mr. Marbury would like to widen your sphere of responsibilities if we can get a typist to take some of the routine work off your hands. It might then be possible for you and Mr. Marbury to be away at the same time. With things as they are at the moment, I'm afraid it's not possible.'

He turned back to the plans as though the matter was closed, and Stella flushed.

'I think you're being very inconsiderate, Mr. Darrington.'

His eyebrows went up as he turned to her, and she felt uncomfortable as his pale eyes flickered over her.

'I'm sorry,' he said dryly. 'I understand that you were not proposing to go away this week?'

'No.'

'Until I came, such an arrangement was out of the question anyway, so no long-standing plans are upset. Marbury himself sees my point of view. I think you're being a little unreasonable, but I see no point in discussing what we think of each other in this connection. As soon as you've decided whether to take next week before Marbury goes, or a later week, perhaps you'll let me know.'

His face was impassive, his tone calm and inflexible. He turned back to the plans, and there was no more to be said. Stella went out quickly before the anger seething inside her could boil over into words which she might repent. Having worked here on such friendly terms with the Marburys ever since she left school, it was not easy to adapt herself now to being no more than an employee of an uncompromising and strictly business-like employer. It was fortunate that she saw little of him during her working hours, and that John was a good buffer. This was her first significant encounter with him, and she did not find it reassuring.

John shrugged his shoulders when she reported failure.

'Never mind, my dear. He's got a point, you know. When will you take your week?'

'I don't know. I don't feel very interested now. Next week, I suppose.'

'Well, as our plans are wrecked, I think I shall see if I can get my passage changed to a week earlier and spend three weeks in France. One or two of the gang are going over early to stooge around, I know. Bill Porter's taking his new Aston Martin. Think I'll get in touch with him and see where he's staying.'

On the whole, thought Stella, John was not unduly disappointed by the loss of their week together.

'Good idea,' she said briefly, and attacked her typewriter with vigour, reminding herself that it was petty to feel injured because John could re-plan their week so happily. His great passion was for cars and his greatest friends were among the rally drivers who shared his enthusiasm. She should be glad that his week was not spoiled, too. Her anger she reserved for Nicholas Darrington.

She decided to go down the lane to Brierley after dinner that evening to confide her ruffled feelings to the sympathetic ears of Cathie Elmore. The Elmore household had always been a source of comfort and happiness to her ever since, at six years old, she was invited to Cathie's eighth birthday party. Stella's mother had died before her daughter was a year old, and Stella's childhood would have been a very lonely one had not Mrs. Elmore welcomed her as one of her own brood. To the only child of a quiet, studious schoolmaster, brought up by a conscientious but rather dour Nanny, the Elmore family was a revelation and an education. At the time of that birthday party, there were three Elmore children: Jimmy, a year older than Cathie, and Mike who was the same age as Stella. Maud Ellen, known as Midge, had not arrived on the scene to complete the quartet until two years later and had miraculously survived the hazards of a late-comer into such a family. Stella's ties with the family were strengthened by the odd friendship which grew up between Mr. Elmore and her father, and she owed much happiness to the occupiers of the large house on the corner of Church Lane, with the gate of which she now wrestled. It always jammed half-way.

The light in the porch swung in the wind. It was a dark, windy night, and a recent heavy shower filled the air with the scent of rotting leaves and wet earth. It was rather a lovely smell, Stella thought as she walked up the drive.

The bell on the front door never rang, and she was about to seize the knocker when an unfamiliar glisten on it deterred her. She touched it cautiously. Wet paint. That probably meant that the Elmores were caught up in one of their father's periodic enthusiasms for home decorating. She walked round to the side entrance and saw a dim shape emerging from the tool-shed with a step-ladder. In the light streaming from the kitchen window, she recognised Jimmy.

'Hullo, Stella, my girl. You're just in time to wield a paint brush.'

'At it again?'

'Afraid so. If you can negotiate the furniture in the hall, you'll find Cathie and Mother incarcerated in the dining-room.'

Climbing over an armchair, Stella caught a glimpse of Mr. Elmore's bald head through the open door of the sitting-room, and she called out a greeting which he returned with a flourish of his paint brush. She had negotiated the main obstacles between her and the closed dining-room door when her eye was caught by a figure creeping down the stairs. It was Mike. He put a finger to his lips when he saw her, pointed to the sitting-room and shook his head, pointed to himself and enacted a pantomime which Stella interpreted as indicating a game of snooker, and slid past her in the direction of the kitchen and the side door as silently as a wraith. She smiled and knocked smartly on the dining-room door.

Cathie's face lit up when she saw Stella.

'Bless you, I was just about to fight my way to the telephone to see if you were still in the land of the living.'

'I'm sorry we're in such a muddle, dear,' said Mrs. Elmore,

clearing a pile of socks from the fireside chair. 'Father's re-painting the sitting-room.'

'I know. I saw him. What's it to be this time?'

'A terrible cyclamen pink,' said Cathie. 'He bought the paint cheaply from a man who'd over-estimated his needs,' she added darkly, but with a twinkle in her blue eyes.

Cathie Elmore, at twenty-six, had much of her mother's serenity and poise, which made her seem older than her years. Even when she was a child, there had been a tranquillity about Cathie which none of the other Elmore children possessed and which had always attracted Stella's more turbulent temperament. Cathie was growing even more like her mother with the passage of time, thought Stella now, as she looked at the two faces opposite her. The same pale complexion, the same dark blue eyes, the same oval-shaped face. But Cathie was smaller in build than her mother and her smooth black hair, parted in the middle and drawn back in a knot at the nape of her neck, threw into relief features that were more finely formed than her mother's. These two, mother and daughter, were the calm centre round which whirled the merry-go-round of the Elmore males and the late-comer to the family.

'Where's Midge tonight?' asked Stella. 'Hasn't R.J. roped her in?'

'She disappeared after dinner without saying a word to anybody after hearing R.J.'s plans for painting, and we haven't a clue where she is.'

'Mike's just performed the same disappearing act,' said Stella, laughing. 'He's gone off to snooker, if I interpreted his mime aright just now.'

'Oh dear,' said Mrs. Elmore. 'I think I'll go and make a pot of tea. Father will be needing it.'

'Mind how you go, Mother. Shall I try to move some of those chairs?'

'No, dear. I can manage.'

'Well, how's life in your comparatively sane world, Stella?' said Cathie, picking up a pair of Jimmy's socks to darn.

'Here, let me have a pair. Good heavens, what are these? Arctic explorers' socks?' asked Stella, holding up an enormous

20

pair of blue socks which appeared to be about half an inch thick.

'Father's. A mail order cheap line,' said Cathie briefly. 'Does he ever wear them?'

'Only for fishing, and then he says they're too hot.'

Stella shook her head, smiling. The strange bargains which Mr. Elmore could never resist were legion, ranging from labour-saving gadgets which never worked to ex-service items of clothing which never fitted and which were ludicrously unsuitable for a man whose life was mainly spent in an office in Ashcombe, where R. J. Elmore, C.A., ran a flourishing accountancy practice with the assistance of his sons.

'Well, you need rug wool to darn these,' said Stella, 'but as there's only one small hole, maybe I can make do with this. I'm browned off, Cathie. My comparatively sane world, as you call it, is far from satisfactory at the moment. Our new chief refuses to let me take my holiday with John.'

'Oh, what a pity!'

'It's absurd. Just one week. Why, I might be ill while John was away and Darrington would manage then. I smelt trouble the first time I set eyes on him. Dictatorial and quite ruthless in getting his own way.'

Cathie looked at Stella with a little smile hovering at her lips. 'I rather like him.'

Stella looked at her, astonished.

'But you've never met him, have you?'

'I was introduced to him the day before yesterday. It's very odd, but Mr. Darrington turns out to be an old friend of Roger Thornton's.'

'Good heavens! How and where?'

'They met five years ago in the Lake District. They were staying at the same hotel, and helped to make up a search party for two young students who had gone climbing and failed to turn up at the hotel that night. Roger used to do a good deal of climbing, you know, and Darrington is an expert on mountains. They discovered a mutual interest in geology, and they've kept up the friendship ever since, mainly by correspondence since they've been poles apart. And Roger thinks very highly of your new employer.'

21

'Well, I'm afraid I can't share his opinion, but Roger probably sees him from a different angle. Taking John's place, he seems intolerable. Where did you meet?'

'In the museum. He had come to look over it, and he stayed about a couple of hours.'

Stella was silent for a few moments, digesting this information. Roger Thornton was the Curator of the Ashcombe Museum, and Cathie was his assistant. Roger would naturally welcome as a friend anybody qualified to share his interests in natural history, and Cathie would set a good deal of store by Roger's opinion of a person. Whether there was more than friendship between Roger Thornton and Cathie, nobody knew, but they had been friends for many years now and Stella suspected that on Cathie's part, at least, there was more than friendship involved.

'John imagines that we shan't be bothered much with him,' said Stella, 'but I think he's mistaken.'

'You'll hold your own, I'm sure,' said Cathie, gently teasing, and Stella smiled and shook her head.

'No sympathy here, I can see.'

Sounds outside the door indicated that their barricade was being removed, and Mrs. Elmore came in bearing a tray of tea, followed by Jimmy and his father. Jimmy, looking huger than ever in baggy flannel trousers and an old cricket sweater that had stretched, placed a benedictory hand on Stella's head as he passed her and sank down into an armchair. He was the only fair member of the family, his sandy hair topping a large, good-natured face which was as comfortable and uninspiring as an old pair of slippers. Beneath his easy-going manner, however, lived an ebullience almost as exhausting as his father's. R.J., as his children usually called him, was as tall as Jimmy, but of leaner build. He had an unusually long face, and his bald dome rose from a fringe of dark hair like an egg from an egg-cup. His features were good and his face creased up into deep wrinkles when he smiled, reminding Stella of a boxer dog that lived close by. He had a booming voice and a baying laugh, was a man of fiery but fleeting enthusiasms, and at fifty-six possessed as much energy as his sons. He was eternally young at heart and had the endearing quality of being able to laugh at himself as heartily as anybody. Stella adored him as warm-heartedly as his family, without having to suffer their frequent exasperation at some of his crazier inflictions. He beamed now at Stella as he took his tea.

'And how's your father? Recovered from that licking I gave him at golf on Sunday?'

'He said you cheated.'

'He's too easily put off his stroke. Funny, I couldn't do a thing wrong. Never played like that before, and probably shan't again. Silly game, really, chasing a little ball along and chivvying it into a hole. Met your new boss today, by the way. Glad to learn that he wants the old firm to look after his money affairs. No monkey business there. Sharp as a razor. Good thing Elmore, Elmore & Elmore are always on their toes. Not that the last two Elmores are so bright. In fact, I get very little co-operation from this family. Where's Mike and Midge? Leaving me to do all the work tonight. It's a good thing I'm a tolerant man.'

'You can't expect the youngsters to share your passion for decorating, dear,' said his wife. 'And you only give them the dull jobs to do.'

'Should think so. Can't trust them with a brush. I'm going to buy one of those rollers tomorrow. A chap told me that they're marvellous for ceilings and large areas.'

Cathie groaned.

'Darling, you're not going to do all the ceilings again?'

'It had occurred to me.'

'Now, Robert,' began his wife, and one of the Elmore family arguments got under way, with R.J. smiling at them all in turn, happily implacable, as impossible to quench as the sun.

Chapter Three

STELLA returned to the hotel after her week's holiday with feelings of slight trepidation about the next three weeks when she would be without the barrier of John between her and Darrington. John had set off for the Continent in high spirits on the previous day, and as Stella watched the red M.G. disappear down the road, she had wished with all her heart that she could have been with him. Now, on a wet Monday morning, she felt a little depressed. She found Bryant in the outer office sorting some papers. He was a small, pale boy of fifteen, and wore horn-rimmed spectacles which added to the seriousness of his countenance.

'Hullo, Bryant. Nasty morning.'

'Hullo, Miss Verney. Nice holiday?'

'Passable, thanks. Is that the post?'

She had barely looked through it before Darrington came in, wished her good morning and asked if she had enjoyed her holiday. It was hardly a tactful question, she thought, as she replied:

'Quite pleasant, thank you.'

'Good. I don't know what arrangement you and Marbury follow with correspondence. You handle a good deal of it yourself, I gather.'

'Yes. All the routine stuff. If there are any that I can't deal with, I hand them over to him at eleven, when he comes in for coffee, and he dictates anything necessary then.'

'I see. Well, I have a good deal of correspondence going on just now with the architect and builders, and a few other business matters. I like to get rid of it early so that I can get down to my book, so from now on would you come along to my room first thing so that I can dictate what's necessary, and bring any letters that Marbury would normally deal with?'

'Very well, Mr. Darrington. I'll come now, shall I?'

'If you please.' His eye fell on Bryant who had sidled in

with some files. 'Don't you usually knock on doors, Bryant?'

Bryant shuffled and murmured something about not thinking it necessary.

'Then think again, my lad. If Miss Verney has anybody with her, it may not be convenient for you to interrupt, and even if she's on her own, it's more polite to knock before you come in.'

'Yessir.' Dick Bryant's mournful eyes looked up at Darrington like a whipped spaniel. He was an unreliable boy and not very much help, but Stellla felt sorry for him now.

'And straighten your tie and wash those filthy hands. You're supposed to be here to learn the business as well as make yourself useful. Isn't that the idea?'

'Yessir.'

'Does anybody see that you do learn anything, or do you just mess about, as you seem to be doing whenever I'm around.'

'I just mess about,' said Dick Bryant, and Darrington grinned.

'I thought so. I'll have to take you in hand, my lad. Smarten yourself up for a start, and come to my room as soon as Miss Verney leaves it. We'll map out a curriculum for you. If your father wants you to learn the business, learn it you shall. At the moment, you don't even qualify for boots.'

His friendly pat on the boy's shoulder robbed the words of severity, and Bryant gave him a shy grin as he slid out of the door. Darrington turned to Stella.

'I gather Marbury hasn't paid much attention to the boy.'

'Wrote him off as pretty useless, I think.'

'He looks fairly intelligent and he's young enough to be trainable. He'll obviously be no good if he's left to himself. We'll see what a spot of discipline and supervision can do. If you're ready, Miss Verney.'

He opened the door for her and followed her out. The man who was not going to interfere with their particular horse was showing a handy aptitude with the reins, she thought, as they went down the wide staircase to his study. He dictated well, with clarity and conciseness, and had finished within half an hour. She adopted her coolest and most business-like manner towards him as she raised one or two matters which she would

25

have to deal with in John's absence, including the supervision of the decorators who were arriving the next day.

'Did you decide on ivory or green for the dining-room, after all, Mr. Darrington? I can't find any reference to it on the files and I'd like to know what was decided. It has been known for Bolsover's to put the wrong colour on and I shall want to be certain before they start.'

'Adam green was the choice. Marbury was going to telephone Bolsover's last week.'

'Right. I'll check on that. Samples of curtain materials came in this morning. Shall I send them down to you?'

'I believe the choice of soft furnishings has been left to you in the past?'

'Yes.'

'Then I'm sure we can't do better than leave the choice in your hands now. It's more a woman's department, after all.'

'As you please, Mr. Darrington.'

'I'd like to see your choice before ordering. Just as a matter of interest.'

'Of course. Will that be all?'

'If that's all you have to raise. Needless to say,' he added a little mockingly, 'I am at your disposal while our manager is absent.'

'Thank you. I hope I shan't have to worry you too much.'

'Miss Verney . . .'

She stopped with her hand on the door.

'May I offer you some advice?'

'If you think I'm in need of it, Mr. Darrington.'

He smiled the crooked smile which was oddly disarming.

'I was only going to remark that learning to bow to the inevitable saves a good deal of useless wear and tear on the human system. I commend the lesson to you.'

His shot went home and brought the colour to her cheeks. He had caught her by surprise, and she had no answer to his perspicacity save a wry smile and a retreat.

There was a great deal to cope with during John's absence, for Christmas was looming ahead, and Stella had quite enough to keep her busy in dealing with Christmas bookings and Darrington's correspondence, without having to keep an eye on the decorators, put the new curtains in hand, draft advertisements for extra Christmas staff and listen to Mrs. Dacres' complaints about the boiler fuel and the kitchen help, both admittedly far from satisfactory.

John was due back on the Saturday, and Stella, still typing at six o'clock on the Friday before his return, was thinking how good it would be to see his cheerful face again, when Darrington came in. During these weeks she had learned to respect his capabilities, even if she could not master her resentment of his ownership of what she still thought of as Marbury property. But to work with, Darrington scored full marks. He never fussed, never dithered, and gave the maximum help and support in the shortest possible time. She could appreciate why he had been chosen to lead an expedition; as a leader and organiser, he was undoubtedly first class. As a person, she liked him as little as a great boulder of rock planted down in the middle of her pleasant garden. He came in now with a sheaf of letters.

'I've signed these. Are there any more?'

'Only this one to your Publishers. I'm just finishing if you could wait one moment.'

'Right.'

He strolled across to the window while Stella rattled off the last few words.

'You've had a hectic three weeks,' he observed as he signed the letter. 'We'll have to get some help for you before the summer season.'

'Thank you.'

'Marbury leaves a good deal to you, doesn't he?'

Stella looked at him cautiously. It was true that during the last year, John had left more and more to her, and Darrington's advent had made no difference in that respect. She liked to feel that John had such confidence in her, and had stifled one or two moments of doubt as to whether he was really pulling his weight. However, she would die rather than voice such doubts to Darrington.

'We run very well in harness together,' she said.

'Well, thank you for managing so well in his absence. I appreciate your efforts.'

27

'I like my job, and I love this place. The Cormorant has always meant more than just a job to me.'

'I wasn't suggesting that your efforts were made out of any regard for me,' he said, his eyes mocking her. 'Nevertheless, as owner of the Cormorant, I appreciate your good service. I have to go down to the town. Can I drop you home?'

'Thank you, but I've still some P.A.Y.E. returns to complete. I shall be half an hour yet.'

'Right. Good night, then.'

'Good night, Mr. Darrington.'

John was not due back until late on Saturday night, and Stella expected that he would telephone her on Sunday, but she heard nothing from him and did not see him until he came into her office on Monday morning.

'Hullo, pet,' he said, flashing a smile at her as he held out his hands. 'Missed me?'

'Terribly,' said Stella as she went into his arms.

Normally they observed the conventions in office hours, with small lapses, but Stella was so glad to see him and he was in such bubbling spirits that their friendly kiss was prolonged, and Stella responded to him with an ardour heightened by his recent absence and the sudden release of the tension of the past weeks. She was so lost that when Darrington's voice said 'Excuse me,' she could not collect herself for a moment, and stayed in John's arms, as though in a dream. Then she straightened up, her cheeks suddenly scarlet as her eyes met Darrington's cool scrutiny.

'I'm sorry to be a nuisance, but the builders have arrived, and the foreman wants to know if we've a spare plan of the lodge extension. I believe I gave you a copy to file, Miss Verney.'

Speechless, Stella went to the filing cabinet and drew out a folded plan.

'Thank you. Might I suggest,' he added, his eyes going to Marbury, 'that this is neither the time nor the place for such ... pleasures. I'd be obliged to you both if you'd confine your private affairs to your off-duty hours.'

For a moment Stella thought that John was going to hit him,

but the door had closed behind Darrington before either of them moved or spoke.

'God, what insolence! Who the devil does he think he is?' said John, his face dark with anger.

'Your boss. You sold out to him, remember?' observed Stella bitterly.

'Well, he needn't think I'm going to stand being treated like an office boy.'

'It was foolish to be caught out like that. My fault. I didn't think. I was so glad to see you.'

'Arrogant devil! If he's going to start that sort of thing, he can find another manager. I've never been spoken to like that in my life before, and I don't intend to start getting used to it now.'

Stella looked at him unhappily. Somehow, he didn't seem to grasp even now the fact that he had sold his right to give the orders. He had sold them both into this man's hands, and it was no use thinking he could sell his cake and have it.

'Has he been coming the iron hand with you while I've been away?'

'Not unduly. But he's had his hand on the reins all right. I don't like it any more than you, John, but we must face the fact that we can't do as we like now, and I suppose it's not unreasonable to jib at necking parties in the office,' she added with a twinkle in her eyes.

John grinned. His ill-temper was always short-lived.

'Probably jealous,' he observed. 'All the same, I don't like seeing this glimpse of a wolf in my sheep.'

'I never thought he was a sheep. In fact, it stood out a mile that he wasn't.'

'I thought he'd be immersed in his book or planning further expeditions. The farther, the better. Wish now I'd held my hand a bit longer. I met a much more attractive potential buyer at Le Touquet.'

'Tell me about your holiday, John. I haven't even asked you if you enjoyed it.'

'Had a grand time, thanks. Came in third in one of the rally events. I'll qualify for the Monte Carlo yet.'

'Splendid! You had a good time with the boys, I guess. Was Rollo there?'

'You bet. He never misses a rally. Goes all over the world. You can do that if your father's a millionaire, of course.'

'Would you like to do that?'

'My idea of the perfect life, ducky. Travel, excitement, good sport and a grand lot of blokes.'

Stella looked at his lively, handsome face, and felt a little chilled by the knowledge that she could not share his enthusiasm as fully as she would like. She had gone to a few car rallies with him, but had found them boring and noisy, and as the weather was invariably bad, the hours spent in the rain or in a keen wind watching cars attempt to get up hills and round tortuous tracks with engines roaring had constituted a feat of endurance on her part. The fraternity on such occasions, too, talked their own jargon, and were of a hearty ultra-masculine type who contrived to make a female feel just an ignorant little woman whose function was to look decorative and cheer the heroes. It was not a world in which she felt at home, and since John no longer asked her to accompany him, she assumed that he had sensed this.

'And who was the potential buyer?' she asked.

'A Mrs. Ridlow. Widow of the owner of a South African mining company who left her a packet, as well as shares in the company. She's quite a driver, too. Won a couple of trophies herself. She's a friend of Rollo's.'

'Does she live in this country?'

'Yes. In London, when she's not travelling. She gets around a bit. I told her about the Cormorant. She said she'd have been glad to buy it. I must say she'd have been a pleasanter proposition than Darrington. However, there it is. I don't suppose the old devil will sell. Not unless he loses a packet over it,' he added thoughtfully.

'I don't think he'll easily admit failure.'

'Oh well, back to the grind, I suppose. By the way, Mrs. Ridlow's coming here for Christmas. I said I'd see that she has the best room we've got. Is number five booked yet?'

'Yes. Miss Mapleton. She always has that room.'

'Well, she'll have to have another this time.'

'But I've already confirmed that she can have her usual room. She likes the view.'

'Tell her there's been a mistake, but she can have number seven. That's almost as good. She won't mind. She's a nice old thing.'

'But she's one of our oldest customers, John. She was a great friend of your father's, and Mrs. Ridlow is a newcomer, after all.'

'A wealthy one, ducky. They're the sort to cultivate. Just compose a nice tactful letter to old Mapleton, and give her my kind regards.'

A knock on the door heralded Bryant.

'Your phone's ringing, Mr. Marbury.'

'Blast! I forgot to switch it through. You didn't think of answering it, I suppose?'

'No. I just heard it across the passage, and I knew you were in here.'

'O.K. Bright boy, aren't you?'

John disappeared. The manager's office was in these days seldom occupied, for John had passed most of the administration over to Stella while his other responsibilities took him out and about the hotel and the grounds. His telephone was switched over to ring on Stella's line in his absence, and at one time Bryant had spent a large proportion of the day running round to find the manager, until little by little John passed responsibility over to her, and now there were few matters which Stella did not handle.

'Everybody seems a bit Monday-ish this morning,' observed Bryant.

He looked clean and well brushed, and had executed commissions with remarkable celerity lately. Darrington seemed to be making his mark there, she thought.

'After all,' went on Bryant earnestly, 'it was more sensible to call Mr. Marbury, who was only a step away, than to dash across the corridor, ask someone to hold on, and dash back. Don't you agree, Miss Verney?'

'Yes. Although you could have taken the call and switched it through here.'

'Yes, but I don't understand that switchboard thing. I cut

someone off last time I tried to do that. I shall have to study it,' concluded Bryant solemnly.

Stella took the cover off her typewriter and wondered how best to phrase the letter to Miss Mapleton. She was conscious again of the uneasy feeling that for all the years of close friendship between her and John, she still did not fully understand him. Otherwise, he could not keep surprising her, as he had done lately. Was he changing, was she obtuse, or was she making too much of remarks of his which jarred? Smothering such thoughts as disloyal, she began to type the letter to Miss Mapleton.

It was a lovely day and to banish the bad start, Stella hurried through lunch so that she would have time to pay a visit to her own private cove. She exchanged a few words with the Misses Corrington, avoided looking at Darrington at his corner table, and slipped out as John came into the dining-room. Solitude and good clean air were what she needed to banish the humiliations and uneasiness of the morning. She walked across the lawns to the cliff edge on the right of the promontory over which the Cormorant presided. A rough, winding track had been made down the cliff face to the tiny cove below, which was inaccessible from land by any other means, and was too small to attract boats. The track was precipitous and, except for one or two of the more intrepid and active visitors, was seldom used, so that Stella had come to look upon the cove as her own domain. It was submerged for a couple of hours at each high tide so that its sands were always fresh and clean, and it was an ideal place for a quiet swim, for studying the wide range of shells which the tide cast up, or for delving into the rock pools at each end. She knew no more healing places for the troubled mind or spirit than this miniature world of sand, sea and rocks, shut away from human intrusion. Rough steps had been made to get down the first vertical drop of about twelve feet, after which the track wound down through the sparse grass and bracken which clothed the cliff face. The recent heavy rains had washed part of the path away, exposing rock, and Stella had difficulty in negotiating it, but she eventually jumped down safely on to the firm sand, although she had slightly grazed one hand on the way.

On that early December afternoon, there was a clarity of atmosphere which the summer sunshine rarely afforded, and it was indeed a clean and sparkling world into which she had descended. She stood at the water's edge, watching the waves curl over and break in shining foam to her feet. She loved the sea in all its moods, but never more than when it tumbled vigorously in sunshine, with white horses flecking its surface as far as the eye could see and spray showering the rocks at each end of the tiny bay. She could watch it, entranced, for ever, she thought, with the world well lost. Some gulls hovered hungrily around her, hoping for food, but she had forgotten to bring any bread, and they wheeled off, their wings arched beautifully against the sky. She lingered as long as she could, and returned unwillingly, conscious of forces at work in the Cormorant which were too strong for her and which she feared. But she was quite unable to put her fears into words.

The climb up was even more difficult than the climb down, for the exposed rock was smooth and steep, and where she had been able to slither down she now had to find footholds and handholds to span the break in the track. When she arrived at the top she looked a little the worse for wear, and decided that she must keep a pair of rubber plimsolls for this climb in future. But she felt better for her escape to that miniature world which she had come to treasure so dearly.

Chapter Four

THE hotel was fully booked for Christmas, and Stella was kept so busy during the preceding weeks that she had little time to speculate on the outcome of the rift which appeared to be growing between Darrington and his manager. John was obviously not putting himself out in any way, and Stella did her best to cover up and take over the duties which were properly John's. The alterations to the lodge were well under way and work had begun on the new garages, which were nicely sited behind a clump of trees. Darrington himself supervised the building programme while Stella organised the Christmas festivities and somehow kept the office routine up to date as well as coping with bookings and cancellations, engaging extra staff, doing John's book-keeping and typing letters for Darrington.

She worked late every night of the week preceding Christmas on decorating the hotel, her last efforts in this respect being aided, unexpectedly, by Darrington, who, finding her precariously balanced on top of a ladder with branches of fir in one hand, scissors in the other and red ribbon hanging round her neck, said:

'Here, come down. I can reach more easily than you if you'll give me my instructions.'

She looked down cautiously and found an unusually friendly smile on Darrington's upturned face. His hand was on top of the ladder, next to her foot, and she was conscious of the length of leg displayed for his eyes. She wobbled and he instinctively shot up his hand, but with no hand free to give him she descended a little rockily and felt his hands on her waist as she came within reach.

'Thank you,' she said hurriedly. 'I thought of putting branches of fir round each of the mirrors and tying them with this ribbon. With the light underneath, it should look rather effective.'

He agreed, looking round the oak-panelled walls of the dining-room from which gleamed, at intervals, small convex mirrors, each flanked by wall-lights in pairs.

'I make it twelve,' he said, his eyebrows raised.

'Yes.'

He looked at his watch.

'Quite an undertaking. It's nearly seven. Are you staying to dinner tonight?'

'No. I meant to get this done earlier, but the day has gone too fast for me.'

'What about leaving it until tomorrow?'

'Christmas Eve? Oh, no. People will be arriving tomorrow. I must get everything finished tonight. There's only the Christmas tree and this room to do now.'

34

'You've made the place look very attractive. Where's Marbury? I haven't seen him today.'

'He was here this morning, but I haven't seen him this afternoon. Don't worry. I'll soon finish this room off,' said Stella quickly.

John had, in fact, disappeared some hours ago with Mrs. Ridlow, who had arrived soon after lunch. Stella had seen the car drive off, but had caught no more than a glimpse of their heads and would not have known that it was Mrs. Ridlow had not the porter informed her, he being agog at the amount of luggage which had been disgorged from the racy-looking car. Stella, however, had no intention of revealing this to Darrington.

'We'll have to work fast to finish before dinner,' said Darrington. 'Hand the stuff up to me and tell me what to do with it. You'd better stay and have dinner here, and Bob can run you home afterwards. It's a wet night. Are you expected home? If so, you'd better telephone.'

'No. I told them that I'd be late. It's always the same the week before Christmas. A little to the right. That's better.'

'You've never fancied living in on the job? A lot more convenient, I should have thought.'

'I couldn't leave my father alone. He has only me. Our housekeeper isn't awfully good company.'

'Your mother?'

'Died when I was a baby. That piece of ribbon wants looping behind the branch on the right.'

'A lonely life for you,' said Darrington, carrying the ladder to the next mirror.

'Not really. I was more or less brought up with the Elmore family. They are very close friends of ours.'

'Oh, yes. I met Elmore and the two sons at their office a short time back, and my friend Thornton introduced me to Cathie, who is your particular friend, I believe.'

'Yes.'

'Nice folk. That girl has a face like a serene Madonna, Italian style.'

Stella was surprised at this from the man who had hitherto seemed as impersonal and unimpressionable as granite.

'She is blessed with a very sweet, serene nature, too. Like her mother. They need to be, for the rest of the family are about as serene as squibs.'

'I can well imagine it. How are we doing?'

'Very well. Three more. We'll have to go easy with the ribbon. I think, after all, I will do the tree tomorrow. I'll come along early, and do it first thing. I really feel too grubby to stay to dinner. I need a bath and a change. It's surprising how dirty one gets doing this sort of job.'

'So I'm discovering,' said Darrington, looking at his hands. 'However, we can provide cleaning facilities, and I'd be glad if you would share my obscure table in the corner tonight. You've had a long day, and you need a hot meal before you go home.'

She protested no more, and found herself sitting down to dinner opposite Darrington's too shrewd eyes just as John escorted Mrs. Ridlow into the dining-room and piloted her to a table for two in the far corner of the room from Stella. Over John's shoulder, Stella glimpsed a much younger woman than she had imagined: fair, classical looks, beautifully turned out in a black dinner dress, and wearing expensive-looking drop ear-rings which glittered with every movement. She was laughing at something John was saying. Stella's eyes returned to her own table to find that Darrington had observed where her attention had strayed, for he said:

'Is that one of our regulars?'

'No. A newcomer. A Mrs. Ridlow. John met her when he was on holiday.'

'No Mr. Ridlow?'

'She's a widow.'

'And a very attractive one, from this distance, anyway. Claret or burgundy?'

'I leave it to you.'

'We're full for Christmas. I gather that's usual here.'

She found herself telling him about previous Christmases, about old Mr. Marbury's love of the place and the enthusiasm which he brought to running the Cormorant according to his own high standards. He had aimed at an intimate but gracious atmosphere, unobtrusive comfort, and, above all, had sought

36

to make the Cormorant a place of peace. 'There was nothing people needed more sorely in this complex modern world, he used to say,' concluded Stella.

'You were very fond of the old man, weren't you?'

'Yes. He was a true gentleman. Kind, courteous, and liking people so much that they couldn't help liking him. He was genuinely interested in everybody who came here, and, of course, the same people came year after year. Still do, most of them. I was very raw when I first came here, but Mr. Marbury guided me with very gentle hands.'

Darrington smiled.

'What a sad falling off now. You're still kicking against the usurper a little, I fancy.'

His eyes held hers against her will, those pale grey eyes which somehow scared her.

'I would have given anything to have kept the Cormorant in Marbury hands,' she said simply.

'You think of yourself as a Marbury, perhaps?'

Her eyes fell.

'My interests and theirs have always been identical.'

'Quite. You're angry with me again. Will it make you more angry if I say that I don't think young Marbury deserves you?'

'Do you know enough of either of us to say that?'

'I think so. Would this place mean as much to you if Marbury were not still connected with it?'

'Why do you ask?'

'Just curiosity.'

'I'm afraid I can't answer that question, because it's something I just can't imagine,' she said, hoping he did not see the fear in her eyes.

'I see. I intend, by the way, to get you some assistance in the new year. You've too much to do. But we'll talk about that later.'

'You're not finding much time for your book these days, Mr. Darrington, arc you?' asked Stella, anxious to steer the conversation from personal matters.

'No, I'm not. I think my idea of finding myself a cosy retreat has misfired.'

Whether it was the effect of the wine or of fatigue, Stella

did not know, but she was aware of a queer feeling of unreality about this scene. The two fair heads in the far corner seemed to belong to a different world, while she was in dark waters, out of her depth, with Darrington. Resolutely, she plied him with questions about the Andes, but when she found herself being driven home by Bob in the hotel car, she could remember little of that part of their conversation. Tomorrow she must have a word with John and warn him that Darrington was quite ruthless enough to fire him if he did not pull his weight. She could not go on covering up much longer, and in any case, she was pretty sure that Darrington knew exactly what was going on. John had persistently underrated this man, and if he thought Darrington would stand aside while the place went downhill for lack of good management, he was miles out of his judgment.

Christmas Eve was a day of pale sunshine and quiet sea. Watching the boats riding gently in the harbour, Stella felt that her fears of the previous night were exaggerated. Probably the result of being tired after the hectic rush of the past weeks. Now she could relax. Everything that could be done to organise a happy Christmas for the visitors had been done. Now it was up to John and the rest of the staff. She always had Christmas Day off and returned to the hotel only for the dance on Boxing Night. It was silly to suppose that John did not know what he was doing. She should have more confidence in him. Under her arm was the parcel containing the white silk scarf she had bought him for Christmas. As she climbed up the winding cliff path, her spirits rose. She would see if John could escape down to the cove with her after lunch. Since Darrington's cutting remarks on the subject of their private affairs, John had taken care not to be caught on the wrong foot again. In fact, she had not been alone with him much since then.

She did not see him that morning until he dashed into the office just before lunch.

'Hullo, sweetheart. Anything for me?'

She discussed one or two items with him, then gave him his present, with which he was delighted. She had found an enormous box of chocolates from him beside her typewriter that morning and she thanked him appropriately, Darrington or no Darrington.

'Can't we lunch together and get away from the hotel for half an hour afterwards, John?'

'Sorry, pet. Booked to eat with Eileen while she's here. She hates eating on her own. But we'll slip away afterwards for a breath of air. O.K.?'

Waiting for him at the cliff edge that afternoon, Stella thought she had never seen the sea look so pearly. She could hardly hear the waves, they were breaking so gently. At the sound of a step, she turned to John with an eager smile.

'Sorry I'm late, Stella. Which way shall we go?'

'Down to the cove?'

'Not dressed for scrambling, ducky. Let's walk towards the golf course. Can't be long. What are you doing for Christmas?'

'Spending tomorrow with the Elmores. We shall try to make it an open-air day on Boxing Day, weather permitting. The men will play golf, and Cathie and I may go walking.'

'Will you be coming to the dance on Boxing Night?'

'Why, of course. I always do.'

'Well, things are different from what they always were, my dear. Don't be too much of a traditionalist.'

'But that's the only time at Christmas that we have a chance to be together, quite apart from the question of my being able to keep an eye on things.'

John shrugged his shoulders.

'That's Darrington's pigeon now, isn't it? Can't say I feel much interest in the place at present.'

'That's fairly obvious. Darrington might turn nasty, John, you know.'

'Let him.'

'Don't you want to stay on here now?'

'On my own terms. Don't worry your pretty little head, sweetheart, and don't be too conscientious. Let Darrington realise that running an hotel isn't all beer and skittles. Let him do the worrying. He might be more ready to sell the business then.'

'Go on.'

'Eileen . . . Mrs. Ridlow . . . likes this place. She'd be willing to buy, or she will be when I've shown her around a bit more and talked to her. She can afford to offer a good price to

Darrington. He probably won't turn down the chance of a quick profit, especially if the hotel is giving him a few headaches. He's never been in the business before, he knows nothing about running hotels and he doesn't particularly want to be saddled with the work. I could kick myself for selling when I did, but I've a strategic plan nicely worked out and I think I can bring it off. So don't be so darned efficient, my dear. I don't intend to be.'

'And if he dismisses you?'

'I don't think he'd dare, but if he did, Mrs. Ridlow could still make her offer and my services as manager would be at her disposal. Trust me, pet. I'm not at Darrington's mercy, as you seem to think. You're making a bogey of him.'

Stella was silent. To her, John's plan did not seem honest. A bargain was a bargain. While he accepted a salary as manager of the Cormorant, it seemed to her that he should execute his duties as well as he could. He read something of this in her expression, for he added firmly:

'I am under no obligation to our high and mighty Nick Darrington. He got this place cheap and gave me to understand that he was not interested in managing it himself. Now that he's poking his nose in and laying down the law, he can jolly well get on with it. I haven't forgotten how he spoke to me that morning. I don't take that from anybody.' Then he smiled swiftly. 'Leave it to me, dear, and don't look so solemn. This is Christmas Eve, and as soon as we're down in that hollow, I'm going to kiss you.'

And in the hollow, he effectively blotted out all thoughts of Darrington and the hotel. But in his arms, looking up at his confident face, she could not help wondering where she stood with him. For years they had been on close and affectionate terms, but he had never proposed an engagement. He seemed to take her friendship for granted, to enjoy kissing her, to assume a continuation of this kind of relationship indefinitely. In this day and age, one couldn't very well ask him what his intentions were, but there was something to be said for the old Victorian approach, she thought. She loved John and wanted to help him. She never held him off, for it was alien to her nature to entertain the idea of rationing herself. But lately, she had felt

40

uncertain, wishing desperately for reassurance that he loved her, refusing to see defects in his attitude and accusing herself of disloyalty for any doubts. But how long did he mean to go on using her without committing himself in any way? It was like being permanently out on hire, she thought, and then once again accused herself of disloyalty. With circumstances in such an unsettled state for him at present, with his own future uncertain until this clash with Darrington was resolved, it was unfair to expect him to commit himself.

They had sat down in the hollow, and John tightened his arm round her.

'I shouldn't bother to come to the dance on Boxing Night, sweetheart. I shall be pretty tied up with Mrs. Ridlow. I've got to make her happy. You understand that, don't you? She's our way out of this jam. I'm darned sorry I got us into it, but leave it to me to get us out.'

'All right. But would you be able to spare me two dances on Boxing Night?' she asked, holding him gently by the ears as she smiled up at him.

'I daresay I could manage that.'

'Then I shall come. You dance superbly.'

'And you always tempt me from my duty. Gold lights in your eyes, copper lights in your hair; there's a sort of incandescence about you that makes other women seem chilly and dim.'

'Would you be referring to Eileen?'

'Jealous?'

'No. Well, perhaps a teeny bit. She's very good-looking, John.'

'I know. And she's got money, too,' he teased. 'But she doesn't glow, like you. I prefer something warmer. She's a good sort, though. I think you'd like her. No fool, and knows what she wants. And she drives a car as well as I do.'

'Well, that's praise indeed.'

'In a mischievous mood, aren't you? I think I must stop your tongue.'

When at last he pulled her to her feet and they walked back to the hotel arm in arm, Stella felt completely reassured and happier than for weeks past. John had never been so loving, and their few jesting remarks about Eileen Ridlow had dispelled the little pang Stella had been trying to stifle since witnessing John's assiduous attentions in that quarter. She was a poor sort of person not to trust this man she had known and loved for so many years, she thought, as she squeezed his arm.

'A happy, happy Christmas, John dear. May the New Year bring you all you want.'

'Going to put your money on me against Darrington?'

'My money's always been on the Marbury stable.'

He chuckled.

'That's my girl.'

Darrington had given the permanent staff generous bonuses for Christmas, and when he looked in at the office just before Stella left that evening, he brushed aside her thanks with a smile and:

'You've earned it if anybody has. I hope you have a very happy Christmas.'

'Thank you. I shall be coming to the dance on Boxing Night. Mrs. Dacres may need an extra hand at the buffet.'

He was on his way to the lodge and Stella found herself walking down the drive with him. It struck her for the first time that his Christmas would be lonely, even if he was surrounded by hotel guests. The lodge extensions were not yet finished and he still lived in the hotel.

'This will be your first hotel Christmas, Mr. Darrington?'

'Yes. Can't say I'm very keen on it. But then I don't like organised fun very much. However, I shall take the opportunity of getting some writing done unless Marbury needs a hand.'

'He's very good at organising Christmas celebrations. You can safely leave them to him. It's rather dim, to work on your own on Christmas Day, though.'

He smiled.

'I may relent and indulge myself with some music.'

'I saw that you had a fine collection of records. What have you a taste for? Classical, I'd guess. I can't see you as a jazz fan. Or would it be opera?'

'Make a guess.'

'All right. I'd say orchestral, symphonic, favourite composer Beethoven.'

He laughed.

'A bull's-eye. I regard that as a compliment, Miss Verney. I thought that as far as you were concerned I was painted all black, but if you guess a liking for Beethoven you concede that I am not all savage, and there is some hope for me. I think I'd bracket Mozart with Beethoven. No. Perhaps a close second.'

'Now there you surprise me. I shouldn't have thought Mozart robust enough for you. He's the dilettante's composer, I'd say.'

'In certain moods, I find him blessedly refreshing. His music is so lucid and gay. Full of spirit, like you, since we're being personal.'

I'm doing well for compliments today, thought Stella. It must be the effect of Christmas. Good will and all that.

'Now I'm chalking up a good mark,' she said, smiling at him. 'How have you usually spent Christmases in the past?'

'When my mother was alive, we had the usual family gatherings. For the last five years I've been abroad at this time of the year.'

'I envy you your travels. I've never been abroad. Dad is such a bad traveller – air, sea or rail, it makes no difference. I'm afraid it's discouraged him. And I've never been able to afford to travel myself. I hope to, though, one day.'

'I don't know whether my kind of travelling would suit you. Rough going, often. Camping out. Well away from tourist routes.'

'In search of?'

'Peace, beauty, a little light on the past. Opportunities to see with new eyes. Time to think, to learn a little more of the world and a little more of oneself, too.'

'What my father calls coming out into the clear by escaping from the pressure of other people's personalities. I wouldn't mind roughing it, as long as there weren't too many insects. I don't mind those underfoot, but I can't bear things buzzing round me.'

'Let me know when you want a route planned. I'll guarantee to avoid the winged pests. Good night.'

'Good night, Mr. Darrington. A happy Christmas to you, with Beethoven and Mozart.'

43

It still seemed a lonely sort of Christmas, she thought, as he waved a hand and went into the lodge to inspect progress. The seasonal spirit must be working on her, too, for she felt that she almost liked the man. Whatever the outcome of the struggle for power between him and John, she would continue to do her job as conscientiously as she could. They must fight it out between them, and dearly as she wanted John to win, she hoped he would keep his weapons clean.

The lights of Ashcombe twinkled below her as she walked down the road to the cliff path. Remembering that stolen half-hour with John after lunch, her heart sang. It would all come right, she thought. Darrington would go off exploring again, John's friend, Mrs. Ridlow, would see the hotel as a good investment, John would be left to run it unchallenged, and he and Stella would live happily there ever after. Smiling at her childish optimism, yet still borne along on it, she ran down the twisting path to the harbour as though her feet were winged.

Chapter Five

THE dinner and dance at the Cormorant on Boxing Night was open to the public, and at the last minute the Elmore children decided to make up a small party and go. Stella, bearing in mind that John would not be available to her, was glad of the arrangement and telephoned him to reserve a table and put aside tickets for them. When she called at Brierley that evening, she found the household in its customary state of upheaval.

Midge, whose first grown-up dance this was, could scarcely contain herself and flew about pestering everybody for a decision on the problem of whether she should wear the rose at the neck of her white net dress or not. The dress had been a Christmas present from her mother and father, and Stella, witnessing this transformation from an untidy, gawky schoolgirl, realised that young Maud Ellen Elmore was going to be a beauty. She had the same blue eyes as Cathie, but her black hair curled and framed a vivacious heart-shaped face, which leaped at you instead of creeping up on you as Cathie's did. In a gym slip, with her unruly hair seldom mastered and long black stockings which were always giving her trouble, she was very much at the awkward stage, but tonight, her cheeks flushed with excitement and her eyes dancing, her coltishness concealed by the full skirt, the tight bodice with its wide neck and little puffed sleeves revealing a delicate figure instead of a badge-plastered box front, the sixteen-year-old Midge trembled on the threshold of maturity with delightful promise. Only her preoccupation with shoulder straps, with the question of whether the dress was a little low, whether the rose looked soppy, betrayed the child.

'You look a dream, Midge, and you want the rose there. It softens the line,' said Stella.

'Well, if you think so, that's all right,' said Midge, who, although she had emerged from the most painful stage of idealising Stella, her emotions having been diverted to a young man in the Public Library, nevertheless still considered Stella's opinion on dress worth all the rest of her family's put together.

'Thank goodness that's settled then,' said Jimmy, craning his chin while Cathie's deft fingers dealt with his bow tie.

'Who's pinched a shoe-lace out of my shoe?' demanded Mike, appearing on the scene for the first time. 'Hullo, Stella. Feeling in good form, I hope. You're the only one in this outfit who can dance. You, Jimmy?'

Mike examined his brother's large feet suspiciously.

'Why should I pinch a shoe-lace, my dear boy?'

'You did,' said Midge. 'At least, I heard you swear when you broke one this evening.'

'Hand over,' said Mike grimly.

'Wretched child. Oh, well, I'll have to use string.'

'You can't!' exclaimed Midge, horror-stricken, for she was at the stage of passionate conformity.

'Don't see why not.'

'You can take the lace out of mine,' said R.J. 'And don't forget to replace it.'

'O.K.,' said Jimmy. 'Is that our friend Roger at the door?

Cathie, my girl, I'm proud of you. You're winkling him out at last.'

'Ass,' said Cathie briefly, as she went to the door.

They had all been surprised when Cathie had said that Roger Thornton would be joining their party, for he was a reserved man who appeared to have no interest in social activities. Cathie attributed this to the fact that Roger's mother was an invalid and claimed much of his leisure time, but the Elmore family regarded him as a queer bird, more at home in his museum than in the world at large. Stella, not influenced by the Elmores' good-natured caution towards intellectual types, rather liked what little she had seen of Thornton and looked forward to learning more about him that evening. He was a tall, thin man, with a pale face, an aquiline nose, and a high forehead from which all but a peninsula of brown hair had receded. A sensitive face. Too sensitive, perhaps, for this world, thought Stella, as they shook hands, for he looked older than his thirty-five years.

'Come along, folk,' said Stella. 'We're going to be late.'

'Did you get any petrol this morning, Dad?' asked Jimmy.

Stella was not surprised when R.J. said that he'd forgotten all about it. Long experience with the Elmores had taught her that three able-bodied males in the family counted for nothing in the exigencies of daily life. The absence of fuse wire when the lights failed, of a bicycle pump when a tyre was punctured, of a key when nobody was at home and the reserve key hidden in the garage had been borrowed: these and dozens of similar cases had now made it seem inevitable to Stella that nothing in this house was where it should be, and that a malign fate ordained that crises should be for ever looming up on the Elmore domestic front, to be solved by the brilliant Elmore improvisation.

'Still,' said R.J. airily, 'you only need a pint or so to get you to the hotel. There'll be enough for that, I dare say.'

'What did the petrol gauge say?' asked Mike.

'Two gallons.'

'Then it's as good as dry. What about the can in the tool-shed for the motor-mower?'

'Of course,' said R.J., smiling expansively. 'I expect there's some in there.'

'Supposing it's wet and I have to walk. I'll ruin my dress,' moaned Midge.

But a small quantity of petrol was unearthed from the tool-shed, after which there was some argument about how they should pack into the Elmore car. It was fortunately capacious, although old, and with Roger in front with Jimmy, and Cathie, Midge and Mike in the back with Stella on Mike's lap, they were finally ready to go.

'Rear light on, Dad?' asked Jimmy.

'No.'

'Give it the works, will you?'

Stella did not know what this might imply, but Mr. Elmore seemed to be banging something behind them, and then his voice announced that all was well, and Jimmy let the clutch in. To Stella's surprise, the car started and they waved good-bye. More often than not, the battery had run down and they had to search for the starting handle.

Unversed in the diversity of life with the Elmores, Roger Thornton said gravely:

'Is it the bulb or the wiring, do you suppose?'

'What? Oh, the rear light,' said Jimmy. 'Dunno. Wiring, I expect. The old car's a bit ribby.'

'You know,' observed Stella, 'I should have thought accountants would have tidy, efficient minds. Do you Elmores fudge accounts as crazily as you fudge the everyday mechanics of life?'

'Exact to the last digit,' said Mike. 'Efficiency is our watch-word. We leave the Inland Revenue gasping at our amazing and intricate knowledge of tax law. But, Stella, dear heart, we must relax sometimes. Where better than in the bosom of our family?'

'You're hopeless,' said Cathie. 'All of you. Mother and I gave you up years ago.'

'How nice and supple you feel, Stella. I'm so glad you don't encase yourself in bones. I can't stand grasping a waist that feels like a bird-cage,' said Mike.

'Couldn't feel worse than your knees,' said Stella blithely. 'It's like sitting on a fence. Oh, no, Mike, angel, don't tickle

47

me. I'll ruin my dress. You have a lovely lap any girl would be glad to sit on.'

Laughing and chattering, they turned into the hotel drive. There was a light in the lodge, and Stella wondered whether Darrington would put in an appearance that evening.

They were a little late and dinner was under way when Stella led them to their table. John was at Eileen Ridlow's table and waved a hand to Stella as she settled her flock. She saw Darrington slip in a few minutes later.

'Ah, there's Nick,' said Roger Thornton.

'Does he know you're here tonight?' asked Stella, who was sitting next to him.

'Yes. Cathie and I met him when we were walking across the golf course on Christmas morning. That was when the subject of this dance came up.'

'It was Nick who persuaded him to come, after I'd appealed to him for help,' said Cathie from the other side. 'I think it was only the bribery of photographs of Nick's last expedition that clinched it. I've a nasty feeling that Roger's going to disappear with Nick for most of the evening.'

'Well, I'm not much of a dancer, Cathie, as you know. Anyway, you're as interested in seeing the photographs as I am.'

'Yes. Nick's such a good talker when he's on the subject of exploring. I get caught up in his enthusiasm.'

Stella, remembering his broadcast, could appreciate this, but she had not realised that Cathie was on such friendly terms with Darrington.

'Have you seen the photographs, Stella?'

'No. Ours is a strictly business footing.'

'Still sparring?' asked Cathie, her eyes twinkling.

'Not exactly,' said Stella doubtfully. 'At least, not at the moment.'

There was a smile on Roger's thin face as he said:

'He's the best chap in the world, but not to spar with. Sooner have him on my side than against me.'

'That's no reason for letting him get away with everything he chooses. That will only encourage him to be a dictator.'

'Oh, I don't think there's any danger of that. Nick's a reasoning creature. He has a trained mind and can be more

48

objective than anybody I know. Dictators are hundred per cent subjective.'

'You can't expect Stella to feel favourably inclined towards the man who has supplanted her John,' broke in Jimmy.

'Ah, now, that *is* being subjective,' said Roger, but with such a kind expression in his brown eyes that Stella could not take offence.

'No, I don't really think I'm letting that prejudice me. I can see that would be unfair. But in a way, I suppose I've always been spoiled here. I do find Mr. Darrington's rule rather less comfortable. He's very appreciative and fair. I grant you that. But . . . Well, perhaps I'm not very good at taking orders and he's superlatively good at giving them. Just a matter of temperament,' said Stella airily, but not quite sure that this simple explanation went deep enough.

She turned to Midge, who was registering distaste at her first experience of wine.

'Don't you like it, Midge?'

'Not a bit what I expected. It's such a lovely colour and sounds so exciting. Wait a minute. I'll try again.'

Midge shuddered.

'It's no use. I don't like it. I do think that's disappointing.'

'Rather have a ginger beer?'

Midge hesitated. She felt she would be losing face by preferring ginger beer. It was incredible to her that something that she had been led to believe was so lovely and exciting, a symbol, almost, of the forbidden joys of the world of grown-ups,, should turn out to be so disagreeable. She hoped all the other entrancing prospects wouldn't turn out to be such a sell. She gave in, thus scoring an early victory for honest thinking.

'Yes, please. I shall never like this. I can't help it.'

'Think no more of it, my child,' said Mike, annexing her glass, and signalling to the waiter.

Darrington came over to their table while they were drinking their coffee, and was introduced to Midge, the only member of the party he had not met. His manner with the child was perfect: neither patronising nor facetious. And when he asked her for the first dance, waiting until the floor was comfortably filled, stars shone out of her eyes as she stood up. That was nice of him, thought Stella as she watched him waltz away. She hadn't credited him with so much sensibility. Then Mike claimed her and she gave herself up to the joy of dancing. She caught a glimpse of Midge chattering away to her partner as they passed, and wondered why it was only she who found Darrington so formidable. He had obviously won Midge's confidence without the slightest difficulty. She wondered what they were talking about, for she saw Darrington smiling at something Midge said . . .

'Maud Ellen. Can you think of any more awful names?' asked Midge.

'Gladys Violet,' said Darrington, avoiding a portly lady with skill.

'M'm. They're pretty bad. Anyway, that's why I'm called Midge. When you come to think of it, I suppose that's really not a very nice name, but it's sort of handy.'

'I like it. Friendly. Do you like dancing?'

'Yes. But this is my first dance. It's very exciting coming to such a lovely hotel as this. I'm sorry.'

'My fault. The gentleman in front is steering a rather erratic course. Ah, that's better, he's giving it up. Or rather, his wife's dragging him off. I'm glad you like my hotel.'

'Oh I do. I think it's super. And how lovely this room looks with all the decorations.'

'That's Miss Verney's work. She did all the hotel decorations.'

'Stella's awfully clever at anything like that. She did a most lovely arrangement of flowers for Mummy's wedding anniversary. She's got an artistic eye. That's why she always looks so nice. You know, just right,' said Midge, earnestly, still a little conscious of shoulder-straps and the fact that the rose had slipped a little to one side. Stella's rose would never have slipped.

'I agree,' said Darrington gravely. 'I suppose, being the youngest, you have quite a tough time of it, holding your own.'

'Two brothers, and Dad. And, of course, everybody tries to boss me. Cathie says that's an ugly word, but I can't think of another one that means what I mean. Oh, I *do* hope we have an encore,' said Midge, clapping vigorously.

Her wish was granted and they circled happily round the room, until her partner brought the dance to an end with a triumphant whirl.

'Oh, that was lovely. Thank you, Mr. Darrington.'

He smiled at her heartfelt thanks, and she said quickly: 'Oh, should I have said that? Anyway, it *was* lovely, and I don't see why I shouldn't say thank you.'

'I'm highly gratified. Not being a very good dancer, I'm not at all sure that I give my partners pleasure unless they're kind enough, like you, to say so.'

'I think you're a very good dancer.'

'Well, I'm not so bad at a waltz. A pretty poor performer at anything else, though.'

'I wish this evening would go ever so slowly,' said Midge, 'so that I could feel every minute.'

The eyes in the vivid face turned to his were the colour of sapphires.

'You know,' said Darrington, 'I think we ought to put you on top of the Christmas tree. But that wouldn't be much fun, would it?'

She shook her head, then added, a little breathlessly:

'I suppose . . . Could I come and see your photographs this evening? I know you're going to show them to Cathie and Mr. Thornton. I would love to see them. It must be so thrilling to be an explorer.'

'And miss some dances?'

'Well, I wouldn't mind missing one or two.'

'Righto. Come along with pleasure,' he said as he escorted her to her seat.

'Thank you. Thank you very much.'

As he smiled and walked away, Midge's eyes followed him, and somehow just then the young man in the Public Library seemed a very pale figure.

For Stella, the evening was dimmed by John's absence, for by the time the interval arrived she had still not spoken to him. She did not lack partners, with Jimmy and Mike looking after her, but she could not stifle a little ache at the sight of John

51

and Mrs. Ridlow dancing every dance together and keeping to themselves. She was aware, too, that John's absence could not fail to be remarked by her friends, who looked on Marbury as Stella's fiancé, although there was no engagement. Their friendship was so long-standing that the Stella-John combination was now taken for granted. She felt unable to explain the business aspect of John's attentions to Mrs. Ridlow, and, indeed, could not see that John's plans demanded such close personal attention to the prospective buyer. At any moment, she felt, one of the Elmores was going to ask her what John was playing at, and she just did not know what to say. Nothing in her gay manner, however, hinted at these uncertainties, and she welcomed Darrington's invitation to her to come to his sitting-room with the others to see his photographs.

It was cosy in that book-lined room with the blazing fire, and they soon became immersed in the photographs while their host dispensed sherry and information when required. The photographs were enlargements from a miniature camera, and revealed that Darrington was a very good photographer. There were few personal photographs: one of a group of five men fording a river, one of a wiry little man in shorts carrying an odd-looking case, who was plant collector and botanist of the expedition, and one of Darrington, pipe in mouth, looking very workmanlike studying a map outside a tent. The rest were photographs of landscape and rock formations, many of them very beautiful.

When they had seen them all, Stella picked out the photograph of that small tent pitched in the valley enclosed by mountains, and studied it again. How wonderful, she thought, to wake up in the morning to that solitary, beautiful world; to watch the sun rise over the mountains to flood the valley; to watch the moon and the stars take its place at the close of day. She was so absorbed that the room ceased to exist for her and she was not conscious of Roger, Cathie and Midge going until Darrington's voice said:

'What are you thinking?' and she realised that they were alone.

'Of some lines of Wordsworth.'

'Tell me.'

> ' "The silence that is in the starry sky,
>   The sleep that is among the lonely hills." '

She still gazed at the photograph, as though it held her in a spell. She was sitting on a low fire-side chair, the turquoise chiffon of her skirt billowing over the sheep-skin hearthrug, the firelight dancing across sequined shoulder straps and bent head, burnishing her hair to copper. Darrington said nothing. The convex mirror on the wall reflected a miniature picture of the girl by the fire lost in a world conjured up by the photograph on her lap, and the man leaning against the mantelpiece looking down at her. The only sounds in the room were the fluttering of the flames and the ticking of the clock, but Stella was not conscious of the passage of time.

Then a piece of coal fell out on to the hearth and she looked up to find Darrington's eyes on her. The magic world of mountains and sun and stars vanished, and she was on the instant back in the world of complex personal relationships. There was something compelling about the quality of that scrutiny and she found it difficult to turn aside and find some trivial remark to dispel an atmosphere suddenly charged with significance. Then he helped her by smiling and holding out his hand for the photograph.

'I wonder if that is your Samarkand.'

It seemed to her that there was an unspoken challenge in his words, and she tried to free herself from this pregnant web which she could not but think was spun by her own fancy.

'I didn't realise the others had gone. Were Beethoven and Mozart good company for you yesterday?'

'Very good, thank you. I had the pleasure of meeting your father on the golf course this morning. He was trouncing Mr. Elmore with great urbanity.'

'They're very old rivals. Dad didn't tell me that he'd met you, but then he immersed himself in his Greek translation this afternoon and hadn't emerged when I left this evening. He was supposed to be attending a gathering of cronies at the Elmores' tonight, but he's quite likely to forget the time and only come in at the death.'

53

'Beethoven or ancient Greece or lonely mountains. There are many escapes.'

'Many golden roads,' she said, smiling as they returned to the dance floor.

'This is a waltz. As I've already explained to Midge, it's the only modern dance I can perform adequately, so may I have the pleasure?'

Stella found him a comfortable partner and they danced well enough together to make talking an intrusion. She noticed above one of his eyes a crescent-shaped scar and wondered how he had got it. A fraction nearer and his eye would have been injured. Exploring wasn't all peace and beauty, she thought, conscious of the firmness of the arm holding her.

John came up to her for the next dance, a tango, and greeted the Elmores with his usual gay charm. In evening dress, his fair good looks were seen at their best. It was no good, thought Stella, as his long stride merged beautifully with hers, you could not be cross with anybody who looked so superb and danced so beautifully as John Marbury.

' "Jealousy". Our favourite,' he said with a smile.

'M'm. Don't talk.'

As dancers, they were perfectly matched, moving as one, and there were many eyes on them as they danced the tango that evening, although Stella was unaware of anything but their unison with the slow throb of the music.

'Lovely,' he said after the encore. 'Never found any partner to suit me as well as you do, my dear. Something to do with those nice long legs.'

'Glad to hear it. Organisation has worked well tonight, John. People really look as though they're enjoying themselves.'

'M'm. Come over and meet Eileen. She's an important star in our firmament just now.'

'And a very bright one.'

'Unfortunately she doesn't dance as well as she drives. She teeters.'

'Too bad. We can't be expected to pass your high standards in all subjects, though.'

Eileen Ridlow wore an oyster satin dress, beautifully cut to outline her slender figure, and the stones blazing at her neck must be diamonds, thought Stella, as John said:

'Eileen, may I introduce my assistant, Miss Verney? She's helped to run the Cormorant a good many years and knows as much about the job as I do. Stella, Mrs. Ridlow.'

'I've certainly taken a liking to this hotel, Miss Verney. I think it's a shame John had to sell it.'

'Yes, so do I.'

'If I'd known, I'd have been only too glad to come in as a partner. I've a lot of friends, and with a big publicity campaign and some capital to spend on a decent cocktail bar and a swimming pool, tennis courts, things to attract more young people, I reckon we could have made a good business out of this.'

It always was a good business in the past, without any more attractions, thought Stella, but she said pleasantly:

'I'm sure you could. I certainly feel that the Cormorant should be in Marbury hands. It was an unpleasant shock to me when John told me that he'd sold it.'

'But one can't live on family sentiment,' said John lightly. 'Still, I agree that the present ownership is not to my taste. I made a blunder there. Maybe we can put that right. By the way, Stella, I shan't be here after ten tomorrow morning. I'll make out the accounts of the departures before I go, but will you do the necessary? Twelve are leaving tomorrow, all before lunch, as far as I know.'

'Right.'

And then the band struck up a quickstep and Mrs. Ridlow looked at John. There was a proprietary air about that look which Stella found disquieting. She imagined Mrs. Ridlow to be about thirty. She had neat, regular features, silky ash-blonde hair and light blue eyes that regarded the world with disconcerting coolness. She had the poise and assurance that grow with wealth, and the assessing eyes of a person whose judgment was based on monetary standards. She nodded with a faint smile at Stella as she and John moved off together. A little smile of dismissal.

And that was the only contact which Stella had with John that evening. He had promised that they should have two dances together, and when the last waltz came, she refused Jimmy on the plea of being booked with John, but, sitting alone, she saw John and Eileen Ridlow waltz by her without a glance in her direction. She apologised to Jimmy afterwards.

'Sorry, Jimmy. John forgot, after all.'

'John's forgotten quite a lot this evening, old girl, hasn't he?' observed Jimmy.

'Oh, he explained to me that he'd have to look after one of the guests tonight.'

'A nice blonde. Let me know if you'd like me to punch his head. Always willing to oblige, you know.'

Stella smiled.

'Thanks, pal, but it's not necessary. Hullo, Midge. You've made a conquest of Mr. Darrington. I don't need to ask if the evening has come up to your expectations.'

'It's been heavenly. And I've danced four dances with Mr. Darrington, and that's more than he danced with anybody else, and *he's* head of all this,' said Midge, indicating all this with a sweeping gesture of her arm which narrowly missed a tray of glasses a waiter was carrying.

'Yes, he's the man at the top,' said Stella, and then they all linked hands as the band played Auld Lang Syne.

Chapter Six

THE first two months of the year were the quietest in the hotel calendar and during that time, improvements and decorations were completed and decks cleared for the summer season, to which Easter acted as a dress rehearsal. The new garages were finished by the end of February, and a week later Darrington moved his quarters to the lodge, now so much improved that it bore little resemblance to the old structure.

During those weeks, Stella had spent little of her leisure time with John, who disappeared to London whenever he could find the time, presumably to see Mrs. Ridlow. In business hours, their contacts were on the surface as friendly and warm as ever, but Stella felt that beneath that bridge of fair words and brief caresses, a gulf was yawning. There was nothing definite to substantiate her fears, only the feeling that beneath the surface John was deeply preoccupied with matters which he did not choose to share with her. Time and again she made up her mind to ask him where they stood, but when the moment came, she allowed his charm to steer her from it.

She was walking across the lawn after lunch one day in early March, pondering how best to tackle John about the shifting sand on which she felt she stood with him, when she saw Darrington helping young Bryant across the lawn. She ran across to them and saw that there was a deep gash on the boy's forehead and the sleeve of his coat was ripped up, revealing a badly bruised and grazed arm.

'He fell down the cliff. Nothing serious, I think, but he's half stunned. Better telephone Doctor Collarton. I'll clean him up at the lodge, but I think this gash may need stitching.'

The boy lurched, and without more ado Darrington picked him up and carried him to the lodge while Stella ran to the telephone. The doctor was there within quarter of an hour and confirmed that there was no serious damage. After he had dealt with the gash, he volunteered to drive the boy home and have a word with his mother, for Bryant lived close to the doctor's surgery.

Stella was dividing her attention between writing out cheques and drinking her tea when Darrington came into her room.

'I've just been to have a look at that cliff path young Bryant came to grief on. He was lucky to escape so lightly.'

'How exactly did it happen?'

'He slipped on the rocky stretch and went tumbling down until he fetched up against a hummock of bracken. If it hadn't been for that, he'd have fallen straight on to the rocks, which wouldn't have been at all funny.'

'No. Poor kid. He's going to feel pretty sore for weeks, I guess. It was lucky that you were walking along there and saw him. Otherwise he might be there now.'

'Yes. He told me that you use that track.'

'Yes. Old Marbury had it cut down to the cove, but it's getting worn away rather badly.'

'Have you used it lately?'

'Yes. Last week.'

'Are you the only person who uses it?'

'As far as I know. I think one or two children have been known to scramble down there in the summer, but I don't know anybody else who uses it. Bryant's never been down there before, I'm sure. It's not safe enough for children now.'

'It's not safe enough for you, either. From now on, that track's not to be used. Can't risk any more accidents.'

'Oh, but that's absurd,' said Stella quickly. 'I know every foot of the track. There's no risk for me.'

'Nevertheless, first-class rock climber though you may be, it's out of bounds. That boy might have broken his neck on the rocks. And every time it rains, more earth is washed off the track. Do you want me to sign those?' he added, drawing a chair up to the desk.

'Yes, please. I've one more to write out.'

She was conscious of her hand trembling under his gaze as she wrote out the cheque, for she was a little edgy these days, and his arbitrary manner was like a rough hand on an aching tooth. She attached the cheque to the account and passed it to him in silence, finishing her tea while he looked at the accounts and added his signature to the cheques.

'Right.'

He pushed back the chair and stood looking down at her flushed face.

'I mean what I say about that track, Miss Verney. It's not to be used by anybody. Understand?'

'I could hardly fail to,' she said icily.

The next day, walking along the cliff in the rubber plimsolls which she kept for the climb, she found that barbed wire had been laid over the rough steps down the first vertical drop on to the track. There was no getting round it, and without the aid of those steps, it was impossible to get to the track. Stella looked down at the cove below, solitary and peaceful in the thin spring sunshine, and was so angry at being deprived of her retreat that she hardly knew how to contain herself. She looked round the cliff face, but it was too sheer to offer any alternative route. Darrington had effectively put the cove out of reach.

A moment's rational thought would have convinced her of the danger of an encounter with Darrington while she was in this mood of angry frustration, but rational thought was as far off as the moon at the moment, and when on striding back to the hotel she met him in the drive on his way to the lodge, she could not let him pass.

'I've just been along the cliff, Mr. Darrington. You have no right to bar people from that cove. You don't own it, or me.'

Darrington's eyebrows shot up.

'But I own access to it. I could put a fence all along the boundary of the hotel grounds a foot from the cliff, but I think the method I chose is less likely to detract from the beauty of the grounds.' He looked at her shoes. 'You intended going down that track today?'

'Yes.'

'I rather gathered yesterday that you had no intention of abiding by my ban. Good afternoon, Miss Corrington,' he added as that lady passed by.

'Good afternoon, Mr. Darrington. A touch of spring in the air today, I fancy.'

'Yes, indeed.' His eyes came back to Stella's stormy face. 'I could almost fancy it tropical,' he added.

'If I care to risk my neck, it is absolutely no business of yours,' declared Stella.

'Well, I suggest that we adjourn to the lodge. I don't think the drive is a convenient place for a row.'

He followed her into his study.

'Now, Miss Verney, let's get this straight. I am responsible for the safety of my employees on my premises. There has already been one accident on that track, and I tried it out myself and found it quite tricky. If I say it's unsafe and not to be used, that goes.'

'You have no right –'

'I have every right, and if you weren't in such a flaming

temper, you'd admit it. It shouldn't be necessary to remind you that I'm in authority here. I fancy, though, that's an unpleasant fact which you've never really in your heart accepted. You'd better go away and cool off. You might like to discuss the matter again with me when you've had time to reflect on your extraordinary conduct. To say that it's childish is letting you off very lightly.'

'Oh, you're impossible,' said Stella. 'I've lived here all my life, climbed those cliffs since I was a child. I know every inch of them. Why should you, an outsider, come in and lay down the law on where I can go?'

'Because I happen to own the hotel and its grounds; because you are my employee, and because access to that particular part of the cliffs is under my jurisdiction. You have miles of cliffs to enjoy as you choose.'

'But there's no other way to that cove.'

He shrugged his shoulders.

'That's a pity. But this coast has plenty of coves that are accessible.'

'But . . . '

She stopped. How explain to him what that cove meant to her? Put in words, it would sound foolish, even if she felt calm enough to try to analyse her feelings about it. Darrington was standing by the mantelpiece filling his pipe, unmoved and unyielding. As well try to argue with the sea. She left him without another word. When she arrived back in her office, she found John there.

'How now, sweeting? You look put out.'

'Our boss has decreed that the cliff path down to the cove is dangerous and forbidden, as though we're all a pack of children. Laying down the law like a policeman.'

'Too bad. I find him a bit irksome myself, but have patience, my dear. We'll get him out yet.'

'It's his quiet arrogance that gets me. Oh, I could . . . '

Stella slapped a file down on her desk, unable to decide what she could do to Darrington to satisfy her outraged feelings. John looked down at her with bright eyes.

'You look attractive when you're in a paddy. If you really want to get your own back, why don't you wait until the summer season is on us, and then give in your notice? That would put his nibs in a jam.'

'Leave the Cormorant? Oh no, not while you're here, John. You wouldn't really want me to, would you?'

When he saw the puzzled expression on her face, he shrugged his shoulders and laughed.

'Oh, it was just an idea. You're too efficient, Stella. I'm out to persuade Darrington that running an hotel is not his pigeon, but you don't help by being so good at the job. After all, why should you put yourself out for a man who orders you about like a naughty child?'

'As long as I accept a salary for doing this job, I shall do it as well as I'm able, John. If I don't want the job, I shall resign at once. Whatever Darrington is, he's straight and I shall be straight with him.'

'All right, sweetheart. Don't be so serious. I was only joking. But you do want to help me get this place back, don't you?'

'Of course I do. But if Mrs. Ridlow does buy it from Darrington, will it be any more yours then?'

'Yes. We should go into partnership. You don't have to worry about that, pet. The only problem is getting Darrington to sell.'

'Do you think he's the sort of man to give up easily? I don't.'

'When his pocket's hit, he'll be as eager to cut his losses as the rest of us. Money, Stella, always has the final word in this wicked world, but you're a child in such matters, and a very nice one, too. Leave it to me.'

Stella twiddled her pencil, then looked up at him.

'John, where do we stand these days? I never see anything of you outside of business hours. If . . . you're tired of our friendship, if you just want to keep things on a pleasant business footing and forget that it's ever been anything more, then please say so. I would much prefer you to be honest about it than to leave me guessing.'

John sat on the corner of her desk and picked up her hand.

'Stella, my dear, how can I commit myself about the future when that future is so uncertain? I've a hell of a lot at stake just now. I've simply got to concentrate on pulling it off. All

61

personal considerations have to be put aside until I know whether this partnership with Mrs. Ridlow can be brought off. Surely you can see how important that aspect is to a man? I want your co-operation and patience and understanding.'

Somehow, he had managed to put her in the wrong. Making it seem as though she was hanging round his neck, trying to distract him from matters of vital importance to his future. But all she wanted, she thought, was some assurance that he loved her, that he was not amusing himself with her when he was in the mood, that he planned a future which embraced them both. That assurance was something she had never had in words from him, although in the past his attentions had surely justified her in assuming as much. His father had taken it for granted that they would marry and had told Stella how happy he was in John's choice. But perhaps she was being unreasonable in taxing him now when his affairs were in such an unsettled state. He would never submit to being an employee of Darrington's for long. That much had become clear. If Darrington refused to sell the business, John would leave the Cormorant and plan his life differently. Was it fair to expect a man to propose marriage when his affairs were at such a critical stage and demanded all his attention and skill in negotiation? The last role she wished to play was the tiresome little woman demanding attention. She smiled up at him.

'Of course, John. I understand. This must be a very worrying time for you. Forgive me. I'm just being silly.'

'You're never silly, sweetheart. Just back me up, that's all. Let's assume that our stumbling block is safely stowed away in the lodge, shall we?'

He ran his hand over her throat and tilted her head up. She wondered why, when he kissed her, she felt as though something inside her was wincing.

'By the way,' he added lightly, as he stood up, 'Darrington said he thought you had too much to do and as Bryant won't be coming back, he thinks you should have a typist in the office to help you. I suggested that we waited until after Easter, anyway. Told him you weren't keen on the idea and promised I'd take a bit more of the office work over from you. We don't want an outsider barging in on us, darling, do we? Spoil everything. Have to be horribly business-like then.'

She seized on this evidence of warmth eagerly.

'No, I don't want anybody sharing this office. I can cope, anyway.'

'Well, I tell you what I'll do. You've got rather a lot on your plate, I know. I'll sort the post first thing in the morning and take out anything that I can deal with myself. I've been shoving it all on to you, but I realise now that you've too much on your plate. You're showing signs of overdoing it, you know. Even the old devil himself has noticed it. And I can't have my supporter falling by the wayside. It's no use asking you to be less conscientious. I've tried that. So yours truly will do a little office work for a change. My typing, although of the two-fingered variety, isn't at all bad. O.K.?'

'O.K.'

'Good. We'll start the new routine tomorrow. I shall be at my desk sharp at nine, so mind you're not a minute later than nine-thirty in future, Miss Verney.'

'And if I am?'

'You'll pay a forfeit. I must go. The man's installing that dish-washing machine this afternoon, and I have to go into conference with Mrs. Dacres before he starts work. She views the whole contraption with suspicion. Not a very progressive soul, I fear. So long.'

'So long,' said Stella.

'How about coming for a spin on Sunday afternoon? Tea at the farmhouse at Coombe?'

'Lovely.'

'Right. I'll call for you at two-thirty.'

*　　*　　*

Stella, agonising over the weather on Sunday morning, saw the clouds break soon after eleven and felt her spirits soar dizzily with the sun. She flew round the house with a duster, prepared the vegetables for Nan, whose arthritis was troubling her that morning, and then went into the garden with two bowls of fading flowers. She found her father at the potting bench re-potting some of their indoor plants.

'Clear a corner for me, darling,' she said.

'Going to be a nice day, after all. May get that round of golf with R.J. this afternoon, if he hasn't embarked on an ambitious programme of carpentry. Since he bought that cheap lot of wood from Manning's when they closed down, there's no holding him.'

'I know. He's fitting the whole house out with window boxes and Cathie says none of them has a clue about growing anything, and that old curmudgeon who keeps the garden tidy has no time for such fancy trimmings.'

'We shall doubtless be receiving some very interesting examples of wood handicraft for presents,' said Mr. Verney in his precise, pedantic manner as he tapped a pot and neatly extracted the trailing plant.

'Aren't the crocuses a picture this year? It was just right scattering them under the trees like that.'

'Yes. What are you going to rob me of now?'

'Polyanthuses, dear. Lovely smell after the rain. I love the spring.'

Stella went off down the garden, trug in hand, feeling as though she walked on air. She had dismissed those odd moments of uneasiness which certain remarks of John had called up recently. She took his words too seriously. He had always been a lively joker. He hadn't really meant what he said about her leaving Darrington in the lurch. It was just a squib of an idea tossed off without thought, much as she had played with the idea of fixing a rope at the top of the cliff just to defy Darrington's ban. Foolish ideas springing like mushrooms from childish anger. She supposed some time she would have to apologise to Darrington for blazing out at him like that. In her present benign mood, she could do it with ease and dignity. The trouble was, when she saw him she always felt the need to be on guard, not to yield an inch. He was right, she thought ruefully. She had never really accepted him as the man in authority. Even now, she felt that the hotel was John's.

As she snipped off the polyanthus flowers, their rich colours glowing against the wet leaves, Stella was remembering the first time she and John had driven to Coombe and had tea at the farmhouse. After tea, they had walked along by the river. She was eighteen and had been working at the Cormorant for six months. John had just come down from Cambridge and was starting to learn his father's job. And that afternoon when they sat down on the river bank, John had kissed her for the first time, and she had fallen in love with him. The handsome, lively young man had come into her quiet life at Ashcombe like a meteor. At an unsophisticated eighteen, she hadn't stood a chance. And although some of the meteor-like glory had vanished in the every-day business of the hotel, there had never been anybody else, and John Marbury was still a shining torch in her life, except that now there was that thin layer of fear in her mind that threatened to dim it. Away with minds, she thought. It's the heart that matters. And that morning her heart sang untroubled.

She was ready and waiting by quarter past two. Another glance in the mirror confirmed the success of the new tweed suit. It was neither blue nor green, but the colour of the sea on a sunny day. She had paid more for it than she could afford, but was unrepentant. At twenty minutes to three she walked to the gate. Church Lane was quiet in the spring sunshine, a picture of Sunday afternoon somnolence. Nan's voice came down the path.

'The telephone, Miss Stella.'

It was John's voice, explaining that he couldn't get away, after all. An unexpected influx of visitors.

'Sorry, old dear. But you know how it is. No time is ever your own in this job.'

'Of course, John. Never mind.'

As she hung up the receiver and stared blankly at the bowl of polyanthuses on the hall table, she knew that one of the unexpected visitors to the Cormorant would be Eileen Ridlow. Her father came out of the dining-room, a newspaper tucked under his arm.

'Anything wrong, dear?'

Stella recovered herself.

'No, Dad. John can't manage this afternoon. Unexpected arrivals at the hotel. I think I'll go for a walk, all the same. I'll give Cathie a ring and see if she'd like to come.'

'Good idea,' said her father, disappearing into the sitting-room.

She had to get out of the house, and she didn't want to be alone with her thoughts. Cathie's calm voice was as good as a life-belt. They arranged to meet at the end of the lane.

'Grand afternoon,' said Cathie.

'M'm. River, cliffs or the heath?'

'It'll be wet by the river after this morning's rain. Let's try the heath. Haven't been that way for a long time.'

They walked across the cricket green, turned away from the river and were soon crossing the sandy stretch of heather and gorse which showed only muted greens and browns now, but which would blaze into a purple and gold glory in the summer. Puffy white clouds sailed across the blue sky, and as they swung along, some of the tension went out of Stella. Cathie pointed out one or two birds, told Stella about the nesting activities that were apparent in their garden. That was the best of Cathie, thought Stella. She was blessed with rare sensibility, and handled other people's feelings with the gentlest of hands, soothing them with her own serenity and never approaching a tender spot unless invited. She would make no reference to John. She had known that Stella was going to Coombe with him, and Stella had explained briefly on the telephone that he hadn't been able to get away from the hotel. But Cathie would not refer to it again.

'Is Midge still in the throes of love-sickness?' asked Stella. 'I haven't seen her since she asked me to take a snap of Darrington with her camera when he wasn't looking.'

Cathie laughed.

'I think it's waning a little from lack of food. Most of her walks take her past the Cormorant these days, I think, but she's only managed to see Nick once since the Boxing Night dance. I'm afraid young Ken Brewer in the Public Library is swimming back into favour on account of being easy of access. She's at that stage. A bit of a handful.'

'With those looks, it couldn't be otherwise. She's going to dent some hearts, I know.'

'Are you getting on any better with her hero?'

'At the moment we are not on speaking terms,' said Stella grimly, and recounted the trouble about the cliff path.

'Well, dear,' said Cathie, 'I don't want to take sides, but

as I really do prefer you with sound limbs and it would grieve me to be pushing you along in a bath chair, I think I'm with Nick on this.'

'Traitor,' said Stella, smiling. 'He's got round you. I don't know how. You were calling him by his Christian name within five minutes of meeting him.'

'Roger knows him so well and we were introduced like that. But I like him, very much. I know what riles you about him. But I think if you'd met him in any other circumstances, his stand-no-nonsense quality wouldn't bother you.'

'Well, the situation at the Cormorant wasn't of my choosing, and I can't say I like it. Somehow, everything's changed since old Mr. Marbury died. The whole atmosphere is different and I find I'm floundering in it,' said Stella unhappily.

'You'll find your feet again in time.'

'Do you think people change, fundamentally, Cathie? Once they're adult, I mean.'

Cathie thought a moment, then said firmly:

'No, I don't think they do. Might get harder, perhaps. More sceptical. Time can do that. But the basic character is constant, I think. Whether you're up against it or whether things run your way can throw into emphasis certain strengths or weaknesses, that's all. But I think they're there all the time.'

It was hard, thought Stella, to accept the fact that somebody whose integrity you had believed in as surely as you believed that the sun would rise every morning, was not to be trusted. And what value was there in any personal relationship without integrity? She wrenched her thoughts away from John to the simpler proposition of Nick Darrington. Why simpler, she wondered, and then realised that he, without question, was a person of integrity, however much his autocratic ways irked her, so that the issues between them were straightforward. He belonged to Cathie's class of integrity. Stella knew this implicitly with her mind. Her belief in John had its roots in her heart, and nourished by his charm, brought to flower by the fact that she had fallen in love with him at eighteen and had seen him ever since through dazzled eyes. Now, against her will, she was seeing him clearly, and her heart ached for her own lost illusions while her mind accused her of cowardice for clinging to them so long.

'I'm going to hate not having that cove to turn to. It's my haven in all the troubles at the hotel. In a strange way, I can find peace there however burned up I feel. It's all very well for people like you, Cathie, who carry peace inside them, but I don't, and I have to find it where I can. That cove was my own secret oasis. But what's the use of explaining that to Darrington?'

'I should think he's one of the few people who would understand, but I guess you only blazed away instead of explaining.'

'Right, Cathie. That's the worst of one's friends. They know you too well. But I'm not going to Nick Darrington with tears in my eyes, explaining my childish little weakness for that cove. I'm not giving an inch to that man, however you and Midge dote on him.'

'Bless your fiery heart,' said Cathie, her eyes brimming with laughter, 'how I'd love to see you two stalking each other. I'm only suggesting that a milder approach might win more ground.'

'Could be. I felt mild this morning, but I don't feel so benevolent this afternoon. Pay no heed to my contrariness, Cathie.'

'I can't help?'

'You do help, by being you. I'm glad you were able to come to my rescue this afternoon. I rather thought you might be booked with Roger.'

'Roger has gone to the lodge to have a nice cosy talk with Nick about metamorphic and plutonic rocks. It seems, Stella, that you and I are just stand-bys,' said Cathie lightly, but Stella fancied that there was a hint of unhappiness in Cathie's eyes, too, at that moment.

'It's a rôle that can pall after years of it,' said Stella. 'A hot-water bottle on chilly days, pushed on the shelf when it's warm.'

Cathie smiled as she said,

'Well, I suggest the two hot-water bottles get replenished with tea. That cottage used to produce a decent

68

pot and it appears to be open.'

'Good idea. Let's rule out the subject of men. They spoil the afternoon.'

And they did.

Chapter Seven

STELLA found the post already sorted when she arrived in her office the next morning, and there were only a few letters left on her desk for her to deal with. She had heard a typewriter clicking in John's room as she came by. If he was going to type some of his own correspondence, her duties would be considerably lightened. She would welcome more time to give to arranging the flowers, to having a few words with the residents, particularly the Misses Corrington, who dearly liked a chat but whom Stella had lately had to avoid for lack of time. To be pulled in several directions at once was tiring, and to neglect the more sociable duties of running an hotel was a mistake, as old Mr. Marbury had always impressed upon her.

She did not see John that morning, and it was not until she was chatting to the elder Miss Corrington on the terrace after lunch that she saw him strolling across the lawn with Eileen Ridlow.

'We see so little of you these days, Miss Verney,' said Miss Corrington. 'I expect you're very busy.'

'Yes. Easing up a little now, though. Isn't the sun lovely? I do hope we have weather like this at Easter.'

'Are you well booked up?'

'Pretty well.'

'A lovely time of the year, Easter, I always think. Daffodils and pussy willow. I remember how the children used to bring me bunches of willow for the classroom every spring.'

'You miss your teaching?'

'Sometimes. But I realise how fortunate Dorothy and I are to be able to retire to such a lovely place as this. Of course, if we hadn't been careful and invested father's money prudently, our retirement would have been very much bleaker. Dorothy was a little inclined to be extravagant, you know . . .'

Miss Corrington's pleasant voice ran on as they strolled towards the dining-room. Blanche loved to pour little criticisms of Dorothy into Stella's ear, and Dorothy found relief in confiding to Stella some of Blanche's idiosyncrasies, to all of which Stella listened gravely. But they were devoted sisters, and Stella liked them both: Blanche with her kind, gentle nature and Dorothy, firm, high-principled, a little lacking in humour.

Stella took her usual walk along the cliffs after lunch. John and Eileen were sitting on a seat beside the croquet lawn and John lifted a hand in salute as Stella passed on the other side of the lawn. She waved back. There would be no apologies for yesterday, no explanation. He would ignore it and be just as charming and affectionate after Eileen had gone.

Sitting on the cliff above the cove, she felt overcome by despondency. The barbed wire mocked her. Cut off. Cut off by Darrington, cut off by Eileen Ridlow.

'Hullo. You look rather forlorn sitting there. Can I join you?'

'If you wish to, Mr. Darrington.'

'Thanks. That's a lovely view of the coast.'

'Yes.'

'Still sore about that?'

He nodded towards the wire.

'Yes. I'm sorry I lost my temper the other day, though. It's your place to give the orders. I'm sorry I've got out of the way of taking them.'

'You'll soon get used to it,' he said cheerfully, and looked so mischievous that her anger died at birth.

'You shouldn't rise to the bait so easily,' he said. 'You must have been put through it by those Elmore boys when you were a kid.'

'I was. I could hold my own, though.'

'Or go down fighting?'

'Yes. Cathie was always handy with a poultice.'

'Did you go down there often?' He nodded to the cove

70

where the waves were breaking silkily into a lacy pattern on the sand.

'Yes. Whenever I wanted to be alone. I found it a comforting place.'

'The equivalent of Cathie's poultices, perhaps?'

'Exactly.'

His eyes met hers and she saw kindness there. Cathie was right. He did understand.

'When I've got time, I'll do a bit of surveying and see if we can by-pass that rocky section. Looks as though there might be a greater depth of earth to the right there. I've a chap coming to live at the lodge, due next Thursday. He's a handy man at that sort of thing. We'll see what we can do.'

'You haven't any ashes handy, have you? If so, I'll throw them over my head.'

He laughed.

'I'll let you off that. You've been working too hard. I have the impression that you're drawn too tight just now, and it's easy to lose your temper then. Relax.'

'I'll try,' said Stella, thinking that the state of affairs at the Cormorant just then was not exactly conducive to a relaxed mind.

'It's a pity the Bryants decided to take young Dick away. He was shaping well and would have been useful to us. Still, I think you'll find Rickie a useful chap to have about the place, if you get on the right side of him. He's a nice little bloke. I've had him with me on several expeditions. He's a marvellous cook, even on a camp fire. And infinitely resourceful. Nothing defeats him.'

'He's not replacing Chef or Mrs. Dacres?'

'Lord no. He's not going to be attached to the hotel. Not officially, anyway. He's coming to look after the lodge and cook a few meals for me when I don't feel like sitting in my corner of the dining-room. In any case, I imagine we can do with the extra table in the summer, and I sometimes feel like a private meal in my own domain.'

'Yes, I can appreciate that.'

'Rickie's had rotten luck since our last trip. He was knocked down by a car and pretty badly damaged. He was in hospital for nine weeks. They've put him together again but he's got to take things quietly, and as I can do with an odd-job man at the lodge, that seemed to me the answer. The hotel staff don't really want to be responsible for looking after the lodge, and I'd sooner be self-contained, anyway. You'll like Rickie, I think. He's quite a character.'

'I think it's a good idea. I've often thought you must be lonely at the lodge sometimes.'

'Really? Am I supposed to be sufficiently human for that?'

'I'm not rising again, Mr. Darrington.'

'Well, I propose to have a little supper-party on Saturday night by way of a house-warming. I've asked Roger and Cathie. Will you make the fourth?'

'Oh. Thank you. I'd like to.'

'Good. Seven-thirty.'

'Right. And now my lunch hour has expired.'

He gave her a hand and pulled her to her feet. As they strolled back to the hotel, he said casually:

'Did you know that Mrs. Ridlow is interested in buying this place from me?'

'Yes. John had told me.'

Darrington's face was enigmatic. She could read nothing from it. She felt compelled to go on.

'Are you interested in her offer?'

'Certainly not at present. I haven't had a season here yet. I've no idea what the potentialities are. And if I start a job, I like to finish it. I'm going to the garage for the car, so I'll leave you here.'

He strode off towards the garage and Stella returned to the office to find John waiting for her there.

'Hullo, ducky. Did I see you walking with the enemy?'

'Yes.'

'Have you signed a truce?'

'Yes. He's going to see if he can make that track safer.'

'Well done! A spot of feminine charm can move mountains.'

Stella said nothing. It seemed to her a silly remark to which there was no answer. John's eyes studied her.

'Don't get too thick with the enemy, Stella. We need you, you know.'

'I think all this talk of enemies is foolish, John. We're not children playing at war. You want to buy the hotel back from Darrington. If you succeed, all well and good. If he won't sell, there's an end of it. I'm not concerned with waging some sort of subterranean campaign. It's a straightforward issue, as I see it.'

'Oh, no, my dear, it's not. You're a child as far as financial affairs are concerned. Each business deal that's made is a campaign with victory to the shrewdest. Tactics play a big part, believe me.'

'Well, I'm no good at tactics. I must leave those to you.'

'You're peeved with me about yesterday, aren't you?'

'I was disappointed, yes.'

'Darling, you've no need to be jealous. Eileen is just a part of the tactics, believe me. She's only interested in the business aspect.'

'Is she?'

He smiled.

'You *are* jealous.'

That idea pleased him, she thought, and realised for the first time how big a part vanity played in his make-up. Although there had been, at the dance and on a few other occasions, an element of jealousy in her unhappiness, by far the greater cause was the cruel revelation of a shabbiness, and shiftiness in John which seemed to drive splinters into her heart. She had admired him so much. She had idealised him. But he would never guess that it was that kind of revelation that was hurting her so badly. To him it was a simple case of jealousy, belittling her not him. She sighed.

'Let's not talk about it, John.'

'But I don't want you to be upset like this. There's no real cause, I swear. Don't you see that Eileen is so important to us, to our future, that I must put her first.'

'Do you really think that Mrs. Ridlow is going to use her money on your behalf without expecting any return?'

'It'll be a business partnership, my dear, and I know how to keep Eileen happy. We shall be, we are, good friends. She's a cool customer, but we get on very well on a purely platonic basis, so you don't have to worry. You're my girl. Give me a kiss and I'll prove it.'

'If you had to choose, John, between Mrs. Ridlow's money and me, what would your choice be?'

She watched him closely. He laughed, but his eyes went to her desk and he picked up the letter she had typed before lunch.

'I don't intend to lose either, pet, and if you play your part, I shan't. I need you in my team. Savez?'

'Yes, I savez.'

He was greedy. He wanted it all, she thought.

'Darrington isn't selling at present, anyway. He told me.'

'He will,' said John confidently. 'By the end of the summer, he'll be glad to cut his losses. I've had a few bills in for decorations this morning that'll scare him.'

'Why? The work was estimated for.'

'Estimate well exceeded, ducky. The few extras I suggested have proved rather costly. Now there's some trouble with the roof. I'm getting Bolsover over tomorrow morning. Could mean a lot of expense to put it right. Don't know how much Darrington inherited, but I doubt whether it's all that.'

'Are you deliberately trying to make expenses mount?'

'No, my dear. But I haven't been able to spend anything on the place since the old man died, you know. And I'm not cheese-paring for Darrington's benefit now. In any case, economy in maintenance is always costly in the end. Remember the old man's pronouncement? It's up to Darrington to jib, if he wants to. He hasn't an idea about the cost of running and maintaining a place like this. By the end of the season, when he tots up, he'll be willing to sell, believe me.'

'Then why should Mrs. Ridlow be willing to buy such a bad proposition?'

'It's not a bad proposition if you can afford to sink a lot of capital in the place and wait for your return. We've been on the wrong tack, keeping this place quiet and old-fashioned. It wants pepping up. Cocktail bar, more dances, swimming pool, tennis courts. Something to attract people with money to burn; what used to be known as the smart set. With a big publicity campaign, people would learn that this was a lively place where you could have a damned good time without going outside the hotel grounds. Look at us now. What have we got? A croquet lawn. That's just about typical. And those doddering old residents occupying rooms at half price. They shouldn't be allowed to stay on during the summer unless they pay full terms. I've known well enough what was needed, but I hadn't the capital. Eileen has.'

Stella could see it all. The chromium cocktail bar which would bring in high profits; dances every night; sunbathing round the swimming pool; everything to attract people with money to spend on the pursuit of pleasure and little appreciation of peace and beauty. It was all very well, but she would not enjoy seeing the Cormorant transformed into a de luxe country club. It offered such rare natural assets that it seemed a pity to scrap them for synthetic attractions of the kind which could be enjoyed anywhere.

'It wasn't your father's idea.'

'My dear girl, you can't run a business with ideas fifty years old. You've got to move with the times. People want to be entertained, they want to have their fun laid on. And there's money in laying it on. You've not got a business head, my dear, for all your competence. You're just not of this age in many ways. If you were, we could have . . . well, never mind. Living in a small place like Ashcombe all your life is a bit limiting. And I guess your father's influence hasn't exactly loosened you up.'

'Loosened me up in what sense?' asked Stella calmly.

'Loosened up those old Victorian principles, my pet. They make life so horribly earnest.'

He spoke jokingly, but she knew that he meant it.

'Well, I suppose it's too late for me to change now,' she said lightly.

'Is it?' He kissed her swiftly, and kept his arm round her. 'Is it, Stella? Think about it, sweetheart. You're not by nature a prig. The reverse. You've a lively spirit and a great capacity for enjoying life. But you could enjoy it even more, we could enjoy it even more, if you buried a few of those old-fashioned principles. Think about it.'

He gave her shoulder a squeeze and then made for the door.

He paused with his hand on the door handle.

'I like that frock. You're far too attractive to be wedded to principles. And there's no need to be jealous, ducky. Duty calls. So long.'

She sat staring in front of her for some minutes after he had left, wondering how it had come to pass that with every encounter, John, who for so long had seemed so close to her, moved further and further away so that the gulf now yawning between them seemed to place them in totally different countries. Had she changed or had he changed. Was she reading more into his relationship with Eileen Ridlow than she ought? Was she subconsciously allowing jealousy to influence her? Was she a prig to find John's tactics with Darrington distasteful? She put her head in her hands, aware of a conflict within which she could not resolve. A see-saw between emotions and mind, between old loyalties and principles. If only she knew what place she held in John's heart. Once she had known. Now she no longer knew. He was like quick-silver.

And then on the Thursday, his attitude seemed to indicate quite clearly that there was no gulf. He breezed into her office after seeing Mrs. Ridlow off.

'Well, that's that. Eileen's off to the Continent for a month, but I've fired her with a determination to get this place in spite of Darrington's refusal to sell. She's set her heart on it, and when Eileen wants anything, she usually gets it.' He rubbed his hands. 'I think she'll be more than a match for our friend Darrington. She's got money, and money is power. At the end of the season, I'm willing to bet he'll find her offer very tempting.'

'We'll see,' said Stella.

'And now I can forget business for a bit and make up to you for my neglect. There's a dance on at the town hall on Saturday. Shall we go?'

'I'd love to, but I can't, John. I'm going to a little supper-party Darrington's giving by way of a house-warming. Myself, Cathie and Roger Thornton.'

'Well, I'm damned! No, Stella, you can't do this. Fraternise with the enemy.'

'I've told you that I can't play at war. You and Darrington

can compete for power here, but I'm only an employee paid to do a job.'

'Yes, but you're playing the friend, now, not just an employee. Can't you see, Stella? He wants to get you on his side. You're useful to him. Might even enable him to dispense with me.'

'Oh, no, John. That's absurd.'

'Is it? If he's thinking in terms of cutting expenses, and he'll soon be thinking in those terms, believe me, that's an economy he might welcome.'

'Is that why you're taking over so much of the work again now?'

'Partly. The main reason, of course, is because you were overworked, and we don't want a stranger in the office. But it did occur to me that I didn't want to be worked out of this job until I chose to go, and that by giving you an assistant, Darrington was taking the first step towards economising on my salary. That's one fast one he didn't manage to pull off, though. Hadn't it occurred to you?'

'No. Not for a moment.'

'Bless your simple heart. Anyway, I want to stay right here until Eileen has brought it off. Nothing like keeping your finger on the pulse. Hence my exemplary discharge of my duties just now. The energetic, pushing manager, that's me.'

'And where do I come in? It seems that I'm being used as a pawn by both of you.'

'Why, you're with me. There's no question of that, is there?'

'Of course not, John. I never liked the idea of anyone else ruling here but you. All the same . . .'

'Don't be enticed into the other camp, my dear. You're too innocent, you know. Darrington's no fool. He's trying to win you over. Business is business. Keep away from any inducements he may offer to change the footing to a friendly one. He's doing it with a purpose that's no doubt aimed at me.'

'Are you sure? I don't think he meant this invitation as anything but a pleasant gesture. Three's an awkward number, and he knows Cathie is a very close friend of mine.'

'Stella, you're either for me or against me. You must choose. If you start getting friendly with Darrington, and by accepting social invitations you make that inevitable, you'll be making a move against me. You must accept my word for that. You're too honest a person to recognise motives of expediency. I surely don't have to ask you, of all people, for loyalty?'

He was looking at her with the old look of tender affection which she seldom saw now, and her heart melted.

'No, you don't have to ask, John. It's yours. It always has been yours. But how can I get out of this invitation now? I didn't realise how you would feel about it. It just didn't occur to me to look at it like that.'

'Well, I'll let him know that you can't come, if you like. I'll say I'd got two tickets for the dance and had forgotten to mention it to you before.'

'I think I'd better tell him myself.'

'Just as you like. But make no mistake, Stella. There's a war on here and I need my lieutenant. It's our future, you know.'

She turned to him, then, and searched his face almost painfully.

'If in your heart you really mean that, John, say it again. I don't want bribing for my loyalty to you. That's yours, as it was your father's, and if I thought I was threatening your position here, I'd leave, however much it hurt me. But if you truly mean it about the future, tell me again.'

He took her in his arms and his lips were brushing hers as he said:

'My future is yours, too.'

A few moments later the telephone rang, jarring and startling them apart. Stella answered it and dealt with the query raised by the printers of the hotel brochures. When she had replaced the receiver, John said, smiling:

'Any doubts, lieutenant?'

'None. Do you know, it's ages since we danced together. I wonder if I've time to buy a new frock for Saturday by way of celebration.'

'You have my permission to take a couple of hours tomorrow morning for shopping, Miss Verney. Be in by coffee time if you can. And don't reckon on dancing with anybody else on Saturday.'

78

'I won't,' promised Stella, her eyes shining.

She was still in a mood of exaltation when she went in search of Darrington an hour later, and tracked him down on the croquet lawn talking to the gardener. Waiting for him to finish, her mood sobered as she considered what to say. It occurred to her that whatever explanation she offered, her behaviour was not going to appear very gracious. Standing behind him, she noted the square shoulders, and the good tailoring of the grey suit, a very fine tweed with a faint blue line in the pattern; she would like a suit of that material herself, but it looked a good deal more expensive than she could afford. She felt uneasy, and stiffened her morale by reminding herself of John's assertion that Darrington was using her with a view to dislodging his manager, that she was a pawn he wanted to take from the other side. When he turned and she met those disconcerting eyes, however, her morale wilted again. She spoke quickly.

'Mr. Darrington, I wonder if you could spare a moment? I've a confession to make.'

'Say on.'

'I'm terribly sorry, but I discovered this afternoon that John had banked on my going to a dance with him on Saturday evening. Will you forgive me if I ask . . . if . . . ' She faltered, then, as he made no attempt to help her out, she added desperately, 'Do you mind if I go to the dance? John will be very disappointed if I don't.'

It was one of Darrington's most discomfiting characteristics that silence never embarrassed him. He could study a person coolly and keenly for some moments without saying a word. And in those moments, Stella felt that he was studying not just the physical form before him but the jumble of thoughts encased in it. She could almost feel him turning them over rather contemptuously just then, like a heap of junk in a second-hand shop.

'Why don't you say what you mean, Miss Verney? You would rather go to a dance with Marbury than have supper with us on Saturday night, and you want to withdraw in favour of the more attractive proposition.'

'I'm sorry, Mr. Darrington.'

She could find nothing more to say. Suddenly John's arguments, which had sounded so convincing, didn't seem to meet the case.

'That's all right. Naturally you won't want to disappoint Marbury. I quite understand.'

She flushed at the ironical note in his voice.

'It is unfortunate that John didn't mention it to me before.'

'Very. Let's say no more about it. I've been having a talk with Bowman to see if he could spare us another day and do something about growing some produce for the hotel. Fruit and vegetables. It would be an economy and desirable in many ways, I think. We've plenty of room behind the garages, and fruit trees could be planted with advantage almost anywhere.'

'Yes, I think it's a splendid idea. Can Bowman put in any more time, though?'

'He's half-hearted about it. I don't think he's much of an asset, somehow. A grudging worker. I'll have to think about it. And Bowman,' he added grimly.

'I forgot to ask you if you wanted your friend met off the six-ten train this evening? Mr. Marbury said you hadn't mentioned it.'

'No, I'm meeting Rickie myself. You might tell Marbury I want a word with him about the roof repairs. I shall be at the lodge for the next hour.'

He nodded and strode off. Stella sighed. She had earned a black mark that afternoon. She would have been surprised, however, had she known just how much that small incident was to tell against her in the future. But nothing could daunt her for long now that John, for the first time, had made it clear that she belonged permanently in his life, that marriage was their goal. And if sometimes his tactics for the future seemed questionable, who was she to judge? John was right; she knew little of the business world and its toughness. He had his way to make and it was no use letting sentiment influence his choice of weapons. She must let him fight for their future in his own way, and enjoy the present with him as much as she could. It was probably her fault that the gulf had ever grown up, for no man liked to feel his actions silently criticised, his style cramped because the time he wanted to devote to somebody who could be useful to him was resented. Remembering his words and the expression on his face that afternoon, her heart felt overflowing with joy and an eager desire to make up for her past scruples. With characteristic generosity, she saw herself as a carping critic, narrow-minded and possessive, and John as the injured party, so that when she went into his office to give him Darrington's message, she added softly by way of postscript,

'Darling, I'm sorry if I've been a bit earnest lately. Forgive me. I'm going to reform from now on.'

He smiled swiftly, pushed his chair back from his desk and pulled her on his lap.

'That's my girl. Told Darrington what he can do with his supper-party?'

'Yes. I don't think he was very pleased.'

'I bet he wasn't. As well to remind him that you're mine, pet.'

An engagement ring would be a helpful and more permanent reminder, thought Stella, but she knew that John wanted to see his future clear before announcing any engagement.

'I shall be glad when this business is settled, between you and Darrington. When do you think it will be, John?'

He shrugged his shoulders.

'In the autumn, I hope. Eileen's coming down again in the summer and we'll discuss the situation then, but I reckon the time will be ripe for another approach at the end of the season. Darrington may have had enough of it by then. He'll have to be full to overflowing from Easter onwards to make out this year, with the extra staff we're taking on, and even then he won't see his capital expenditure back for a good many years. This place just isn't a paying proposition, run on its present lines. He'll find that out by the end of the summer. Meanwhile, we'll enjoy ourselves, Stella. Leave it all to me and don't bother your attractive little head about the business. You just do as I tell you. I'm your immediate boss, you know,' he concluded with mock severity.

'This is hardly conducive to good discipline, sir,' she said, her eyes laughing at him.

'You're dead right. And I'd better go across and have a

81

little talk with Lord Darrington about the roof. He's not going to laugh much over that.' He kissed her and put her on her feet. 'Run along. I don't want to get the sack, yet. It's a treat to see you looking so happy. Nobody quite blazes with it as you can. Definitely warming.'

Chapter Eight

As Stella ran up the stairs of the hotel the next morning, she could hear the telephone ringing in her room. With the box containing her frock under one arm, her handbag and mackintosh hanging on the other, she flew round the corner at the top of the stairs straight into the arms of Darrington. Her handbag flew in one direction and scattered its contents round three pairs of feet, the box was neatly fielded by the little man beside Darrington, while the latter held firm against her impact and restored her balance, by which time the telephone had stopped ringing.

'I'm so sorry, Mr. Darrington.'

'That's all right.'

They gathered up the contents of the bag: note case, powder compact, keys, a diary, handkerchief, two bills, fountain pen, nail file, a card of darning silk . . . there seemed no end to the contents of one small handbag. Darrington rescued the last item, a lipstick, from the top stair, then said calmly:

'May I introduce my factotum, Ken Rickall? Rickie, this is Miss Verney, our secretary.'

Feeling that she hardly depicted a competent secretary at that moment, she held out her hand with a friendly smile.

'How do you do.'

'Pleased to meet you, Miss Verney.'

He was dark and so thin that he looked cadaverous, but his smile was perky and his eyes as alert as a bird's. He had the sort of skin which always looked in need of a shave, and Stella thought she detected a faint hint of a Welsh accent when he spoke.

'Lovely place, this. The chief's just been showing me the layout.'

'Yes. The Cormorant's a gem, I think.'

'I'll see you back at the lodge, Rickie. I just want to have a word with Miss Verney.'

Darrington followed her into her room.

'I came across earlier to have a talk with you about how you were placed for work just now.'

'I'm sorry I wasn't here. I had time off for shopping this morning. I forgot to switch my telephone through to Mr. Marbury's office last night. I usually do that when I'm not here.'

'I see. Well, I had a chat with Marbury, and he tells me that you're not so busy now that he's more time to give to the office.'

'That's true.'

'Then I wonder if you could take on some typing for me. An article for a geographical magazine and a paper I'm reading at a scientific meeting in London the week after next.'

'Of course.'

'Thank you. It's just a case of copying the article. I've written it out. The lecture I shall have to dictate. I shall want them both by the end of next week. Can you manage that, do you think?'

'Oh, yes.'

'Right. I'll send the manuscript of the article across. I'll rough out the lecture this weekend and dictate it on Monday. Thank you.'

His manner was strictly formal. The vein of friendliness which had been evident at their encounter on the cliff top had vanished. She had scotched it by her withdrawal from his invitation, and she felt sorry until she remembered John and the dance. The dress she had bought was a honey; yards of ice-blue tulle and a bodice glittering with rhinestones. It would mean no more new clothes for a long time, but it was worth it. She wanted to do John credit.

And John's reaction the next evening confirmed her in her

extravagance. The evening was a joy from first to last, with John the perfect dancing partner, as always, and certainly the most distinguished-looking male in the room. It seemed impossible, dancing with him, that she had ever felt that there was a gulf between them, that she had ever doubted his devotion to her, that it had ever crossed her mind that his mental stature did not match his superb appearance. The Elmores laughingly referred to John as Stella's Apollo, and although she protested, since their intention was not altogether complimentary, the reference was in fact not inept, for John's looks were of the classic Grecian type.

It was a full moon that night and he took her for a drive after the dance. He gave her a hair-raising example of how well he could handle the car at high speeds, and a blood-heating example of how well he could handle her. The church clock was striking two as she crept up to bed, the exhilaration of the evening still with her so that she could not imagine she would ever sleep . . .

Some of the exhilaration was still with her as she walked to the hotel on Monday morning. There was a fresh breeze blowing, and the sea tossed and sparkled in tune with her mood. She met Mr. Bolsover at the gate of the Cormorant.

'Good morning, Miss Verney. You can save me a walk up that drive. I've brought along the estimates Mr. Marbury wanted. Sorry I couldn't get 'em done by Saturday, but I worked on them this weekend and thought I'd drop them in, as Mr. Marbury's in a hurry for them.'

'Yes. The work will have to be done before the summer season. Can't have workmen about the place when we're full up.'

'Well, perhaps you'll give these to Mr. Marbury. He said he wasn't interested in patching up, but I've made out an alternative in case the complete job's a bit too steep. Must say the cost's come out pretty high, but with labour so dear, I can't cut it.'

'Do you think patching up would meet the trouble?'

Mr. Bolsover shrugged his massive shoulders.

'It'd serve for a few years. But for a long-term policy, of course, the complete job's the answer. Anyway, there are the estimates. Might ask Mr. Marbury to let me know as soon as possible.'

'Right. I will.'

Mr. Bolsover climbed into his car and drove off. Stella took the envelope straight to John's office. He whistled when he saw the price.

'Hullo! This is going to make his nibs sit up.'

'What about the other suggestion?'

'Not worth considering. It would be a waste of money, and only postpone the main job for a short time.'

'Is Bolsover competent to judge? I should have thought it might be advisable to have an architect to look into it.'

'That's up to Darrington. Adds to the expense. Bolsover's quite competent to judge a straightforward job like this. Not worrying over Darrington's pocket, pet, are you?'

'No. It's his business, not mine.'

'It was a good evening, Saturday, wasn't it?'

'Heavenly. I haven't enjoyed myself so much for ages.'

'Nor me. We must have more fun, Stella. Life's to enjoy, my girl. Thought any more about my suggestion?'

'Which one?'

'About a weekend.'

'I thought you were joking.'

He was watching her, and suddenly, he smiled mischievously.

'Perhaps I was. I can't resist aiming a small arrow now and again at the Ashcombe bourgeois outlook.'

'Sorry,' she said lightly. 'I'm afraid it's too late to do anything about my upbringing and environment now.'

'Never too late to learn, sweetheart. I shall be happy to be your teacher and guide.' He grinned up at her wickedly as he added, 'Here's your quota.'

He handed her a few letters, tore up a sheet of paper, and stood up with two unopened letters and the builder's estimate in his hands.

'Well, I must see Darrington about this. Not much for you today, Stella. See you for coffee. The new brochures have come. On top of the telephone directory. You'd better take half of them.'

He went and Stella investigated the parcel of brochures.

Before she left his office she picked up the pieces of paper he had thrown into the waste-paper basket. As she thought, it was the alternative estimate from Bolsover which he had torn up. She collected the brochures and letters she had to deal with and walked slowly to her room. The exhilaration had evaporated. It occurred to her that her relationship with John resembled a topping of sparkling froth on cloudy water.

She did not see him for coffee, after all, because Darrington spent the whole morning in her office dictating his lecture, and they broke off for only a few minutes when Mrs. Dacres brought their coffee in. She found the lecture interesting and was glad to have something impersonal on which to concentrate. In spite of the geological terms, many of which she did not understand, she received a sufficiently clear picture of the nature of the country he was describing to say, as she flexed her cramped fingers at the end of the morning,

'It sounds a fascinating country, South America. I envy you your wide horizons. Makes me feel as though I've been living all my life in one small room.'

'You'd like to travel?'

'Yes. I've always wanted to. Not just as a tourist, though that would be pleasant, but to explore lesser-known parts of the world, as you have done.'

'It means discomfort as well as excitement, you know.'

'I don't think that matters if your surroundings are new and absorbing. Comfort only looms large when what is around you isn't new or stimulating enough to push comfort into the background. A question of relativity.'

'Yes, that's true.'

'I don't think I'd be interested in the geological aspect very much, though. I think I'd rather help the botanist look for new plants.'

'Well, everything is related, you know. Geology, botany, biology, and so on, are all inter-dependent, all make up the whole. It's the whole that appeals to me. I just happen to know a little more about geology that the rest, but I'm not really a specialist in the narrow sense. Lately, in fact, photography has tended to take up more and more of my time on these trips. Perhaps, though, that's just an insurance for my old age when I shall only be able to indulge in armchair travelling. Colour photography enables you to capture foreign countries so magical. You get the atmosphere, as well as the physical record.'

Watching that strong, rather ugly face, she found herself wishing that she had met this man in other circumstances, on another footing. On neutral ground, she thought it possible that she would welcome his friendship. Cathie was right. Their relationship was bedevilled by the fact that he had usurped the Marbury position; that as an employer she found him too dictatorial after the friendly footing which had always existed between her and her employer in the past; that she was inevitably involved in a conflict of loyalties, drawn into a coil of politics which she did not like. She thought of the estimate John had destroyed. She wanted to tell Darrington about its existence, but loyalty to John kept her silent.

He glanced at his watch and stood up.

'Nearly lunch-time. Rather a long session I'm afraid. By the way, has Bolsover always been the builder employed here?'

'Yes. Ever since I've known the Cormorant anyway.'

'Old Mr. Marbury relied on his judgment always?'

He was watching her closely, she felt, or was it her uneasy conscience that made her feel this?

'As far as I know. Why do you ask?'

'I had the estimate for the repairs to the roof this morning. It seems to me that he's making rather a meal of it, that's all.'

Now, she thought, was the time to tell him. But it would be awkward for John if he had not mentioned Bolsover's alternative. Perhaps he had, and they had both agreed that patching up was not worth considering. Drowning her scruples in this thought, reminding herself that it was not her business to interfere between Darrington and his manager, Stella gave a non-committal reply and Darrington left her. But after he had gone, she propped her head between her hands, feeling that her world was becoming too complicated, that she was enmeshed and couldn't see clearly any more.

Easter came and went. John was charming and attentive, and Stella resolutely banished introspection and enjoyed the outdoor activities which spring had brought. They played tennis, went riding and driving together, and on the surface the old carefree footing appeared to be re-established. And if Stella sometimes felt that she was skating on thin ice, that something fundamental had changed in her feeling for John, she quickly dismissed such thoughts.

For the first time in her experience at the hotel, she found after Easter that she had not enough work to fill the day. With extra staff engaged for the summer season and everybody geared up, bookings were lamentably slow in coming in. By nature an energetic person, Stella suggested to Darrington that she might start a small flower garden next to the vegetable garden which Rickie was developing with the grudging aid of the gardener.

'It will save on our florist's bills,' said Stella, 'and I can easily spare the time if the gardener will get the hard digging done for me.'

They were walking along the beach of the little cove. The path down the cliff face had been re-made and pronounced safe two days ago, and Stella had followed Darrington down for the first time that evening.

'It sounds a good idea. We certainly can do with some economising somewhere. I'll speak to Bowman about it. A bit late in the season to start, though, isn't it?'

'Too late for seeds, of course. But we can buy plants, and it would still be much cheaper than the florist's. I know a very good nursery. Dad gets all his plants from them. If Bowman could get a bed or two ready in a week or so, we could produce quite a lot for this season.'

'You're a gardening enthusiast?'

'Yes. My father's influence. And I love to be out of doors. This will give me a cast-iron excuse for being out of the office,' she added, with a smile.

'All right. You have my permission. I hope the project won't have the same economic results as my sister's efforts to save pounds by growing strawberries. By the time she'd paid for a wire cage to keep the birds off and straw mats to keep the mud off, the strawberries cost her about ten shillings a pound.'

'I'll keep accounts and we can compare the results after a year.'

'Right. This is certainly a delightful little cove. I can appreciate your wrath at being deprived of it.'

'Thank you for giving it back to me, anyway.'

He gave her a brief smile.

'That's all right. You know, you're growing up.'

It was so unexpected that she looked at him in astonishment.

'I should have thought I was old enough now to be considered an adult.'

'I wasn't thinking of years. Lots of people never really grow up. Never mature. Just keep their childish egos.'

'And what are the signs of growing up which you detected in me just now? I'm curious.'

'An old friend of mine, an Oxford don, once said to me that growing up was learning humility. A simple statement, but the more you think about it, the truer it is.'

'Humility never sounds a very attractive virtue.'

'You're not confusing it with weakness, are you? It's the reverse, you know. What it boils down to, I suppose, is a true sense of proportion, so that your own importance isn't magnified and you're not everlastingly suffering from wounded pride or trying to boost your ego to the world. That's immaturity. My friend reminded me of that when I was feeling a little peeved at a particularly cutting criticism of an essay I'd produced for him. I've never forgotten.'

'It must make life a lot happier once you've achieved it,' said Stella, thinking of all the pricks to pride which would no longer hurt. 'And of course,' she went on, 'that's where the strength comes in. I begin to see what you mean. But I think growing up, in that case, is a slow business!'

'Takes all our lives,' said Darrington cheerfully.

'Then I've really made quite an early start,' observed Stella, smiling.

'Yes. Already, you can laugh at yourself – that's always a good indication.'

They climbed up the path and stood for a few moments on top of the cliff to get their breath. The sea was a deep blue, flecked with white. The weather that spring had been poor, but on a day like this, clear and fresh and sparkling, Stella felt that she could forgive the climate anything. She felt happy and at ease with Darrington as they walked back. In the cove they had re-established the friendly footing which had been shaken by her withdrawal from his supper-party.

John was not very enthusiastic about her gardening scheme, but Stella went ahead and found a keen ally in Ken Rickall, now known to everybody as Rickie. Perhaps it was because she was such a good listener to the stories he told of his travels with Darrington, stories which lost nothing in the telling, she was sure; perhaps because she was always ready to discuss cookery with him, the next dearest subject to his heart; the fact remained that within five minutes of Stella's arrival at her plot of ground, Rickie invariably appeared to attend to the vegetable plot next to her. She liked his cheerful common sense and defended him against John's criticism.

'I don't know why you're so suspicious of everybody these days, John. Rickie's a perfectly ordinary, decent little man, grateful for an easy job after a tough time. It's ridiculous to think of him as a spy for Darrington.'

'He keeps his eyes peeled and his ears wide open, my dear, and I've no doubt everything goes back to the chief. I should watch your tongue when you're with him, that's all.'

'You do make the world a dark forest.'

He smiled swiftly.

'I know more of it than you, pet. Come away from the window. I want to kiss you.'

'I'm feeling strictly business-like this morning,' said Stella, putting files back into the cabinet.

'Come here and I'll soon dispel that.'

He was sitting on the corner of her desk, swinging one leg, and his blue eyes danced as he watched her face.

'No. Not in office hours.'

'You're looking awfully chastened this morning. Did you get into a row for being so late last night?'

'Not exactly, but Nan called out good night to me just as I was creeping past her room, and when I explained this morning that we'd have a puncture and the jack wouldn't work properly, she obviously didn't believe a word of it. I don't think she quite approves of you, John. You're too handsome to be good.'

'And I've always exerted my charm in her presence. Can't get over that Presbyterian core, I'm afraid. She must have given you a hell of a time when you were a kid.'

'Oh, she's a good soul, really, but a bit narrow and awfully sin-conscious. "Who sups with the devil, Miss Stella, needs a long spoon." That's her favourite maxim, dished out to me at regular intervals since I was in socks.

'Did you get it this morning?'

'I did.' Stella didn't add that Nan's parting shot that morning had been, 'Anyway, Miss Stella, it's time that young man bought you a ring.'

John chuckled delightedly.

'In this day and age! It's a knock-out. Well, come and sup with the devil for another few minutes.'

'I've told you, I'm busy, John.'

'All right,' he said, coming across to her. 'If you don't mind chancing on-lookers, I'm sure I don't. You know, you present an irresistible challenge to me, Stella. There's just one little bit of you that escapes me. The bit that Nan's cultivated, perhaps. But I mean to have it.'

'No, John.'

'Yes, Stella.'

She struggled in his arms for a moment, then gave way and was lost to the world.

'I think,' she said shakily, when he released her, 'you really are a devil, John.'

He laughed, pleased with his triumph.

'What's wrong with making love to your girl? Especially when she's being foolish and pretending to be above all that. There's friend Darrington and his henchman.'

Stella turned quickly to see the two men for an instant on the gravel drive below, before the hotel entrance hid them from her. If they had walked up from the lodge, they could hardly have failed to see her in John's arms.

'Oh,. dear. Are you trying to get me the sack, Mr. Marbury?'

'Don't worry. You can't be spared at this time of the year.'

91

'As a matter of fact, I think I could. Bookings are very poor so far, John, aren't they?'

'Yes. Early days yet, though. Rotten weather puts people off. Get a good spell, and they'll start feeling holiday-minded. By the way, I had a letter from Eileen today. She's coming down in June for the rest of the summer.'

'Oh.'

'And what does that signify?'

He was bent on teasing her, and Stella was not going to let him get any satisfaction out of her reply.

'Nothing in particular. I hope the hotel will fill up by then, or she'll think it's a bad business proposition.'

'Not Eileen. She'll itch to get her hands on it and shake it up. She's a good business woman and she realises that the Cormorant will never do well on its present old-fashioned lines. It has great potentialities, though, and she's already spotted those. Are you going to be a good girl over Eileen?'

'John, please don't talk as though I'm a silly jealous child. It's . . . humiliating and untrue. I hope I'll have a chance to get to know Eileen during the summer, since she's so important to our future. But don't try to play us off against each other to please your vanity. It . . . hurts.'

'I'm sorry, darling. I was only ragging. But we can't afford to neglect her, you know. And I did think you were a wee bit green-eyed when she was here before. Now confess. Just a tinge of green?'

She smiled.

'Perhaps. But you hadn't made it clear then that it was our future you were thinking of. Now you have, I promise I'll co-operate in any way I can.'

'And trust me?'

'You shouldn't have to ask that, John.'

'I know. But it's bothered me a little these past months. Ever since Darrington's taken over, in fact. I've felt at times that you were critical, not really with me.'

'I was a bit captious, perhaps, over Eileen, because I didn't understand, but I thought I'd made it clear enough lately that I stand with you. I always have.'

'And you trust me to handle this business of Eileen and the

hotel, even if sometimes you don't understand or see the point of what I'm doing?'

'Yes, I trust you, John. I know I'm a noodle about the business world. Out of my depth. Only keep a little space for me this summer where business can be forgotten and I can be reminded that what is between us isn't business.'

'That's my girl.'

Her heart was in her eyes as she looked at him. Of course she trusted him. She loved him, and you loved for better or worse. And it was a horrible thought that she might be guilty of too readily sitting in moral judgment, as Nan did. Self-righteousness was to be avoided like the plague. John had faults, as she and every human being had faults. She would not want a plaster saint. She was so glad to hear him talking openly and seriously about their relationship instead of skating gaily along, ignoring any cracks, that she could not do enough to make up for them, and her heart leaped to take the full blame for those cracks.

'Forgive me, John, if I've seemed critical. My only excuse is that uncertainty made me nervy and foolish. Now I've no longer any excuse. And I promise that you won't be bothered in that way again.'

'Bless you, Stella. You're a grand girl. Small wonder if we're both a bit nervy sometimes. Being in love is rather a nervy business, after all.' He took her in his arms, and his lips brushed her cheek. 'I think it will have to be a rather special birthday present for you in July. A little piece of jewellery. Just to help settle those nerves.'

And by then his lips had found hers again, and all doubts and fears and promises died in that embrace.

Chapter Nine

THAT season looked like being the worst the hotel had ever known. It was about a quarter full in June and unless there were a lot of last-minute bookings, things would be little better in July and August. Stella felt sorry for Darrington, but her own personal happiness shut out any other serious concern. She spent a good deal of time in her flower garden, which promised well, and although she saw less of John outside office hours once Eileen arrived, she accepted the state of affairs with happy equanimity, took every opportunity of cultivating Eileen's acquaintance, and counted the days to her birthday, for which she made careful plans. For this birthday was, indeed, a special one.

She took the opportunity of raising it with Darrington one day early in July when he came into her office to borrow her *Pears Cyclopaedia*.

'Mr. Darrington, I want to ask a favour of you.'

'Ask away.'

'It's my birthday a fortnight next Saturday. Could I hire the dining-room annexe for a small supper-party?'

'That's what it's mainly used for,' he said. 'Why should I object?'

'Well, that's not all. If it's fine, I thought of arranging a picnic tea-party in the afternoon and I wondered if we might have it in the cove. It's lovely for bathing and the other beaches are getting crowded now.'

'Of course you can. I assume your party will all be able-bodied souls not likely to break ankles.'

'The picnic contingent will be. Just the Elmore family, I expect. The elders will probably prefer to join us at supper.'

She wanted to invite him, but wondered whether John would be annoyed. Then it occurred to her that on this occasion, when her alignment with John would be made public, he would probably like Darrington to be there to witness it.

'Would you be able to join us for supper? I'd be very glad if you could,' she added.

He eyed her thoughtfully and she felt her colour rise, remembering her treatment of his invitation.

'Thank you. I'm expecting my sister and her husband down next Saturday for ten days. They'll be staying with me at the lodge. But I'll be glad to look in and drink your health on the evening in question. Is it impolite to ask how old you'll be?'

'Twenty-five. This is rather a special day, though.'

He shot her a quick glance.

'You and Marbury?'

'I'd better not say any more. It's all very hush-hush, if you don't mind.'

'I am discretion itself. I think it would be suitable if I brought some champagne, don't you?'

'Very suitable. And very nice of you.'

He looked at her desk.

'Much in today?'

'Afraid not. One enquiry for the last fortnight in August. That's all. I don't know what's happened to everybody this summer. Even our regulars have let us down, except the faithful Miss Mapleton.'

'Is this summer exceptional?'

'Yes. I've never known it so bad. Of course, the weather hasn't helped.'

'No. I must confess I'm a bit worried about it. Our overheads are heavy. I expected better results than this. Were we much fuller last summer?'

He was wondering whether John had misled him about the business, she thought, and said quickly:

'Much. We weren't full all the season, as we used to be in Mr. Marbury's time, but we were full from the middle of June to the middle of September.'

'I see. Well, make what arrangements you want with Marbury for your birthday.'

'Thank you. How is the book getting on?'

'I'm on the last lap. Expect to finish it this month. There'll be a spot of revision, and then I think I shall take a holiday.

Writing is harder work than I thought, and I'm tired of being chained to a desk.'

He nodded and went. Stella went to the window and pushed it open. It was a humid, grey day and there seemed no air in the room. She watched Darrington walk back to the lodge. He stopped half-way to light his pipe, then went on, unhurried but with the purposeful air which always enveloped him. She wondered why she had felt compelled to give him that information about her engagement, for she had not intended to do so. She had not even gone so far with Cathie, since John himself was treating it as a secret understanding between them. The fly buzzing on the window-pane distracted her, and she was looking round for a weapon of destruction when John came in.

'Hullo, pet. Have you finished with the Cash Book?'

'Yes, John. I've just been arranging my birthday celebrations with Mr. Darrington. I had a bright idea. Thought we'd have a little tea-party in the cove in the afternoon, weather permitting, and then follow on with the supper-party here.'

'Good idea, but I shan't be able to join the afternoon party, my dear.'

'Oh, John, why not?'

'I've entered for the car rally over at Bollington. Only a friendly little affair.' He saw that she was disappointed and he came across to her. 'Sorry, darling, but you did say the celebrations would begin at seven on Saturday evening, didn't you?'

'Yes. The picnic was an afterthought. We all like swimming and I thought it would give us a good appetite for the evening.'

'You'll enjoy it with the Elmore crowd. They're not really my cup of tea, dear, and a whole afternoon and evening of them would be a bit much.'

'Is Eileen going to the rally?'

'Yes. She's entered her car for one of the events. Only six in her class, and she's a good chance of winning.'

'You'll be back by seven, won't you?'

She saw the look of irritation which crossed his face, and was sorry that she had spoken. She knew he hated to feel tied.

96

'Oh, yes, ma'am,' he said lightly, but there was an edge to his voice.

'Sorry, darling. I didn't mean to sound possessive, but it's a special day for me, after all.'

'So it is. Don't put reins on me, though, Stella. I've never liked the feel of 'em.'

'I'm with you there. I hope you both come back with prizes, and that will make a bumper evening of it.'

He smiled wickedly as he took her in his arms.

'Well done. You shall have a prize for that. I think emeralds are your stones, all the same.'

'Brute,' she said, half laughing until his mouth stopped hers.

She found it difficult to turn her attention to work after he had gone, and got no further than putting a piece of paper into her typewriter. Her thoughts were on the future. She would always have to handle him carefully, she thought. He would never want to feel bound by possessive love. She must learn to love him and let him be free of her when he wished. He was restless, full of vitality, with a questing temperament, enjoying any sort of challenge, any risk. That was why he enjoyed driving as he did: it offered him the challenge, the excitement, the release to his nervous energy which he needed. She must learn to make no demands; only be happy in his love and not try to change him.

It was this resolution which kept her contented when she saw little of him during the next two weeks. He was busy in his office most of the day and was never able to make arrangements to be with her after her office hours. She could understand this, for discounting Eileen's presence, the manager of an hotel could never call any time his own during the season, even a slack season. She did ask him again if she could help more with his correspondence, for he spent a lot of time at his typewriter.

'I'm getting a first-class typist,' he said, grinning at her. 'Surprising what you can do with two fingers.'

'But I've time to spare these days, John. You should let me do some of it for you.'

'Oh, they're only odds and ends not worth dictating. I got ninety out of Eileen's car last night.'

Stella repressed her instinct to say do be careful, darling, and expressed suitable admiration. She thought there was an air of suppressed excitement about him. He always looked twice as alive as anybody she knew, but that morning she sensed something more, and wondered whether Eileen had made any progress in persuading Darrington to sell the hotel. She had seen them talking on the terrace together when she arrived that morning.

'Run along, sweetheart. You always have a sadly distracting influence and I've a load to do. If you really want a job, take those cheques down to the lodge for Darrington to sign, will you? He's taking his sister and brother-in-law out for the day and I want to get the cheques signed before he goes. Have you seen them? His sister and her husband, I mean.'

'Only in the distance.'

'As you might expect, she's not exactly pretty. Lively, though. Her husband's something in the City. They run rather a nice Alvis. Darrington's taking them in his car, so I'll have a chance to inspect that Alvis some time today.'

Stella took the cheques down to the lodge, and after Darrington had signed them he went out into the hall with her and introduced her to the couple who were waiting there, studying a map.

'Felicity, my dear, this is Miss Verney, our secretary. My sister, Mrs. Crayne.'

She was small and slight with a dark skin, dark brown eyes and black hair. Her heart-shaped face puckered up oddly when she smiled and she reminded Stella of a vivacious monkey. She wore a dark green jumper over a green tweed skirt, and a brilliant, flame-coloured silk scarf was knotted carelessly round her neck. Stella thought she was about Darrington's age, but the only family likeness which she could detect was the set of the head and shoulders. They both carried themselves with complete assurance. Her voice was deep and attractive, and she shook Stella's hand with a firm grasp.

Her husband was considerably older, a tall, heavily built man with greying hair. He greeted Stella with courteous gravity, investing their meeting with the formality of a state occasion.

'I hope you have a nice day,' said Stella, smiling. 'We've lovely country round here. Perhaps you know it.'

'No,' said Felicity. 'We've never been in these parts before. We either go south in search of the sun for our holidays, or north to Scotland and rain. My husband insists on calling it mist, though. His mother was Scottish and that explains his passion for that dour, damp country,' she added mischievously.

Her husband smiled at her but said nothing, and Felicity turned to her brother.

'I'd rather walk round that bit of coast, Nick. Can't we leave the car somewhere here?' she asked, pointing to a spot on the map.

'Well, I know you can't sit still in a car for more than an hour, so perhaps we'd better. Can't bear fidgety passengers.'

'It will do Hector good to walk. He's putting on weight. It'll ruin the set of that kilt, dear.'

'I haven't worn it for over a year, and probably shan't for another five, if you have your way about holidays. Anybody would think, Felicity, that I pranced about in a kilt and sporran every day, from the way you talk.'

Felicity gurgled.

'I've never forgotten you at that ball, darling. And the terrible woman with the red hair who insisted that you were members of the same clan and dragged you into that reel. It's a memory I shall recall with joy to my dying day.'

'If I were you, I'd take a stick to her,' observed Nick. 'Women have no gallantry.'

Stella left them arguing over the map, and rather envied them their day.

She had another encounter with Felicity at the end of the week. Stella was picking some sweet-peas from her garden and Felicity hailed her and asked if she might help.

'Do. I'm hoping to get enough for all the dining-room tables.'

'Nick tells me this garden is all your work.'

'I didn't do the first digging. That was the gardener's work. I like looking after it. A nice change from my office desk and it's useful, too. I can grow the kind of flowers I like arranging. Are you interested in gardening?'

'Very much. We've frightful soil, but I do a lot of pottering and get some fair results. We live in Surrey. On chalk.'

They talked on happily about gardening until Stella's trug was full, when Felicity turned her attention to the weeds.

'It's a phobia with me. I have to pull them up wherever I see them. My hands are never presentable, and I'm always ruining my best stockings. A hopeless grubber, that's me. And very conscious of it when I see anybody like that,' she added, as Eileen Ridlow strolled past, every fair hair in place, her tailored grey suit faultless, her court shoes gleaming and unspotted although the gravel paths were wet from a recent shower. 'It's odd,' went on Felicity, 'but I always get unexpected visitors like that when I'm at my grubbiest in the garden. Fortunately, Hector is used to bringing home important people in the business world and finding his wife on hands and knees in a windcheater and slacks hauling convolvulus out of a muddy bed.'

'Doesn't he give you any warning?'

'Sometimes. But he doesn't mind, bless him. He's not nearly so conventional as he looks, and sometimes I really think he enjoys catching me out. This is my most hated enemy,' added Felicity, tugging ferociously at some ground elder.

Watching that small, intent figure, Stella decided that there was something very appealing about Felicity Crayne.

'You want a fork to tackle that,' she said.

'No, I'll get it,' said Felicity with such grimness that Stella laughed.

'You share your brother's determination, I can see.'

'Hector's less polite. He calls it the Darrington obstinacy. Do you like working for Nick?'

Stella found this sudden shot a little disconcertaing.

'Yes. Yes, I do, now I'm getting used to him. Not that I see much of him. His book keeps him very busy.'

'M'm. He's a bit worried about this place, I think. Doesn't say much, but it's not doing too well just now, I gather.'

'No. We're having a shocking season. I'm sorry about that. I can't understand it. We've never been as quiet as this.'

'It's a delightful place. Ideal for holidays, in my opinion. I'm sorry we have to go next Tuesday, but our child arrives home on Wednesday.'

She spoke in an unusually detached tone for a parent, and Stella said:

'Somehow, I didn't imagine you had any children.'

'Peter's our only child. He's nearly fourteen. Away at school in Sussex. He's bringing a friend home with him for a fortnight. Hector and I like to have a holiday to ourselves before the school breaks up. We seem to get so little time alone together, and I think that's bad, so we always make an effort to have one holiday on our own each year. Never marry into big business, Miss Verney. Not unless you're very lukewarm about your husband. Your personal life is apt to get swallowed up. Hullo, darling,' she added as her husband came up, followed by Darrington.

'I might have known I'd find you here. I wondered if you felt like a swim.'

Felicity scrambled to her feet, brushing the soil from her hands.

'Rather. Have you brought my things?'

'Nick has.'

'I've just been asking Miss Verney how she liked working for you, Nick. I don't think she's sure.'

'Really?'

'She's probably like me. Doesn't like to be organised too thoroughly.'

'If you're going to undermine discipline among my staff, you won't be invited here again, my girl,' said Nick good-humouredly.

Felicity surveyed her husband and Nick as they stood side by side, and her eyes sparkled.

'Lords of creation,' she said softly. 'I wish I had my camera.'

'Take her away, Hector. I want a word with Miss Verney.'

They went off arm-in-arm, and Darrington turned to Stella.

'Who is taking charge in Marbury's absence tomorrow afternoon?'

'Bob will look after the arrivals. He's quite capable if he's well briefed beforehand. There are only four coming in and two going, but Mr. Marbury will be here in the morning to see the departures off.'

She didn't think he liked the idea of the porter being in

charge in the afternoon, but he only said:

'I see. You've arranged everything satisfactorily for your birthday?'

'Yes, thank you. Confess that my garden's a success,' she said, holding the trug out for his approval.

'You get full marks. I'll see you tomorrow evening, then.'

He nodded and went. She had a feeling that he was displeased about something, but could not think of any reason. She dismissed the thought and went back to the hotel.

She was in a quiver of excitement the moment she woke up the next morning and saw the sun streaming in through the window. This was her day. She imagined her father's dry satisfaction, Nan's relieved approval, and Cathie's quiet pleasure at the news they would be given that evening. Although she did not deeply mind about the world's opinion, it had pricked her many times to read criticism of John into Nan's observations, and it was not exactly soothing to one's pride to appear in the eyes of the world as the girl John Marbury amused himself with when there was nothing better to do. That was how the Elmores, fierce in their loyalty, had interpreted John's behaviour at the Christmas dance, and Stella's lips had perforce been sealed. Now she was proud that John would kill such ideas once and for all. They had been through rough patches, as all couples doubtless did. There were faults on both sides. But she loved him and was sure he loved her. And understanding grew with love. He had a spirited, unusual temperament, and love would teach her the wisest way to handle it. Ordinary, easy-going people like the Elmores couldn't be expected to understand the more complex nature of a person like John. He was so different. He glittered in comparison. That was why she loved him, she thought, as she watched the motes hovering in the sunbeam which slanted across her bed.

He telephoned that morning to wish her many happy returns of the day, and said that he would bring his present with him that evening. He sounded excited.

'Are you going to bring two cups back?' she asked.

'Tankards, dear. This is only a small club affair, you know.'

It was, she knew, a speed hill climb for various classes of

cars, and she had attended similar trials with him before. She knew better than to express any fears.

'Well, remember me to the gang. And I wish you both the best of luck, darling.'

'Thanks, Stella. Until tonight.'

Jimmy and Mike Elmore, nobly giving up cricket, joined Cathie, Midge and Stella for the picnic. It was like old times when they were all children, thought Stella, lying back on the hot sand in that delicious pause, half trepidation, half joy, before plunging into the sea. The weather was perfect; the first really hot day of that miserable summer. The sea was choppy and inviting, and she felt happy and relaxed with these friends who were as comfortable to be with as a pair of old slippers; who were simple and jolly and kind, and glad to share in her happiness.

Cathie sat down beside her.

'Midge is overcome at the thought of seeing Nick tonight. Heaven knows how long we'll have to wait for her now. She insisted on going right to the end of the rocks to undress for fear of being overlooked.'

'It's a funny age. Takes you different ways. What a heavenly day, Cathie. A day to remember.'

'I'm so glad, dear.'

Stella turned her head and gave her friend a smile, then resumed her study of the sky between half-shut eyes. No need to put it in words for Cathie. She had a sixth sense where Stella was concerned, anyway. The sky was a pale, pale blue, and an aeroplane, high up, was tracing beautiful white patterns across it. The sand was burning the backs of her legs and her shoulders. Jimmy came up, shaking his head like a dog, the water trickling down his hairy legs like snails' tracks.

'When are you two girls coming in? It's damned cold, I may say.'

'We're waiting for Midge. She's gone nearly to Wibley Bay in an effort to find security from the public gaze,' said Cathie.

'Quaint child. Did you know that the old man's going to a pottery demonstration this afternoon, Stella?'

'Oh, no!'

'Oh, yes. Mark my words, we'll be setting up a kiln in the

house next. Come on, Midge. Who do you think is interested in watching you undress?'

'There's no need to be coarse,' said Midge with dignity, but the dignity broke down as Jimmy chased her into the water.

'It sounds cold,' said Cathie, as Midge squealed.

'Come on. Let's do it together.'

Cathie took Stella's hand and they ran in, as they used to when they were children, not separating until they were beyond the breakers, when they both plunged at the same time and began to swim steadily out to sea. They were good swimmers, and they moved easily together for about a hundred yards before turning over and floating. It was blissfully peaceful, being gently rocked on the waves, thought Stella, moving her hands lazily. Now and again a small wave chopped up against her face in a friendly manner. She half-closed her eyes against the sun . . . When she turned over and began to swim back, Cathie was already on the rocky ledge from which they could dive.

They had the cove to themselves all the afternoon, and it was a sun-soaked and happy party that trudged up the track to the hotel just after six o'clock.

'I'm ravenous,' said Mike. 'Hope you've laid on a good supper, Stella.'

'I have.'

'My hair's sopping, and I did want to look nice tonight,' said Midge tragically.

Stella looked at the mop of wet black curls which shone like coal.

'Looks all right to me.'

'No, it'll all frizz up when it's dry. And it's terribly sandy. Your hair always looks so silky and good-tempered, Stella. Mine so often seems in a kind of rage.'

'Nobody's going to mind what sort of mood your hair's in, my child. Gosh, this is a steep climb. People drop dead doing this sort of thing, you know,' panted Jimmy.

Stella took Cathie and Midge off to her office to repair the ravages of sun and sea. They were few in Stella's case, for she was the fortunate possessor of a skin which was unaffected by the sun, and, glowing with happiness and physical well-being, she was looking her best in the flower-patterned nylon frock which fitted the brightness of that summer day.

The Elmore car arrived with a good deal of noise just before seven, depositing Stella's father, Nan and Mr. and Mrs. Elmore at the hotel entrance. Stella and Cathie had walked to the gate to meet the car, but had been forced to leap for their lives as Mr. Elmore swept the car round and through the gates as though he were rushing a hill. They arrived back at the hotel entrance, slightly puffed, just as Mr. Elmore was discussing with Bob the most convenient place to leave the car. From Bob's expression, it was obvious that he did not consider the car a good advertisement for the hotel, but Mr. Elmore's expansive geniality was unabashed.

With her tribe stafely gathered in the small room next to the dining-room, which she had decorated lavishly with sweet-peas and roses the previous day, Stella helped her father to dispense sherry.

'I do hope John's not going to be late,' she said, as the clock struck seven, and then she turned eagerly as the door opened. But it was Darrington who came in, followed by Charles, the head waiter, each bearing champagne in ice buckets. Darrington wore a light grey suit and sported a red carnation, and Stella warmed to him for this festive participation.

It was the first time they had met that day, and he came across to her and offered his congratulations before greeting the party, all of whom he knew with the exception of Nan.

'Another one at this end, Charles, I think,' said Darrington as he accepted a glass of sherry from Stella.

They all chatted merrily until half-past seven, when Stella, feeling a prick of anxiety, said that they would not wait any longer for John as he might well be delayed for some time if the rally took longer than expected.

'His was an early event,' she explained, 'but sometimes the order has to be changed, and he could easily be held up for an hour. As it's a cold supper, he can join in quite well when he gets here.'

'Wouldn't mind having a shot at some of those hill trials,' said Mike.

'What, with our car?' asked Midge, incredulously.

And laughing, they sat down at the long table, well launched on the subject of cars. With the Elmores one never had to fear lapses in the conversation, thought Stella, shouting to Nan above the boom of Jimmy's laugh. The trouble was to get a word in edgeways. They were all of them interested in everything, ready to argue about anything, and the best company in the world, she decided as Darrington threw back his head and roared at some sally of R.J.'s. It just needed John to make the circle perfect for her.

She knew that it was foolish to worry and that these friendly little car rallies were not dangerous, but she had never forgotten seeing a small car turn over at a bend and roll down a steep slope to crumple up against a tree. The driver had been thrown clear and sustained nothing more serious than a broken collarbone, but since then, Stella had never been able to stifle a faint uneasiness, knowing how reckless John could be when he was behind the wheel. He would never mind taking a chance.

At half-past eight they were sitting over coffee, still without John, and Stella was finding it difficult to keep her mind on her guests. He could surely have telephoned if the proceedings had delayed him so much. She had pictured him seriously injured, on his way to hospital, until she remembered that Eileen Ridlow was with him and could telephone in such an emergency. It was hardly likely that they were both injured.

'I guess your young man's stranded with a puncture somewhere, Stella,' said Mike cheerfully, noticing Stella's expression as she stirred her coffee. She smiled.

'Seems like it.'

She looked at the empty champagne bottle in front of her and felt that her smile was glued on. They had drunk her health, wished her well, but the toast which should have been proposed had remained unspoken. Perhaps only Darrington and Cathie knew with certainty the news which Stella and John were to celebrate that night, but there had been an air of expectancy about her friends which indicated that the news would be no great surprise. Why should it be? She and John had been linked for years now, and she had had enough hints about it, in all conscience. For one dreadful moment, when

R.J. had proposed her health, she thought he was going to refer to John, but he had tactfully confined himself to Stella only, and that with merciful and unusual brevity. The coldness which had put a finger on her at that juncture increased its hold with every minute that passed, and when nine o'clock struck, she felt that she was caught in a frozen nightmare, and her mind was blank so that she could not think how to bring the evening to an end. The empty chair beside her now seemed as large as a tomb, engulfing her. She heard her voice and laughter as though they belonged to a stranger. There could have been no accident. Such news travels fast. As this realisation slowly dawned on her, she felt humiliation seeping into every pore, melting the frozen misery, until she felt as though she were on fire.

At some time, she had no clear idea when, she caught Darrington's eyes on her. Then he leaned across to Cathie to say something, and in a moment got to his feet. Stella would never have suspected that he could act with such charm and tact, but she blessed him from the depths of her heart for discarding his blunt staff in favour of a delicate wand.

'Ladies and gentlemen,' said Darrington after Jimmy had knocked on the table to quieten the company, 'I am sorry that I have to be the first to leave the party, but I'm afraid that's unavoidable, so may I, on my own behalf, and I am sure on yours, thank Stella for inviting us to share her birthday celebrations. I am very glad she chose to do so at the Cormorant, and would like to express the hope that we may share many more birthdays with her in this very pleasant manner. Good wishes, Stella, and thank you.'

And after that, it was easy. Cathie said that the wine had made her sleepy. Mrs. Elmore declared that Midge ought not to have a late night because she was starting off early the next morning on a treasure hunt with some school-friends, and Jimmy reminded them that there was no guarantee that the car would start, and, anyway, some of them would have to walk and they'd better decide who.

In the end, the older generation went by car, with the addition of Midge. The two boys and Cathie were waiting on the terrace for Stella when the red M.G. roared up the drive, closely followed by the green Aston Martin.

'Where's Stella?' asked John, as he climbed out.

'In her office, I believe, putting her coat on. We're just going home,' said Cathie coldly.

'So early? Good lord! Thought we'd be in at the death.'

'Did you?' asked Jimmy, and Cathie put a restraining hand on his arm as Eileen Ridlow joined them and was hurriedly introduced by Marbury.

'We've won a tankard each,' she said triumphantly.

'Congratulations,' said Mike. 'A nice job, that car of yours.'

Wearing dark, well-tailored slacks and a wind-cheater showing a bright scarf tucked in at the throat, Mrs. Ridlow looked a trim and competent figure as she walked round the car with Mike, talking about the competition. Marbury went into the hotel to look for Stella, and Cathie and Jimmy sauntered down the drive.

'I could wring his blasted conceited neck,' growled Jimmy.

'I know. But it wouldn't do any good, laddie. The kindest thing for us to do is to ignore the whole thing. If only somebody had removed that empty chair tonight!'

Jimmy dug his hands into his pockets and mooched round, kicking the gravel savagely, his kindly nature outraged by this callous public insult to Stella, whom he regarded as one of the family.

Stella had her coat on and was just summoning up courage to join the others and appear bright and normal when John came into her room.

'Stella, pet, I'm terribly sorry. Eileen's event had to be postponed because of two late arrivals, and then we simply had to celebrate with Rollo and the boys when we walked off with a tankard apiece. A double victory. I mean to say. Just couldn't get out of it. Thought we'd be back before you broke up, though.'

'The supper was at seven. It's now just gone ten. There's a limit to the time one can wait for an absent guest.'

'I knew you'd be angry, but it was a bit of an achievement, dear, winning both events against stiff opposition.'

He was speaking quickly, the words tumbling out, his face

flushed and his eyes avoiding hers. He was acting, she thought, and wondered why.

'You know what this party was meant to celebrate, didn't you?'

'Your birthday, my dear. What else? And you're quite right to feel cross with me for not turning up. I'll just give you your present and beg forgiveness again on Monday when you've had time to get over it. It really was exciting, Stella, today. I was the last competitor in my event so I knew what I had to beat . . .'

He went on talking quickly as he walked about the room. She did not take in what he said about other competitors, Eileen's race, the people there whom she knew. Watching him, she knew that he was acting for all he was worth. He had known exactly what her party was to celebrate. He had meant to buy her an engagement ring. She knew that she had not misunderstood his words on the day of their reconciliation. At some time since then he had changed his mind, and remembering that he had not used the actual words engagement ring on that occasion, he had seen the way out. Now he was acting with consummate skill to make her think she had been mistaken, banking on her pride to keep her silent on the chief issue, paving the way for her to be annoyed at his failure to be present at her birthday party, pleading guilty and giving her time to adjust herself to this new version and save her face by ignoring his backing out of an engagement. Now she understood why she had seen so little of him during the past weeks, why there had been no further mention of a ring. There had been a loophole through which he could wriggle without the specific unpleasantness of putting his *volte-face* into words, and he was wriggling with all the skill and charm at his disposal.

'I'm tired, John, and the others are waiting for me. Good night.'

'I'll go down on my knees again on Monday. Meanwhile, take your present, Stella.'

She picked up the little box he had put on her desk and opened it. Inside was a pair of emerald ear-rings. He remembered that he had mentioned emeralds, she thought dryly, and felt a hysterical desire to laugh. If she had opened this present at the supper table that evening, Nan would have been quite convinced that Stella was in moral danger. It was a handsome pay-off, she thought. Whether it was reaction from the devastating emotional storm she had been through that evening, or the effect of his play-acting on her, she did not know, but her mind seemed suddenly clear and cold, and the stark truth came away from the soft wrappings of the past so that she had no hesitation in saying calmly:

'Thank you, John, but rich gifts wax poor in these circumstances. I shall follow Ophelia's example and hand it back. Good night.'

He looked a shade uneasy for all his dash.

'No kiss of forgiveness? Perhaps on Monday, then.'

She left him without another word.

Chapter Ten

WALKING to the hotel on Monday morning, Stella wondered whether she could see the season out at the Cormorant. In fairness to Darrington, she felt that she ought to stay until the summer season was over. Replacements were difficult at this time of the year. But the thought of working with John now seemed impossible, and after the humiliation of her birthday evening, she felt that she never wanted to have to meet Darrington's eyes again. Pity would shrivel her up.

She stopped from force of habit and watched the gay little boats bobbing in the harbour, but without taking in what she saw. Not one word had been said at home about John, and on Saturday night the Elmores had talked feverishly all the way home about every other subject under the sun. Really, she thought, the pointed avoidance of the topic was more painful than discussion would have been. Now she had to face John again, and she prayed that he would not stage a reconciliation.

Surely he had humiliated her enough. This hope, however, was not realised, for he appeared before she had her coat off that morning.

'Any hope for me today, pet?'

'As far as I'm concerned, John, our relationship is a strictly business one from now on. I'm sure that won't really be any hardship to you.'

'Now come, Stella. I've said I'm sorry. You know what I am where cars are concerned. Let's be friends.'

She looked at him with puzzled eyes. Why, if he did not want to be involved with her, did he not seize the escape she offered? What did he want of her? She felt that there was something behind it which she did not understand, and had little hope that he would enlighten her.

'Your actions and your words don't line up, John.'

'You're making too much of it, my dear. I behaved badly, thoughtlessly, I know. But surely to goodness that doesn't mean that we're to be enemies from now on.'

That rang a little bell, but the connection eluded her and she said quietly:

'Not enemies. That's childish.'

'You'll come round, Stella, I'm sure. We've known each other too many years to let a little thing like this break up a pleasant friendship.'

She almost smiled at his careful choice of words.

'You might as well know now that I've laid a wreath on that . . . pleasant friendship. It's finished, John. I shan't change my mind.'

He looked at her, hesitated, then came to her swiftly and took her in his arms. Somehow, that was the biggest insult of all. She remained rigid and passive in his arms as he kissed her, and when he released her he knew that it was all over. He shrugged his shoulders.

'I'm sorry. Do you intend to stay on here?'

'I haven't decided. I ought to stay until the end of the season. It's difficult to find secretaries just now, at the height of the holiday season, and I don't want to make things awkward.'

'Well, I hope you'll see reason and change your mind, but

111

if you won't, I don't see any point in making a martyr of yourself to save inconvenience. I could probably cope myself for that matter. We're not very busy.'

He would like her to leave and increase Darrington's difficulties, she thought, her mind still working with that cold clarity which had taken possession of her on Saturday night.

'I'll have to think about it. I shall probably resign at the end of August. Meanwhile, there is no reason why we can't work together in a normal business manner. Is that the post you wish me to deal with?'

'Yes. Well, it's your choice, Stella. I shall be only too happy if you change your tune.'

He went and Stella uncovered her typewriter. It was odd, this cold feeling that had gripped her. It was as though her heart had received a dentist's injection.

Sitting on the window-seat with her coffee that morning, she saw John walking down the drive with Eileen Ridlow. His arm was in hers and they were both laughing. They made a handsome pair. His fair hair gleamed in the sunshine, and he moved with the grace which had always appealed to her so much. He was a superb physical specimen, she thought, and wondered how he would treat Eileen. She seemed much better armoured than Stella had ever been, but appearances were not an accurate guide to the condition of the heart. Eileen and John were both good at hiding what was in their hearts. She remembered with a sudden pang the laughter she and John had shared, the joy of dancing in perfect unison, the leap in her blood when he took her in his arms.

As the past came up before her eyes, in spite of her efforts to shut it out, the comforting numbness of the injection began to wear off. Painfully she examined that past to see if she had read more into John's attentions than she should. She remembered the many occasions during the past year when his attitude had troubled her and she had withdrawn from him, and always he had gone out of his way to win her back, to stifle her misgivings in his arms. She remembered her plea for frankness about their relationship, and he had said, with his lips brushing hers, 'My future is yours, too.' She had surely been justified in believing that he loved her and wished to marry

112

her. He had either changed, or else had never wanted her for anything more than amusement. Perhaps it was as a mistress, not a wife, that he hoped to win her.

She leaned her head against the wall, feeling mangled and ashamed. For six years she had loved and admired a handsome, pleasure-seeking, self-centred young man, who was not too scrupulous in the means he used to attain his ends, and during the past months she had allowed his love-making to soften her mind and gain her loyalty against her better judgment. Now it was all over. Her mind was clear. But it was a shabby end, and all the more painful for that reason . . .

The next two weeks dragged miserably by. Stella saw little of Darrington, who was immersed in the last chapters of his book, and her encounters with John were brief and businesslike.

As she walked back from the cove one grey, chilly day which would have suited November better than August, she reflected that in ten days' time she would be handing in her resignation to Darrington, and she wondered what to give as her reason. He could hardly fail to understand the real reason, she thought, so perhaps no explanation need be given. She was absorbed in her thoughts so that Miss Mapleton's greeting jolted her.

'Hullo, Miss Verney, the weather doesn't put you off your constitutional, I see.'

'No. I like to get a walk after lunch to blow the cobwebs away. I'm sorry you're so unlucky with the weather this year, Miss Mapleton.'

'Yes. I've always had sunshine here before, but then I've never come in August. September is my month. Still, the Cormorant is just as nice as ever, and I'm feeling a lot better for the change of air.'

Miss Mapleton, a robust looking woman in her late fifties, strode along beside Stella talking about her health, always a favourite subject with her. Stella smiled and replied sympathetically where necessary, but was only giving half her attention to their conversation until she heard Miss Mapleton saying:

'Of course, I told them to write early, but I thought they'd be bound to get rooms in June if they wrote at Easter. I was so

8   113

sorry because I know they would like it at the Cormorant. To tell you the truth, they thought it was odd that I should get in during August when you were full up for June, seeing that we both wrote within a week of each other. I explained, of course, that I might be privileged as a very old friend of the Marbury family. But I see you're not full now, anyway.'

'I'm so sorry, Miss Mapleton, I didn't quite catch what you said at the beginning. Two friends of yours wrote here for accommodation in June, did you say?'

'Yes. Miss Twining and her friend Miss Greatorex. It was Miss Twining who wrote, though. Two old friends of mine, both civil servants. They went abroad last year, on a tour, and had such an exhausting time that they wanted to make sure of a quiet, peaceful holiday this year. "You can't do better than the Cormorant at Ashcombe," I said, and told them all about it. They were so disappointed when they heard you were full up for June. They went to Cornwall instead, and struck rather a poor hotel. They were always hungry, poor dears, and the hot water was seldom hot.'

Stella frowned. They had not been completely full at any time that season, and in June they had been half empty.

'Are you sure they wrote here, Miss Mapleton?'

'Quite sure. In fact, I posted the letter for them, I remember. It was on Easter Monday. I'd spent the afternoon with them and posted the letter on my way home to save them the trouble of going out.'

'Twining. I don't remember the name. Did they want any particular rooms, facing the sea?'

'No. They would have taken any two single rooms available, or even a double room if there had been one.'

'I can't understand it, then, because we weren't full up in June. There must have been some mistake. They did actually receive a letter from us saying that we were full? It wasn't a case of not getting any reply?'

'Oh, no. They had a letter.'

Miss Mapleton was looking a little put out, and Stella said quickly:

'Then it must have happened when I was off duty, and Mr. Marbury dealt with it. I suppose it was the one date we couldn't manage,' said Stella, hastily trying to retrieve the situation.

'It seems like it.'

'Have you seen our new flower garden, Miss Mapleton? I know you're interested in horticulture, and I'd like to show you a most unusual gladiolus I've grown. It's nearly black, streaked with purple.'

Stella led Miss Mapleton to her garden and here kept her chatting for ten minutes, during which time she had hoped the subject of her friends and their holiday had faded from her mind.

Back in her office, she tried to sort out her confused thoughts, and could arrive at only one answer. At no time during that disastrous season had the Cormorant been fully booked up. She had never seen a letter from a Miss Twining. John had sorted the post since before Easter. She found it hard to believe that he had deliberately refused people accommodation, but the more she thought about it, the clearer became the explanation of this extraordinarily bad season. He had passed on to her the regulars and a few others, and had answered the remainder of the enquiries himself, in the negative. That explained the amount of typing he did. That explained, too, why he had tried to avoid a break with her, to keep her in his camp at all costs. As an enemy, she could be a danger to him, for nobody was in a better position than she to discover what had been going on.

She sat there, shaken and horrified by this evidence of plotting and deceit but unable to disbelieve it, since it tied in with John's whole attitude to Darrington and the hotel. As her own predicament became clear, her dismay grew. What should she do? Although she had finished with John, she had always felt in her bones that this hotel belonged to the Marbury family, and all the affection and loyalty which she had felt for John's father tugged at her. The past, too, in a sense bound her to John, even though their personal relationship had foundered. But the only honest thing to do was to tell Darrington.

She walked up and down her room, wishing desperately that Miss Mapleton had never raised the subject. In a few weeks she would be leaving here and need never have known of John's dishonesty. She thought of Darrington. He had always treated her fairly, been straightforward with her. She could not be a party to this trickery, and if she said nothing she would be just as guilty of dishonesty as John. She stopped short at the window. Below her, Miss Mapleton was talking to John. Stella went to her desk, and found herself trembling as she sat down. He would be here in her office within five minutes, she knew.

Any doubts that she might be mistaken about the conclusions she had drawn vanished when she saw John's face. His eyes were alert, his manner wary.

'Stella, I've been talking to Miss Mapleton. She's a bit put out because there seems to have been some muddle about a booking for friends of hers. She said you seemed rather confused about it and she thought she'd better mention it to me. What happened?'

'According to Miss Mapleton, a Miss Twining wrote in June for two rooms and received a reply from us to the effect that we were fully booked at that time. I never saw any letter from a Miss Twining,' she concluded, looking at him steadily.

'Oh, the old girl's probably got things muddled up.'

'I don't think so. Miss Mapleton is a very clear-headed person and she's quite certain of the facts.'

'So what? We can't do anything about it now, can we?'

'I'm wondering how many people had the same letter from us as Miss Twining.'

He looked at her as though weighing her up. Then he smiled and said:

'I shouldn't worry your head about it, Stella. Not your pigeon.'

'Have you been deliberately swindling Darrington, then, John? For that is what it means.'

'I'm afraid I can't take you into my confidence any more. Your loyalty always has been shaky on this issue. But to set your mind at rest on the question of swindling, our offer to Darrington for this place is a very generous one and will more than off-set any small losses through carelessness on the part of the staff in making bookings.'

'A typical John Marbury wriggle,' said Stella, her eyes

116

scornful as she looked at him and wondered how she could ever have admired him.

'I would advise you to leave it at that.'

'Has Darrington agreed to sell?'

'Mrs. Ridlow's offer is in his hands now. He hasn't replied yet. There's little doubt that he'll accept. It's a far better offer than he could hope to get from any other source.'

'I see.'

'It's a good way out of a bad business investment for him.'

'Quite,' said Stella dryly.

John picked up a pencil from her desk and looked at it as he said casually:

'It would be foolish to interfere in things which you don't understand, my dear. You're rather fond of making mountains out of mole-hills, but a little confusion over one summer booking is a very small mole-hill indeed. I think it would be most unwise of you to exaggerate it. You've not changed your mind about resigning at the end of the month?'

'No.'

'I'm sorry. But you'll have a good reference from me. It shouldn't be difficult for you to find another job. One that would pay you a good deal better than this, probably. You're an excellent secretary.'

'Thank you.'

'If I can do anything to help, I hope you'll let me know, Stella. However badly you think of me, I'm still fond of you. We've had good times together and been friends for many years. The old man was fond of you, too. Can't wipe those ties out just because of this split between us. Anyway, I haven't given up all hope of that split mending, and I'd like to see you settled in a good job. I feel responsible to that extent, and the old man would want me to keep an eye on you. So any influence I can bring to bear is at your disposal.'

'Thank you, John,' said Stella, and for once her face revealed nothing to his scrutiny.

His hand was on the handle of the door when her next remark brought him spinning round.

'When does Darrington get back from London?'

'Late tonight or tomorrow morning.'

'I see,' said Stella, and began to type.

He hesitated, frowning, and then went.

Stella had little sleep that night. She knew what her own course of action must be. John's veiled threats had only strengthened her decision. But the shock of this discovery and the thought of the unpalatable role of informer which she had to play kept her mind in a fever of restlessness. Her conscience allowed her no other way out. Darrington was being manoeuvred into a forced sale by dishonest means. To be an accessory after the fact was impossible. But she felt as though her heart was being mangled. The last drops of her love were being wrung out in an agony of mind which she could hardly endure as she lay in bed watching the clouds move across a pale, moon-washed sky, which looked as cold as Darrington's eyes. It was not going to be pleasant facing those eyes.

The sun was shining next morning when she walked down Church Lane, and the trees were already beginning to hint at autumn. The mountain ash berries glowed in coral clusters and the leaves of birch and hawthorn showed touches of gold. The beautiful, bell-like berries on the yew trees by the church were pink and glowing as though lit from within. But Stella had no eyes for them that morning, and she crossed the cricket green and walked through the gardens, quite unconscious of her surroundings. Even the raucous cry of the gulls round the harbour failed to penetrate the wall of leaden misery that imprisoned her. She was a long time climbing up the winding cliff path, and her legs felt as though she had walked miles by the time she reached the hotel. She managed to smile at the porter.

'Good morning, Bob. Did Mr. Darrington get back last night?'

'Yes, Miss Verney. He's been across here once this morning, asking for you.'

'Oh, has he? I'm rather late, I'm afraid. Any message?'

'No, Miss.'

Propped up against the telephone on her desk, Stella found an envelope, across the back of which was written:

'Please come to the lodge immediately you get in. N.D.'

Had Miss Mapleton herself, then, gone to Darrington? That

was a way out which she had not anticipated. Rather odd, though, for in Miss Mapleton's eyes, the hotel was run, as always, by a Marbury. Perhaps it was for some other reason that Darrington wanted to see her. He had taken the manuscript of his book to his publishers the previous day. Perhaps something urgent had cropped up in connection with that. She was still wondering how to broach her own disclosures when she knocked at the door of the lodge and was shown into Darrington's study by Rickie. Immediately she saw his face, she knew she need worry no more about how to broach the subject. He knew. She felt the impact of his anger like a physical blow.

'Sit down, Miss Verney.'

He nodded to a chair. His face was as grim and bleak as any Arctic waste, and Stella felt suddenly frightened. He spoke with cold deliberation, as though making a police statement.

'Just after I got back from London last night, Marbury brought Miss Mapleton across to see me. She said that friends of hers had been refused accommodation here in June because we were full up. After she left us, Marbury reluctantly expressed the suspicion that you had been turning away applications all this summer, and that this accounted for the appalling season we've had. Just a moment,' he said, holding up his hand at her ejaculation. 'Hear me out. Your reason for doing this, Marbury thought, was to induce me to sell the hotel to Mrs. Ridlow and himself. He said that you had always bitterly resented the fact that he no longer owned the Cormorant, and he had himself unfortunately made it clear that if the hotel didn't return to his hands, he would be leaving at the end of this summer as he and Mrs. Ridlow were going into partnership and would buy another hotel if I didn't sell this. He was afraid that you had behaved in this incredible manner in a desperate determination to keep him here. What have you to say, Miss Verney?'

His eyes had never left her face while he was speaking, and she felt that they were boring into her.

'That it's completely untrue. Miss Mapleton told me about her friends yesterday. I challenged Jo – Mr. Marbury, and he tried to pass it off as a mistake. He knew I intended to tell you as soon as you got back, and he stepped in first. You can't

119

believe that I would do a thing like that. Swindle you. Surely you can't!' she exclaimed desperately.

'I am investigating the facts. We'd better have Marbury over,' he said, picking up the telephone.

This was rock-bottom, thought Stella, as they waited in silence for Marbury. She felt sick and shaken by his treachery.

When John came in he turned first to her.

'I'm terribly sorry about this, Stella. But I had to do it.'

'Had to lie your way out at my expense?' she asked bitterly.

'I'll conduct this, if you please,' rapped out Darrington. 'Miss Verney says she knew nothing of this matter until Miss Mapleton told her about her friends yesterday. Then she suspected that you had turned people away and she challenged you with it. You said it was all a mistake, and Miss Verney thinks that you have come to me with this accusation to forestall her disclosure to me.'

'Good lord, Stella! This really is going a bit far. There's no need to panic. I've asked Mr. Darrington to be lenient with you, because, in a way, I'm the cause of it all, and I'm sure he won't be harsh. But don't start telling lies. That isn't going to help any of us.'

How convincing he was, thought Stella, looking at him with wondering eyes. He turned to Darrington before she could speak.

'I do hope you'll be lenient with her, Darrington. I feel I'm much to blame because she did it for me. And women aren't very rational in such circumstances. Stella's devotion to me has always been . . . a little obsessional. I don't like having to say such things. Embarrassing to all of us. But it may help you to take a more lenient view of her behaviour.'

'I have been swindled out of a considerable sum of money. How much, I suppose we shall never know. I am not inclined to be lenient because it was done for love of you, Marbury, or anybody else, although I agree that there's been far too much mingling of business and . . . pleasure.'

'The personal relationship between Mr. Marbury and myself has nothing to do with this business,' said Stella quietly. 'He wanted to make sure that you would accept Mrs. Ridlow's offer. He's been plotting for that ever since she first came here.'

120

'This doesn't sound like devotion, Marbury,' observed Darrington.

'I'm afraid Stella has been a little touchy about Mrs. Ridlow for some time, and last night we had a rather unpleasant scene. I told her that Mrs. Ridlow and I were engaged to be married. I was damned sorry. I knew it would be a blow. But Stella has rather assumed possession of me for years now, and because I'm fond of her and we're old friends, I suppose I haven't been quite brutal enough in making the limits clear. I'm to blame there, perhaps. But I didn't think spite would make you attack me like this, Stella. You're still upset about last night, and not yourself. You wouldn't behave like this otherwise, I know.'

It was fantastic, thought Stella. He really believed every word he said. He had worked out his part and put himself inside the skin of it as an actor does. Her face burned with humiliation and she wished the floor would open up and swallow her. She could not cope with such bare-faced lying, and although she opened her mouth to speak, the words stuck in her throat and she shook her head helplessly.

'I think we've heard enough about personal feelings,' said Darrington curtly. 'Let's get back to the facts. Who opens the post?'

'Stella,' said John. 'I leave it unopened on her desk each morning and she sorts it and gives me what I have to deal with.'

'That's leaving rather a lot of responsibility to Miss Verney, isn't it?'

'Stella is very capable and has been in the business even longer than I have. I had every confidence in her. If she was in doubt about anything, she discussed it with me over coffee every morning.'

'And Miss Verney signed her own letters?'

'Naturally.'

'And bookings were Miss Verney's responsibility?'

'We discussed them together, but Miss Verney wrote and signed the letters. I kept the records of the bookings as Miss Verney gave them to me.'

'And what is your version, Miss Verney?'

'That was the procedure until Easter. Bryant used to leave the post on my desk and I sorted it, as Mr. Marbury has said.

But when it was suggested that I needed help, Mr. Marbury offered to take over more of the office work, and he collected and sorted the post before I arrived in the morning. He brought me the letters he wanted me to deal with, including the applications for accommodation. But I only had what he gave me.'

'I see. Well, this is deadlock, isn't it? One of you is lying and there is no way of proving which,' said Darrington grimly.

His eyes went from one to the other of them and he said nothing for a few moments. The Darrington silences, thought Stella, were always hard to bear. Then he squared his shoulders and said briskly:

'Well, whether you were directly involved or not, Marbury, you must, I think, accept a certain amount of responsibility for the staff under you. It is your job to know what is going on. I shall take over the management of the hotel from today. Our agreement was to the end of September, I believe, and you will be paid accordingly, but you are free to leave at once. There is no question of my selling the Cormorant to Mrs. Ridlow, so you will doubtless wish to make other plans as soon as possible. That's all.'

He nodded a dismissal, and Marbury's lips tightened, but he made no protest. Indeed, thought Stella, he had got off lightly.

'And Miss Verney?'

'I think you had better leave Miss Verney to me. I'll see you in your office at eleven.'

When the door had closed behind John, Stella looked up at Darrington.

'You believe him, don't you?'

'Not altogether. He had quite a lot at stake, too, and I've never had much confidence in his integrity.'

'Or mine, apparently.'

'I'm up against an unknown factor with you,' he said unexpectedly. 'I don't know to what lengths being in love will drive a woman. Basically, I think you are an honest person. But I know you are, or were, very much in love with Marbury.'

'Does being in love make you untrue to yourself?'

'I've told you, I don't know. I'm not an expert on the subject. But I do know that when he chose, he could influence you quite strongly. I think it's remotely possible that you were in this together, and that Marbury ratted on you when he saw that Miss Mapleton was going to let the cat out of the bag.'

'And you think that if that were so, I would accuse John and try to get out of it myself?'

He spoke carefully.

'If he had played fast and loose with you, and gave Mrs. Ridlow the ring he had promised you, I think it would be expecting a lot of you to take the rap for this and let him wriggle out.'

'I see. Well, you're going to dismiss me, of course, but I would like to try to explain a little more about John. I can take a lot from him, but not the suggestion that I've tagged on to him and am now acting out of jealousy of Mrs. Ridlow. I did love John, for years. At least, I loved the man I thought he was. He swept me off my feet when I was eighteen and I never found out what was under that handsome surface. Anyway, there's been enough mud-slinging this morning, and I don't want to indulge in any more. For the last year, the foundation of our happiness has been cracking. I found that underneath the surface attraction, the fun, there was no substance. I felt we were fundamentally strangers. And I wouldn't accept it. I stifled all sorts of doubts and scruples over John's attitude to you and the hotel, and his blowing hot and cold with me. In that I was dishonest with myself. I despise myself now for compromising over certain principles, in making excuses for him because I was too cowardly to face the truth. But my birthday finished that. I faced the truth then and it was all over between us. I was going to resign at the end of the month because I couldn't bear to go on working with him. I had to make a fresh start. But however I have let John influence me in the past, I do ask you to believe that I've never been disloyal to you. I've done my job as well as I could, and except for one incident, which did bother my conscience, I've never let him influence me against you.'

'What was that?'

She told him of the estimate for the repairs.

'I knew John held one back. I wanted to tell you, but I smothered my conscience by telling myself that it was not my department. I'm guilty of that. But I've never been disloyal in any other respect. I suppose I can't expect you to believe me. John's picture of me this morning was pretty convincing, I must say. But I just wanted to tell you. I'd like to go now.'

'I haven't finished with you yet. I didn't say I believed you had tried to push me out of business in this way. I said I didn't know, but that it was remotely possible. I've a suggestion to make. You heard me say that I'm taking over the management of the hotel forthwith. It's going to be very inconvenient if both you and Marbury go. I shall need a secretary to carry out instructions. Are you willing to stay on in that capacity? You will have no responsibility apart from carrying out my instructions. Your salary will remain the same. It's up to you.'

'Is this your idea of punishment or lenience?'

'Neither. I'm offering you the opportunity to prove your case. I have an open mind on it. If all this job meant to you was Marbury, then you probably won't care to stay on without him, and I shall draw my own conclusions.'

'And they wouldn't be right, even then,' cried Stella passionately. 'Do you think it's easy for me after the cheap picture John drew of me just now to face you at all?' She pressed her hands to her burning face. 'I feel I never want to set eyes on either of you again. I'd like to disappear completely. How can I work for you, knowing that you see me as he painted me? The man-hungry girl stalking him, obsessed with him, willing to rob for him, and jealous of any other woman who approaches him. It's unendurable, to be so humiliated.'

'Not pleasant, I agree, but nothing about this affair is pleasant. Any man who could say the things Marbury said about you, true or not, is a pretty low specimen, but it's up to you whether you sink your pride and work your way out of the mess he's put you in.'

As his eyes held hers, she wondered whether she could bear to stay at the Cormorant where everything would remind her of this unsavoury business. Stay on as a typist under Darrington's eye, on probation; the girl whom Marbury did what he liked with. And yet, she thought, unless she could clear herself here, the bad smell of it would linger with her always.

'I'll stay,' she said.

'Good. I shall take over Marbury's office. I'll see you there at two o'clock to discuss the daily routine. I shall be doing a lot of reorganising. That'll be all for now.'

And quite enough, too, thought Stella as she left him. She couldn't have stood much more. The shock of that morning's revelations coming on top of the restless night of worry and distress made her feel ill. Her legs would hardly carry her, and her head throbbed in a peculiar dull, thudding manner as though John was literally wielding the club which had that morning metaphorically hammered her heart to death.

Chapter Eleven

STELLA had one more encounter with John Marbury before he went out of her life. She hoped that she would not see him again, for when she went into his office to talk to Darrington at two o'clock, the latter took one look at her and sent her home, arranging to see her the next morning. By then, she thought, John might have gone, but when she arrived at the hotel the next morning, she met Eileen Ridlow in the drive, who informed her that they were leaving in half an hour.

'Can you spare a moment, Miss Verney? I'd like a few words with you before we go.'

'I really don't see the point, and I'm due to see Mr. Darrington very shortly.'

'Just five minutes on the terrace seat here. Please.'

Stella hesitated, and then sat down. She could not think what Mrs. Ridlow had to say.

'I'm sorry about this business, Miss Verney. John told me about it last night.'

'I don't want to discuss it.'

'No. I can understand that. But what I wanted to say was, don't be too unhappy over John. He isn't the man for you, my dear. He never was. You've idealised him, I suspect.'

Her cool, calm voice might have been referring to the stone urn at which she gazed, so detached was her manner. She wore a grey suit, black hat, gloves and shoes, and her profile was cold and lovely. An invulnerable face, thought Stella, and envied her that invulnerability. She found it an effort to reply.

'I heard of your engagement yesterday. I hope . . . it will work.'

'I'm sure it will. We've a lot in common, John and I. And I shan't expect as much as you. I know John's marrying me mainly for my money, and because I share his passion for cars.'

'And that seems to you a good foundation for marriage?'

'Certainly. My money makes me completely independent. We can each lead our own lives if we want to, but I think we shall get a good deal of enjoyment together. We intend to travel, do a lot of driving. John has a hankering after racing, and I'd get a kick out of that, too. And as I hold the strings of the biggest purse, I fancy I can call our John to heel if necessary. Tactfully, of course. He's quite mettlesome.'

'I don't see what you get out of it, if that's all you feel about John. Why get married?'

'For companionship, an escort when I need one. A husband performs a useful function socially, especially one as handsome and charming as John. Besides, I'm fond of the young man, but not so fond that I can't keep it in hand. I advise you to keep your affections in hand, Miss Verney. Biggest mistake in the world to spill your all. No man is worth it, and they'll take all if they can and do it as a matter of course. Like greedy children. And here comes my particular greedy child.'

Stella was face to face with John. He stood in front of them and it was difficult for her to slip away.

'Ah, Stella, I wanted to say goodbye.'

'I have nothing to say to you, John. I think you're utterly contemptible.'

'I was afraid you would. But, my dear girl, what else could I do? There was still a chance that Darrington would sell, but I knew he'd see me in hell first if he thought I'd been doing a bit of rigging. I didn't think it would hurt you to take the blame. After all, if he had sold, I'd have seen that you were all right, and if he didn't sell and I left, I couldn't see you wanting to stay here under his ownership. So what harm did it do? I'll give you a reference.'

'What harm did it do? You think it's a trivial matter to be shown up as a swindler of one's employer?'

'Oh, lord, off on the old hell-fire principles again. You do make such mountains out of mole-hills, my dear. Darrington will get somebody to take your place and will have forgotten all about you in a few weeks. I shall give you a good reference and you can get another job that will suit you a lot better than staying on here after I've gone. I've been a pretty agreeable sort of boss, after all. Darrington would be quite a different proposition.'

'I'm glad to say. He hasn't told you, then, that I'm staying on?'

It was his turn to look surprised.

'No. Are you?'

'Yes. I didn't have time to congratulate you yesterday. I do so now. I think you've met your match.'

John laughed a shade uneasily and Eileen's smile held a mocking little gleam.

'Well, we're thinking of buying a hotel in the south of France now. If you can live where you like, why choose this appalling climate? On the whole, perhaps, I'm not so sorry Darrington's refused to sell.'

'Excuse me, but I've an appointment with Mr. Darrington. Goodbye, Mrs. Ridlow.'

'Goodbye, Stella,' said John, holding out his hand.

Stella ignored it and went, dumbfounded by his effrontery. Darrington was at his desk when she went in.

'Good morning, Miss Verney. Are you all right today?'

'Yes, thank you.'

'Well, you don't look it,' he said bluntly, 'but let that pass. Now, about the rest of the staff . . .'

She was surprised at the thoroughness with which he set about reorganising the administration, and was reminded of his sister's remarks about his love of organising. With economy and fool-proof efficiency his aims, he went into the duties of each member of the staff, listing them and jotting down all Stella told him against each name. When only her name remained to be listed, he paused, and frowned at the paper now covered with his square handwriting. Then he turned it over and wrote 'Miss Verney' at the top.

'I shall have a bell rigged up between your room and mine. I'll ring for you in the morning when I'm ready. I'll dictate the letters and have them back for signing about five o'clock. Nothing will go out unless it is signed or seen by me. Understood?'

'Yes,' said Stella, flushing.

'And I don't like this filing system. I want to be able to lay my finger on everything.'

He outlined the filing system he wanted, and then went on to the book-keeping, which he proposed to take over himself.

'I presume,' said Stella icily when he had finished, 'that I am still to keep the postage book, or are you taking that over, too?'

'That will hardly be necessary. I'm taking over all this as much to get myself into the picture as to check on you. I've never done this job, and I want to know it from the bottom upwards so that I can keep an eye on it if I ever install another manager.'

'I'm sorry. It's difficult for me to get used to being a junior again.'

'Promotion will depend on you,' said Darrington, and she looked up to find him trying to stifle a smile.

'I'm afraid I can't find this state of affairs amusing.'

'Forgive my eccentric sense of humour. Lord knows I've little to smile at over this business. How much money I've lost, I don't know, but more than I can afford, I guess. Cheer up. I shan't stand over you with a whip. We shall work well enough together, I'm sure. But . . . I'm giving the orders. If I go broke next year, it'll be my own doing, and nobody else's.'

'Would it help if I took less salary? I mean, I shan't be worth what you pay me. I shall only be doing the work any junior could do. I could take less.'

He smiled then, the smile that transformed his ugly face and invariably made Stella sheathe her sword.

'That's nice of you. No, the margin isn't as narrow as that. It can stay as it is. I want to whip in some advertisements for

128

late holidays and for winter residents. We'll get down to drafting those today. Then I think I'd like you to take a week's holiday. You're looking all in.'

'No, I'd rather not, Mr. Darrington. Please. I want to work. The more work the better. A week at home is the last thing I want.'

'The rest might be good for you.'

'Rest? You don't know Nan's tongue. I told her last night that John was engaged to Mrs. Ridlow. I had to tell her to stop her probing. And Nan can go on saying "I told you so" in a thousand different ways.'

'Why not go away?'

'I can't go away from myself.'

To her horror, she found her mouth trembling and her face broke up as she turned away and put her head in her hands. Anger and disgust had kept her dry-eyed the previous day. She had endured Nan's remarks with a stony control, and had lain awake most of the previous night in a state of frozen misery. Now, out of the blue, her control cracked and splintered, and she sat there helplessly while the tears poured down her face and the sobs shook her body. Darrington pushed his chair back and put a hand on her shoulder for a moment.

'All right. Let it rip,' he said, and walked across to the window, staring out until Stella mopped up her eyes and said, with a catch in her voice:

'I'm sorry. I'm all right now.'

'I'll go and fetch some coffee. Stay there.'

When he returned with two cups of coffee on a tray, she had repaired her face as best she could and had herself in hand.

'Please forgive me. I won't do that again,' she said.

'It probably did you good. You know, at the risk of following Nan's terrible example, I can't help saying again what I said to you once before. He isn't worth it. He never was.'

'I'll never let anybody do this to me again. Never,' she said passionately.

'I doubt if you're the kind of person whose heart is easily put into cold storage.'

'I've learned my lesson,' replied Stella grimly. 'I shall follow Mrs. Ridlow's example in future: look after myself and never let my feelings deflect me from that.'

'My dear girl, haven't you learned yet that you're saddled with your own nature and that you'll never be able to change it? You'd have a better chance of turning a monkey into a fish than yourself into a second Mrs. Ridlow.'

'Experience can change you.'

'Not fundamentally. In small ways, yes. You'll undoubtedly be more cautious now in giving your affections. But Mrs. Ridlow is out of your ken, believe me.'

'Do you admire her?'

'In a way. She knows exactly what she wants and goes for it coolly and confidently. Rather rare in a woman. And she has no illusions about the world.'

'She might have started off by being like me.'

He shook his head, smiling.

'Never. Her blood has always run cold.'

'And so does mine, now. I'm putting my own interests first in future.'

'Are you? Even now, when you're raw from the beating you've taken from Marbury, you're acting true to form in staying on here. Why did you?'

Stella studied her coffee and was silent.

'Come on. Let's work out this argument. Why did you?'

'I had to stay to try to prove to you that I haven't deceived you and been a party to this swindle.'

'There you are, then. It can't be very pleasant for you, staying on here, eating humble pie, in surroundings that must constantly remind you of the past. Do you think the Mrs. Ridlow type would do what you're doing? Not on your life. She'd be away to fresh fields, not caring two hoots about the reputation she left behind. You can't escape from yourself; only get a little thicker armour with the years.'

'I don't find that very comforting now.'

'You were unlucky in coming up against Marbury when you were so young. He has an amazing personality, and yours won't be the only heart he damages. I don't think I've ever seen a finer-looking man.'

'I suppose you think there will be plenty of others, too, who will lie, and, if necessary, steal for him?'

'It's possible.'

'I wish you didn't think that of me.'

'I've told you, I have an open mind about it. I mean what I say.' He glanced at his watch. 'I think I've time to see the rest of the staff before lunch. I'll see them individually. Perhaps you'd ask Mrs. Dacres to come up first. I shan't want you until after lunch. I think it would be a good idea if you went and dibbled about in that garden of yours. And when you feel like taking a holiday, let me know.'

Stella paused at the door, and hesitated.

'What is it?' he asked gently.

'Oh . . . just, thank you.'

She went out to her garden, as he had suggested. The flowers in the hall needed replacing, and she had some gladioli in bloom. It was a still, warm day, and the sun had broken through the morning mist. Her plot of ground was infested with weeds, evidence of her unhappy preoccupation with other matters for the past month. She felt a little better for her talk with Darrington. He had let some fresh air into the situation, she felt. Or perhaps the tears had released some of the tension. There was kindness behind his bluntness; the truth, however unpalatable, was more stiffening than soothing platitudes. Somehow, she thought, she was going to convince him that she had known nothing of John's treachery . . .

*   *   *

In the garden of Brierley, the peace of the summer evening was broken by a loud yell, a crash and the tinkling of glass. Cathie and Stella, about to go into the garden, stopped for a second, transfixed, then Cathie said, 'Dad', and flew around the house.

Mr. Elmore was lying groaning on his back beside a fallen step-ladder, a hammer still clutched in one hand. He was surrounded by nails and screws, half of which had showered the grass around him while the other half had gone with the tin box which had contained them through the top of the cold frame and had come to rest among the lettuces.

'Dad, are you hurt?' asked Cathie anxiously.

'Hurt? Of course I'm hurt. I've just come off the top of

131

a step-ladder on to hard ground and I'm not made of Dunlopillo. I'd better not move. Fetch your mother.'

R.J. refused to budge, convinced that he had broken something. Stella ran to fetch Mrs. Elmore while Cathie persuaded her father to move each of his limbs gently to see where the damage was. When Mrs. Elmore arrived on the scene, he was sitting up rubbing his back.

'You've been a long time, Lou. I might have been in agony,' said R.J. aggrieved.

'I was bottling some plums, dear, and had to seal them. Are you in pain?'

'I don't know. No, I'm not. But I've done something to my back, I'm sure.'

Cathie and Mrs. Elmore helped him up. He moved everything gingerly and seemed almost disappointed when he found that he was uncrippled. The shock resolved into anger.

'Who mended the ladder with that idiotic piece of string?' he demanded.

'I believe Midge did when she picked the pears.'

'Might have been killed. I sometimes think this is a family of lunatics.'

'What were you trying to do, dear?' asked Mrs. Elmore mildly, and Cathie's eyes twinkled.

'Do? Aren't we supposed to be making a pergola down this side of the garden?'

'Oh, I didn't know you were starting that this evening. I thought you said you hadn't got the wood. Here, dear, sit down on the seat until you get your breath.'

'I shall have to get some more wood, of course, but I found enough to get the first two supports in.'

Stella and Cathie looked at the two posts leaning towards each other in a friendly manner, and said nothing.

'Bottling plums!' exclaimed R.J. 'I've a completely heartless family, Stella. There's Midge up there at the window. She must have seen what happened. Doesn't even come down to enquire if her father's crippled.'

'She's washing her hair, dear,' said Mrs. Elmore.

And at that, Stella had to turn her face heavenwards.

'And Mike's fiddling with the wireless set. All more important things than their father's safety. They must have heard that crash. It could have been heard a mile away.'

'But you're all right, dear.'

'How do they know? How do you know? I might have some internal injury. Nobody cares. Bottling plums. Washing hair. Jimmy's probably finishing the sports column of the paper. What do I matter?'

Cathie laid her head for a moment on her father's shoulder, and said, with a smile:

'Just the old bread-winner, R.J.'

He looked at her suspiciously, then his long face broke into a grin as he said:

'It's a good thing I'm so unselfish.'

And at that family saying, they knew all was well, and Mrs. Elmore led the victim away to have a cup of tea.

'Oh, dear,' said Cathie. 'That pergola's going to look dreadful. R.J. won't have the patience to make the supports really strong, and you can imagine what will happen after a gale.'

'What put it into his head?'

'We went to see the garden of an old country house last Sunday. A beautiful place. And there was a pergola. So now we must have a pergola. But it won't look anything like the one we saw on Sunday.'

'Dear R.J. How dull you would find it without him.'

'He's incorrigible. Nobody minds a handyman if only he's handy, but Dad's all enthusiasm and no staying power. He's terribly impatient, and he can't wait to do things properly. He can always think of a quick and cheap way to copy what he sees, and the result's usually shocking. That pergola, if it's finished, will look like a drunken man's nightmare.'

'Oh well, that's life at Brierley,' observed Stella, smiling.

'And how is life at the Cormorant?'

'Reduced to the ranks, as I am, pretty grim. I thought Darrington might ease up after the first week or two, but he hasn't. I'm right back where I started with old Mr. Marbury when I was eighteen. It's the feeling of not being trusted that I can't get used to. I do things instinctively off my own bat, and then get told off for it.'

'What kind of things?'

133

'Well, today, for example, I found we were running low in stationery and telephoned an order to Bowmary's for some more. Darrington happened to come in while I was on the telephone, and told me off for not consulting him first. How can I put the clock back and act as though I know no more about running the office than Midge? I could have thrown something at him.'

'I'm glad you're feeling better. I was getting really worried about you.'

'Well, I don't feel half dead any more, but in a way coming to life is more painful. I feel so angry. I feel angry most of the time. You know, Cathie, I wonder whether I was right to stay on. Whether I'll be able to stick it. Everything about my life at the Cormorant reminds me of John's treachery, and I'm paying every hour I'm there for his dirty trick. The injustice of it burns me up.'

'I know it's a wretched position for you, Stella. But if you've got the grit to see it out, I'm sure it's the right thing to do. I wish you'd follow Nick's advice, and take a short holiday. I still have a week to come and I've got to take it next week. Couldn't we go away for a week together?'

'But I thought Roger was going away next week and you had to be his stand-in?'

'It's changed.' Cathie looked at her hands. 'Roger has been offered a post in North Wales and is going there at the beginning of October. He wants me to take my holiday next week because the new Curator arrives after that and I shall have to be there.'

'Cathie!' Stella turned to her in surprise. 'How long have you known this?'

'Since the beginning of the month.'

'That's a blow, isn't it?'

'Yes. There are always letters, though. What do you say about a holiday? We always meant to go back to that little inn on Exmoor and spend a week walking there.'

'I think we'll go, Cathie, and put all wretched men out of our minds for a week. I must ask my boss, of course, but as it was his suggestion in the first place, I shall undoubtedly have his judicial approval.'

'Stick it out, Stella. He'll come round in the end.'

'But why can't he accept my word that I knew nothing of that beastly business, Cathie? You believe me. Why can't he?'

'He doesn't know you as I do. Put yourself in his place, Stella. You've resented the fact that he succeeded John as owner of the Cormorant. You resented that from the first and you didn't hide it from him.'

'I'd like to know what you could hide from those eyes.'

'Moreover, you were in love with John and everybody expected that you would marry him. Is it so very unreasonable of him to entertain the possibility that, loving John, you would do a lot to help him keep the Cormorant? Remember, he doesn't know you as we do.'

'Cathie, you've been talking to him about me.'

Cathie met the accusation in her friend's eyes with her customary serenity.

'Yes.'

'When?'

'Last week, the day after you told me what had happened.'

'Why?'

'I wanted to plead your case. I felt I had a right to,' said Cathie simply, and Stella was disarmed.

'I see. Well, I'm in no position to jib because of pride. It was good of you, Cathie, but it won't have done any good. Darrington isn't easily influenced.'

'He doesn't say that you did it.'

'No. He has an open mind,' said Stella drily. 'That means, he believes that at best I was under John's influence.'

'We are all, up to a point, influenced by the people we love.'

'And Darrington doesn't know where in my case that point came, but he thinks it came jolly late. It's so unjust. He hasn't a shred of evidence to show that I followed where John led.'

Cathie was silent, and Stella looked at her.

'Well, has he?'

'He thinks he has.'

'Go on. Tell me.'

'It'll make you angry.'

'That is my natural state at the moment. Tell me, Cathie.'

'He reminded me how John had called you to heel over that

invitation to his supper party. And . . . '

'Go on.'

Cathie picked her words carefully, like a cat walking on thorny ground.

'He said that, against his orders, you allowed John to make love to you at any time he chose, and he had the impression that . . . that at such moments, John could have taken you to hell with him had he wished. I'm sorry, Stella.'

'I asked for it. Oh, Lord, what a mess! It could have looked like that. But that point did stop short of any disloyalty on my part to Darrington. I made that clear to John very early on. Even so, maybe I compromised more than I should. Let's not talk any more about it, Cathie. The harm's done, and heaven knows if I'll have the patience or the humility to live it down.'

'You will. And Nick's not a fool or a tyrant. It's getting dark. Shall we go in and fish out the map to plan our holiday?'

'Good idea. Cathie . . . '

'Yes?'

'I'm sorry about Roger. So wrapped up in my own affairs that I forgot yours.'

'It's a better job for him, and there's never been any question of more than friendship between us, you know. That will go on, I hope, across the miles. I suppose I'd better collect that ladder before we go in.'

They crossed the lawn and Cathie examined the ladder. The piece of string between the steps and the support was no thicker than a violin string. Stella took one end of the ladder, Cathie the other.

'It's remarkable,' said Cathie, 'how this family survives. I'll ask one of the boys to come out with a torch and collect the nails before Father ruins the mower with them.'

They put the ladder in the toolshed and went into the house to begin an exhaustive search for the map.

As Stella had foreseen, Darrington approved of her decision to take a holiday.

'Do you a world of good to get away from all this for a week. Where are you going?'

'To a little village on Exmoor with Cathie Elmore. We

136

came across it on holiday two years ago and fell in love with it. Ideal for riding and walking.'

'An excellent prescription for over-wrought nerves: exercise, unspoilt country and Cathie Elmore. Guaranteed to restore anybody's equanimity.'

He leaned back in his chair and looked at her. She had just finished taking down the letters and she closed her shorthand notebook with a snap and collected up the necessary papers. Since her breakdown in this room three weeks ago, no reference had been made of the past. Darrington maintained a strictly business-like attitude and had been as impersonal as a rock. She felt that the old friendliness which had always been ready to spring up between them and warm the unsettled landscape of their relationship was now no longer there. He had been sympathetic and helpful at the sight of her tears, but since then she had been banished into a cold, impersonal land which she found hard to endure with the equanimity which he appeared to think desirable. He was never angry, never lost his temper. He confined his remarks to business, gave his instructions clearly and if she had been a dictaphone she could not have been treated more impersonally. His observations about her proposed holiday were the first signs of a human approach for three weeks.

As he looked at her now, the anger smouldering inside her was fanned by the recollection of his remarks to Cathie, and her hand clenched round the papers. If only her feelings didn't ride her and put her at a disadvantage. Darrington was all too right. She could never be an Eileen Ridlow, and she would have given all she possessed just then if she could have achieved a quarter of that lady's control of emotion.

'I think you're making things more difficult for yourself than you need,' said Darrington unexpectedly.

'In what way?'

'Your old failing – not being able to bow to the inevitable. You will waste your energy by kicking. Maybe your holiday will calm you down.'

'Perhaps it will even persuade me that this situation is enjoyable.'

'I don't see why it shouldn't be . . . tolerable. You have no responsibilities to worry you, this hotel is a pleasant enough

137

place to work in and I don't think I'm an unreasonable person to work for. Why can't you accept it at that?'

'Because the injustice of it all burns me up.'

'You chose this course. If you can't stick to it, say so. But it's no use flaming away at me about injustice. If there is any, it must be laid at Marbury's door, not mine. And as I don't like employing people who suffer from a sense of injury, you must either get rid of it or go. For these past weeks you've been like a volcano, threatening to erupt at any moment. I won't have it, Stella. Either you accept the situation with a good grace, and I don't see why it should be so difficult, or you must go.'

'You don't see why it should be so difficult!' echoed Stella bitterly.

'Aren't you making me responsible for Marbury's crimes? He's put you in a damnable position, but it's no good jibbing against me because of that. Isn't that what you're doing?'

'You're not helping me at all.'

'How should I?'

'You make the atmosphere so cold and accusing.'

'I think in the past it's been a good deal too warm. Maybe that's why you notice the difference. I've told you before that business and pleasure don't mix. The emphasis here is going to be on business.'

'I think that's hitting rather low,' said Stella, her face burning.

'It's the truth.'

Stella looked down, unable to deny it, and then, finding it impossible to sit there under his gaze, she walked across to the window and stood staring out, her hand tapping her pencil restlessly against her notebook. The sun through the window lit up the coppery tints of her hair and quivered in patterned bars across her brown dress. There was such an air of caged and desperate energy about her that she reminded Darrington of a young leopard he had once seen caught. Her voice sounded strangled.

'Is ice the only alternative to warmth?'

He swung his chair round.

'You've been consumed by two fevers since Marbury went.

138

Damaged pride and self-pity. You haven't whined. You've just got more and more furious. Furious with Marbury, with yourself, with me. A mixture of all three, perhaps. I can do nothing to soothe your pride. You've just got to come to terms with that yourself and accept the position here. If you can't, as I've said, you must go. And sympathy isn't an effective cure for self-pity. It's not that I haven't any sympathy for you. What stands out as clear as the Eiffel Tower from all this mess is Marbury's rotten treatment of you. I'm sorry for you. But you know as well as I do that sympathy only piles on the agony. You've got to climb out of it yourself. I can't help you. If I've been more chilly than you like, it's because I think a cool wind can be bracing. It seems to have braced you a good deal too much,' he added drily.

'I'm sorry. I just feel that I can't contain myself. I want to do something violent. And just sitting at a desk all day taking orders from you like a child back in the schoolroom makes it worse and worse. You're so unmoved and cool about it. That infuriates me, too.'

'Would you rather I lost my temper and got out a cane?' he asked, half smiling. 'I think one temper flaring about is quite enough.'

'I don't know what's got into me,' said Stella, despairingly. 'I feel as though acid is gnawing at all my bones.'

'Sounds horrible.' He came across to her and put a hand on her shoulder. 'Go away and work it off on a horse. Violent exercise can be an excellent purgative. When you come back, we'll see if we can maintain a more even temperature all round. If you drop eighty degrees, I'll rise a couple, and that should do the trick. What do you say?'

'I'll try.'

'Good.'

'What makes it so hard is the fact that I'm helpless. If I could do anything about it, I'd feel better. I've wondered if I could possibly find out from Miss Mapleton who signed that letter, but even if I was able to prove that it was John's signature, that wouldn't mean that I knew nothing of it or that I hadn't sent others. It would only prove that he'd been in it with me. It wouldn't let me out. It's that feeling of never being able to prove to you that I knew nothing of it that is burning me up more than anything.'

'More than losing Marbury?'

Her eyes met his.

'I'd been losing John for months past. The gulf grew wider every week, but I wouldn't face it, and he was clever at throwing a temporary bridge over it. For that, I despise myself. But there were no more bridges after my birthday. It was all over between us. I finished it, and John knew it was no use trying those bridges after that. I was desperately miserable about it, in a cold, numb sort of way, but that has nothing to do with what I'm going through now. I want you to know that. I can get over John. He's not worth any grieving. But how can I wash out the picture he painted of me for your benefit? I can't prove anything. And appearances were against me.'

'If you think I believed everything Marbury said, you take me for a mug. And there are more ways of proving something than one. You've made a start by staying on here. That's not an easy way or a quick way. As far as I'm concerned, we start again from scratch. And you must stop this burning-up process. Try to follow the advice which my Oxford don once gave me: accommodate your ego to your destiny.'

She thought a moment, and then said slowly:

'That's not a philosophy I find easy to accept.'

'Egos are the very devil,' he said, smiling. 'Now, Miss Verney, are you going to get those letters done for me? I'm going up to London this afternoon, and I shall want them to sign before I go.'

'I'll do them straight away, Mr. Darrington,' said Stella briskly. 'Will you be coming back tomorrow?'

'No. I shall get back about midday on Friday. You can take over until then, and I shall expect a detailed report from you on Friday. If anything goes wrong in my absence, heaven help you. After that you can take your furies to Exmoor and bury them in the bogs there.'

'I'll come back so demure and good that you won't know me,' she said, smiling her gratitude at him as she went.

Chapter Twelve

THAT week on Exmoor, riding and walking with Cathie, did much to help Stella exorcise the devils which had been consuming her and accept her fate. The physical exertion eased the nervous tension, and Cathie's serene presence was like a cool hand on her tormented mind. Whatever Cathie might be feeling about Roger, nothing in her manner suggested stress or anxiety.

They walked for miles along the wild streams and coombes of the Doone country, often seeing no other life but scattered groups of ponies or an occasional stag, from the time they set out from the village in the morning until the time they returned in the early evening. And, as if to make up for the sins of the summer, September gave them a perfect week of mellow sunshine in which the countryside stood still and breathless, clad in all the warmth of its autumn beauty, poised on the threshold of the darker days as though inviting them to take this gift of a repentant summer before it was too late. And some of its peace entered into Stella's heart.

It was not until they were riding home on their last evening that Stella mentioned the Cormorant again. Tacitly, the subject had been dropped as soon as they had left Ashcombe behind.

'Back to the valley of humiliation,' she said, sighing. 'I wish we could stay on here for ever.'

'M'm. I can't say I'm returning with great zest. I hope the change-over at the Museum won't be as difficult as the change-over at the Cormorant has been.'

'Do you know anything about the new man?'

'Only what Roger told me. He says he's very pleasant. Quiet, a good deal older than Roger, with a couple of books on archaeology to his credit. He's married, I believe. I don't feel that this horse and I are in perfect harmony,' added Cathie as her mare stopped to chew a piece of bracken from the high-

141

banked lane and ignored Cathie's efforts to move her on. Stella smiled and waited. She had found an ugly, raking bay at the stables who suited her very well and had been able to hire him every day they rode, but Cathie had tried three different hacks without finding a comfortable ride. It was Stella who had taught Cathie to ride, but although adequate, Cathie hadn't been born with that feeling for horses which Stella possessed, and when they rode together, Cathie preferred to amble along at a modest pace and Stella was content to fall in. She had been taught by John, who was an excellent horseman and had fired Stella with his own enthusiasm.

'How is Roger's mother going to take the move?'

'Not too well, I'm afraid. But as a better salary means that Roger can have a full-time companion for her, she can hardly refuse to go. Her life is a terrible burden to her, poor soul, and I'm deeply sorry for her, but she does make things even more difficult for Roger by her attitude. It's so hard to keep a companion for her, she has such a biting tongue and she complains so much. Of course, she suffers a lot of pain, and one shouldn't judge her by normal standards.'

Coming from Cathie, this meant that old Mrs. Thornton was quite impossible, thought Stella, and remembering Roger's sensitive face and patient manner, she said impulsively:

'What a hell of a life for a man. Is he the only child?'

'Yes. His father died ten years ago. Roger has had to look after his mother ever since.'

'Wouldn't Mrs. Thornton be better off in a nursing home?'

'Roger couldn't afford it. And Mrs. Thornton would refuse to go, anyway. It's a tragedy for both of them. And so little can be done to relieve arthritis.'

'Is she getting worse?'

'She's crippled with it. She can't use her hands and she can't walk more than a few steps. She's been like that for years. I don't think there's much change.'

'I feel rather ashamed of the fuss I've been making about my own affairs when I hear of cases like that.'

Cathie gave her a quick glance.

'I don't think you've been making a fuss. Other people's misfortunes can't take away our own or lessen the hurt. Only

. . . I can't help feeling relieved that you found out about John before you married him. I never thought he was the man for you. I couldn't believe he would bring you the kind of happiness that endures. You would have been unhappy, sooner or later. I think it makes it easier to get over it if it's sooner.'

'Perhaps. I don't know whether he would have married me if Eileen Ridlow hadn't turned up. I think it was at the back of his mind, but he hated committing himself. He would have preferred . . . a less irrevocable relationship.'

They rode on, the silence broken only by the creaking of leather and the horses' hooves. Stella looked straight ahead, but saw nothing of the leafy lane. She saw John's laughing face, the intense blue of his eyes, the vitality which, combined with his classic good looks, made him irresistibly attractive, until one came up against the ruthless selfishness behind it. But how his high spirits had lifted hers until they soared together in a bubbling, intoxicating atmosphere which seemed to have no connection with the sober workaday world around them. What fun they had had together! Dancing, riding, swimming, teasing, kissing. Light and lively as champagne bubbles. If it could have ended there a year ago, she would have cried her heart out, but she would have remembered it afterwards as a happy iridescent bubble of her youth. This year of betrayals, when the light touch had been invaded by something more urgent, when lies and deceit had eaten away her love, had spoiled even the bubble of happy memories, since thinking of it only led her to the bitterness and humiliation of the present. Whenever she looked back at the past, her thoughts ended at that empty chair beside her on her birthday.

They turned off through a gate and took a track across the heather towards the village now visible below them.

'This has been a good week, Cathie. I'm feeling a lot better for it. Ready to accommodate my ego to my destiny, which was what my chief recommended to me. Meaning, of course, toeing his line.'

Cathie smiled.

'I'm not worrying about you suffering at his hands. I have a great respect for Nick Darrington.'

'So have I. That doesn't mean to say that I like bowing to

his leader-of-the-expedition technique. I prefer to organise my own life, even if so far I have made a howling mess of it. But I give you one thing, Cathie. When you've been treading on shifting sands for a year, it's a relief to be standing on rock, even if it is darned hard and cold. I'm starving. I wonder what's for dinner?'

'Roast pork. I saw the butcher arrive this morning.'

'Gorgeous. I can hardly wait. I hope the crackling crackles. As it's our last night, I think we should have a bottle of wine. We'll drink a good riddance to being in love.'

'You don't mean to say that you've done with the disease?' said Cathie, laughing.

'Indeed I do. I don't intend ever to catch it again. The senses are not to be trusted, Cathie. Take warning from me.'

'And you never intend to marry?'

'No. Not unless I can make a judicious, cool and carefully considered match with a man I like. I'm having no more of this heart-pounding, knee-jellying sickness which clouds your mind and paralyses your will and does shocking things to your heart. As far as that disease is concerned, I've had it, and I shan't get another attack. Think you can shake your horse into a canter? We're not going to have much time for our bath.'

'I'll try, but she seems to be of a somewhat lethargic disposition.'

The mare responded to Cathie's heels with a reluctant canter which soon subsided into a trot, whereat Cathie reined back to a walk.

'Sorry, Stella, but I can't trot this animal. Our bumps won't coincide. I believe she has an unaccommodating nature.'

'Like Nick Darrington's,' said Stella, smiling. 'If you can't rise and fall with me, you jolly well take the consequences.'

They jogged on down the track, a hot bath and roast pork hovering invitingly before them. Stella took the lead as the track narrowed and steepened in its fall to the bridge across the river, and as she leaned forward to pat her horse's neck, Cathie admired the slender, supple back presented to her. Stella, with her boyish figure and long legs, looked well on a horse. She seemed to belong to it, whereas Cathie felt all too clearly that she and a horse were two separate bodies likely to part com-

144

pany very easily and moving together as awkwardly as a tall man dancing with a small child. But from her youngest days Stella had always possessed a beautifully co-ordinated physique, thought Cathie. Running, dancing, climbing, riding or swimming; it was all the same. She did it with an easy, supple grace that seemed to involve no effort. None of the Elmores could approach her in that respect, and Jimmy had always maintained that she could have won many medals if she had gone in for athletics.

Stella had crossed the bridge and turned to wait for Cathie. The week's sun had given her a slight tan and she looked fit and bright-eyed as she smiled at Cathie's efforts to push her mare along. She was over the worst of it, thought Cathie, who had been very worried by the numb, inert version of Stella which had followed the birthday party and the angry, bitter version which had succeeded that. And then she gave a little sigh. Stella was right. Loving was a painful business, and she, too, faced a blank return to Ashcombe . . .

*   *   *

Stella found life easier at the Cormorant after her return. Instead of fighting against it, she settled into the new routine and found Darrington a good deal more lenient and friendly as a result. Their advertising campaign brought them a fair number of late holiday-makers, and the winter residents increased to eleven, which was encouraging. They were fully booked for Christmas, and as the holiday approached, Darrington began to pass more responsibility over to Stella. He was always businesslike in his attitude to her, but she felt a more human warmth creeping in as the weeks passed. She mocked at herself a little for feeling so pleased. You've been a good girl and done all you were told to do, so you're being given a few sweets as a reward, she said to herself one day just after Darrington had left her laughing at a joke he had cracked. But pleased she was, and it was no use denying it. And her pleasure soared still higher when he came into her room that afternoon with the letters he had signed.

'I've switched the phone through and I'm packing up here for the day, Stella. I want to get a quiet couple of hours on the proofs of my book before dinner. A tiresome job. I'd like to get it finished before we're up to our eyes in Christmas activities.'

'Can I help you at all? I can probably spot printers' errors for you.'

'But not any errors I may have made. No, I'm afraid it's a job I'll have to do myself, but thanks for offering. What I'm going to suggest is that you take over all the office work for the rest of this week so that I can concentrate on the proofs. I ought to get them off by Saturday if I can spend most of the day on them. Will you do that? If you're in doubt about anything, you can either ring me or pop down to the lodge.'

'Of course. There's nothing I'd like better. Shall I bring letters down to you at the lodge to sign?'

His eyes met hers.

'No. Sign them yourself unless you're in any doubt. I'll see the copies at the end of the week to bring myself up to date. We look like having a goodish winter season.'

'Yes. I'm so relieved about that. I think we could easily get back to the success old Mr. Marbury had. We really did well then.'

'Here's hoping, then.'

'Oh, by the way, Mr. Darrington, do you want me to do the Christmas decorations and if so, how much can I spend?'

He looked at her with an odd little smile twitching his lips.

'You know, I've taught you your lesson almost too well, haven't I? Of course you must do the decorations. You're extremely good at it, I remember. And spend the usual.'

Her cheeks were a little flushed as she said:

'I think we ought to grow our own holly. It costs the earth at Christmas. That would be a simple economy.'

'I admire your practical mind. But isn't holly rather a long time growing?'

'Yes, but we can plan for the future. Anyway, holly bushes look very nice and we could make room for several kinds in the shrub border along the drive.'

'I leave it to you, Miss Verney,' he said gravely.

He was rather fond of poking sly fun at her now and again,

and she smiled at the deferential air he had now put on for her benefit.

'You're in a dangerously meek mood this morning, Mr. Darrington. You're probably going to spring something horrible on me.'

'Such as?'

'Clearing out hundreds of dirty old files from that cupboard in your room and making a list of them for your benefit. I felt I'd never get clean again after I'd finished last Friday.'

He laughed.

'It was you or me. Not being gallant, I gave the job to you. I thought you'd enjoy it.'

She shook her head as he turned to go.

'Mr. Darrington.'

He turned and cocked an enquiring eyebrow in her direction. 'Madam?'

'I'll see that nothing goes wrong this week. And . . . thank you. Thank you very much.'

'You've earned your stripes,' he said with a brief smile, and left her.

And no amount of self-mockery could prevent Stella from picking up a file and waltzing with it to the filing cabinet.

That Christmas proved more than usually hectic, as two of the kitchen staff succumbed to influenza a few days before Christmas and one of the two waiters engaged specially for the holiday failed to turn up. Rickie stood in for the waiter and managed the job with a dexterity which won even faint commendation from Charles, the head waiter, whose standards were nothing short of perfection. Charles was something of an institution at the Cormorant. He had been head waiter there for the past ten years, descending on them early in May like a visiting monarch and leaving at the beginning of October for the Continent where he combined business with pleasure for a couple of months. It was customary for him to return to the Cormorant for the Christmas and Easter holidays, but after the previous bad summer, Stella had feared that Charles might contemplate leaving the sinking ship, for failure and Charles were incompatible. However, Charles was giving them another chance, for he appeared in all his glory that Christmas, a handsome, commanding figure who charmed and impressed the visitors and intimidated the rest of the staff.

It was Stella who flung herself heroically into the breach in the kitchen, helping the chef and Mrs. Dacres to keep up a smooth service and putting in a good many hours attending to the dish-washing machine. Apart from a short interval at home on Christmas afternoon, she worked at the hotel throughout the holiday, and the Boxing Night dance found her behind the buffet serving refreshments. Darrington, too, had worked like a Trojan and had found little time to spend with his sister and brother-in-law who had brought their son with them for the Christmas holiday. When he came to collect a glass of lemonade from Stella for his nephew just after ten o'clock on Boxing Night, it was the first time they had been together that day, for Stella had worked behind the scenes and Darrington in the front of the house.

'Heaven knows how that boy contains all this fizz without blowing up. This is the fourth this evening, so Felicity says.'

'I can't do it as well as Charles. He manages such a gorgeous flourish with everything he hands over.'

'I've asked Rickie to take over from you. He'll be across in a minute. You look tired out.'

'No, I'm not. A bit of a back-ache, that's all.'

'Peter's just off to bed. Come along and join us when Rickie arrives. Felicity will be disappointed if she doesn't see you before they go, and they're off early tomorrow morning.'

'Righto. I'd like to.'

When Stella joined them at their corner table, Felicity welcomed her with a warm smile.

'I was beginning to think we'd never get together. Nick tells me you've been shut up in the kitchen all day. That seems a bit hard.'

'You never know what you may be called on to tackle in a hotel,' said Stella. 'Crises are apt to loom up in all departments.'

'It must make you a very versatile and useful person.'

'It does,' broke in Nick. 'Stella, to my knowledge, is capable of being secretary, gardener, decorator, kitchen help and plumber. Believe it or not, we should have been flooded out

148

the other day in one of the bathrooms if she hadn't produced by magic the right size of cork for a certain tap.'

'The resourceful type,' said Felicity, adding with a twinkle, 'That makes a pair of you. I've yet to see Nick at a loss. He thrives on difficulties, and would far rather improvise a bridge across a raging torrent with nothing to hand but what nature provided than walk a mile or two to a nice, safe, stone bridge.'

'That,' declared Darrington, 'is a slight axaggeration. The bridge was three miles away, the raging torrent was little more than a stream, and the tree trunk I found was quite adequate. The fact that you stooped down to watch a fish when you were half way across was not my fault.'

'The reference, Miss Verney, is to an incident on the moor during our holiday here last summer,' observed Felicity's husband solemnly.

'And what happened?' asked Stella.

'The trunk rolled, Felicity executed a sort of war dance, and fell in. It wasn't very deep,' said Nick, grinning.

'Three feet of icy water is quite deep enough to be treated with respect instead of being used for Red Indian games with tree trunks. That's the worst of being an explorer. You thrive on discomfort,' said Felicity.

'Not at all. Hector found no difficulty in negotiating that tree trunk. It would have been absurd to go three miles out of our way to cross by the bridge.'

'It was a torrent,' maintained Felicity. 'Anyway, it would have been just as pleasant meandering along without crossing it.'

'But, my dear girl, we were aiming to get to that waterfall. It was your choice. We would never have made it if we'd crossed by the bridge. We saved about two hours crossing where we did, and you soon dried off.'

'I wouldn't have minded if we hadn't seen the waterfall. I can always adapt my plans to circumstances.'

'Well, if I have a goal, I like to make it,' replied Nick calmly, 'whatever's in the way.'

'Neither of them will let the other have the last word,' said Hector. 'Would you like to dance, Miss Verney, and leave them to it?'

149

'Before you go,' said Felicity, 'whose side are you on, Miss Verney?'

'Well, I'm afraid, like Mr. Darrington, I'm obstinate. I don't like being beaten. I think I'd accept the hazards to reach my goal.'

'No compromise? Well, well. Two of that kidney under the same roof. That could mean trouble,' said Felicity, looking at her brother with merry eyes.

'You've just said that our sort thrive on trouble,' said Darrington, and at that point Hector moved off with Stella.

When they returned, Felicity was alone and Darrington was on the far side of the room saying goodnight to Colonel Wright and his wife, two of the Cormorant's regular visitors.

'I find it amusing to see Nick doing his duty to his guests. I must say he's better at the job than I would have imagined, since he's not at all the sociable type and abhors small talk.'

Stella, too, had been surprised at Darrington's success in this sphere of his responsibilities. John, with his easy charm and his good looks, might have been born for the job. In that respect he had been a tremendous asset to the hotel, for nobody, young or old, could fail to respond to his brilliant and attractive personality. Darrington, with his blunt tongue and his entire absence of camouflage, presented as great a contrast as one could find. And yet, people obviously liked him and engaged him in long conversations at all times of the day.

'Oh, I don't know,' said Hector. 'There's an honest, re-assuring kind of solidity about Nick that goes down well with most people. Reliability is a good selling point in this kind of business.'

'I never thought he'd have the patience, though. He's the lone type by temperament, and not awfully fond of the human race. He'll never settle to it permanently,' said Felicity.

'He never intended to, and still doesn't, I guess. He'll be itching for the wilds before long.'

Stella watched him walking back towards them, looking less solidly built in evening dress but still giving an impression of bull-dozing strength. No, he would never deviate from his goal, and the hotel would never be big enough to contain him permanently.

150

She enjoyed the rest of the evening with them. Felicity had a lively tongue, and the obviously warm affection between brother and sister invested their frequent sparring bouts with a good humour that never slipped into irritation. But when the band played Auld Lang Syne, Stella became aware of the fact that tiredness had dropped down on her like a heavy blanket. She said good night, and went to fetch her coat. Nick met her in the hall when she came down.

'I'll run you home, Stella. Just wait while I have a word with Bob, then I'll get the car round.'

The night air was cold and she shivered as she slid into the seat beside him. He pulled a rug off the back seat and gave it to her.

'I'm afraid this has been rather a Cinderella Christmas for you, Stella. I'm very grateful to you for your hard work, but I feel a bit guilty of robbing you of your fun.'

'I've quite enjoyed it, and fun isn't very much in my line these days, anyway.'

'Dear me. That sounds a bit grim.'

Stella was remembering the Boxing Night dance of the previous year; the evening she had sat and waited for John to dance with her. She had enjoyed this evening more.

'No,' she said. 'It's a relief, in a way. And if you work in a hotel, you expect to forfeit any personal Christmas.'

'Well, thank you, anyway. You know,' he added gently, 'I don't expect you to work yourself to skin and bone to make up for Marbury's deficiencies.'

'It eases my conscience,' she said simply.

He was nosing the car out of the entrance and as they moved down the lane, the harbour swung into view below them, peaceful under a crescent moon, the assorted craft with their riding-lights diminished to toys. It was a still night and there were few signs of late festivities as they drove through the town. The church clock struck half past twelve as they went along Church Lane. Stella, accustomed to John's dislike of being distracted by talk when he was driving, kept the question that was in her mind until Darrington had drawn up outside her home.

'Mr. Darrington . . .'

'Yes?'

'There's something rather personal I want to ask you, and I don't know quite how to put it, or, indeed, whether I should put it. It's not really my business.'

'Go ahead.'

'When you spent that weekend with Roger Thornton at the beginning of the month, did he . . . mention Cathie at all?'

'As a matter of fact, he did.'

She looked at him quickly.

'Could you tell me what he said?'

'Why do you ask?'

'Because I know Cathie's eating her heart out over him.'

'Has she told you so?'

'No. Cathie never talks much about herself. But I know. She didn't have a card from him this Christmas and he hasn't answered two letters she wrote him. She says she expects he's too busy to think of anything but his job. But her eyes give her away. I wondered whether Roger was deliberately cutting all ties between them, or whether . . . he thinks there aren't any ties.'

'I'm sorry, my dear, but I'm afraid I can't repeat confidences. Cathie had better forget him.'

'Cathie isn't the forgetting sort. You can at least tell me what you did and how he was that weekend. Cathie asked me yesterday, and I had no information. If I could tell her that he's well and happy in his job, it would be something.'

'He is well, and he likes his job. We spent most of the weekend at some excavations in the neighbourhood which have thrown up some interesting Roman remains.'

'I see. You've nothing else you can tell me, without betraying any confidence, that might comfort Cathie?'

Darrington was silent for a moment, then:

'Stella, if you had to dig up a plant that had grown in the wrong place, would there be any point in waiting until it was bigger, or half doing it and leaving it to die off slowly?'

'It's like that, is it?'

'That's all I can say. Interference in affairs of this kind is fatal. The best thing is for Cathie to forget him, believe me.'

'It's so easy to say. So difficult to do.'

'Is it? Are you desperately unhappy still about Marbury?'

152

'No. A little sore, still. That's all.'

'And that was broken off less than six months ago.'

'But . . .'

'But what?'

'With John and me it was different. We had a lot of fun together – dancing, riding, swimming. And then . . . after . . . What I'm trying to say,' she went on desperately, 'is that what bound John and me together was that sort of thing. On the surface. It never went to deeper levels, and that's where it fell down, because there we didn't meet at all. It was . . .'

'I don't know why you're finding it so difficult. It's nothing to be ashamed of. I take it that what you mean is that it was mainly a physical bond between you and Marbury.'

'Yes.'

He looked at her, but Stella's eyes were on the dashboard. He seemed amused as he said:

'Well, don't sound so abashed about a perfectly natural state. You were two young, healthy, attractive people with more than average vitality, in constant proximity. If the out-door sports spread to sport of another kind, it's really what one might expect. Few people with red blood in their veins haven't experienced the heady delights of being in love, and in a good many cases besides yours, being in love hasn't grown into loving. The lesson that the one doesn't of necessity follow the other is one of the more painful pills we have to swallow, but there's no need to feel ashamed about it.'

'Well, I am. Ashamed that I allowed my judgment to be kissed away. I'll never be so feeble again. I've done with all that.'

'Don't be so fierce. You know, there's something of a Don Quixote streak in you. I'm known to like a challenge, but upon my soul, I've never been rash enough to challenge the fundamental laws of nature.'

'I think,' said Stella sternly, 'you're trying to side-track me. We were talking of Cathie. I only mentioned my own follies to prove your comparison between us a wrong one. Cathie isn't like me. She'd be far more likely to fall in love after she loved someone than the other way round. She's never run around with the opposite sex. Never been aware of them

153

in that way. You know, there are people like that, and you can always sense it, even if you can't put it into words. I do wish you'd take me seriously.'

'My dear girl, I am taking you seriously. I agree about Cathie. Midge will be the reverse, I'd say. Now you're going to tell me that Cathie won't be able to forget Roger, if you're right in assuming that she cares for him, because her feelings, as distinct from her senses, are deeply involved. That it?'

'Exactly.'

'I'm afraid, then, we shall have to hope that even deep feeling will fade without sustenance.'

'Is it that Roger doesn't care, or because he feels he's not in a position to care? I know his circumstances are difficult, and I think he's a very conscientious and serious-minded person.'

'I'm sorry, Stella, I'm just not at liberty to say. Roger talked to me in the strictest confidence. I have enough faith in his integrity and in his intelligence to accept his decision as the wisest in the circumstances. You must leave it at that.'

'I understand. It's such a shame that it should happen to Cathie, of all people. She's such a good person. I know that sounds priggish and old-fashioned, but it's the only word I can use about her. It's natural to her to put everybody else before herself. Perhaps I deserved what I got. But not Cathie.'

'And nor you. If you weren't so tired, I'm sure you wouldn't be so displeased with yourself. Perhaps Nan, like dripping water, is having more effect on you than you think.'

'Oh, Nan's not too bad. She's stopped behaving as though my soul is in mortal danger, anyway, which is a relief, although in some respects I'm not exactly her prize pupil. Too self-willed, headstrong and obstinate.'

'Well, perhaps we won't quarrel with that. Substitute bossy for headstrong, and I'm tarred with the same brush, according to my sister, anyway, and she's had more opportunities of judging than most.'

'She's nice, Felicity. I like her very much.'

'It's mutual. Well, we'd better not sit here any longer discussing our sins, or Nan will be putting your soul in mortal danger again. We can't do anything about them, anyway. One is saddled with oneself, like it or not. Good night, Stella, and thanks again. Shall I give you one laurel leaf to put in your crown of thorns?'

'Would it be that I'm a useful girl in the kitchen?'

'That's true, but not what I had in mind. No, I'll present you with a laurel leaf for being the most generous person I've ever come across. It's a very warming quality. Good night.'

And she found no reply to that before he drove off with a wave of his hand.

Chapter Thirteen

THE New Year found Stella happier and more at peace with the world than she had been for a very long time. Under Darrington's hand, the hotel ran smoothly and the Easter bookings were heavy. Gradually she was given more and more responsibility until she was back in her old position, and in the spring a young typist was brought in to help her in the office. Miss Bromley was a bright, intelligent girl and soon slipped into the routine. The only cloud in Stella's sky was Cathie's unhappiness. Cathie seldom mentioned Roger Thornton, and on the surface appeared as serene as ever, but Stella was conscious of a strange inertness about her friend which she could not stir. It was as though a light had been switched off inside her, and the effect of this on a personality which was always quiet and self-effacing was curiously deadening. The passing of winter into spring made no change in her and Stella could still not find the old Cathie.

It was Mrs. Elmore who put Stella's own disquiet into words when they met in the town one morning.

'Hullo, Stella. Playing truant?'

'No. Shopping for the hotel. I've just been ordering some more china, and thought of having a cup of coffee before I go back. How about it?'

'A good idea. Distinctly chilly for May. Coffee will be very welcome.'

They found a corner table in a café, and after stowing away her shopping basket and several parcels, Mrs. Elmore began to talk about Cathie.

'I'm worried about her, Stella. I don't know whether it's Roger Thornton, or whether there's something wrong with her health. She looks so pale and pinched up. Do you know? Has she talked to you about what's wrong?'

'No. Not directly. But I'm pretty sure it's Roger. I don't like to ask her outright, but I'm not at all happy about her, either. I so often feel when I'm with her that she's not there.'

'That's it. It's all so intangible. She goes about at home just the same as usual, and the others don't seem to notice anything amiss, but I sometimes feel that it's all automatic, as though it's not Cathie but a puppet walking about the house. It quite frightens me sometimes. But she denies that anything is wrong when I ask her.'

'I wish she would talk about it. I'm sure it would ease things. Cathie's so terribly self-controlled.'

'Yes. But it's not good to shut yourself in with unhappiness.'

'I'll see if I can get her to talk about it. I'm sure it's Roger and not ill health that's the trouble.'

'Yes. She watches the post so closely. I've noticed that. Oh, well, my dear, we can only give her kindness and our love, and hope it will soon get better. You've had your own troubles to get over, and mustn't worry too much about Cathie.'

'We don't either of us seem to be very fortunate in our choice, do we? If I can do anything to help, you know I will.'

'Yes, dear, I know.'

And there they left it. When Stella and Cathie were together a few days later, however, Stella decided to bring the subject into the open. They were walking along the beach on Sunday afternoon. It was a warm, friendly day; propitious, Stella considered, for delicate matters to be aired. The sand was firm beneath their feet, washed clean by the receding tide, and gulls were paddling in the shallow fringes of the waves, their cold cruel eyes alert, yellow beaks stabbing.

'Roger is coming down to spend a weekend with Nick at the end of the month.'

'Is he?' Cathie had turned quickly.

'M'm. Do you want to see him again?'

'It's more a question of does he want to see me.'

'You didn't answer my question, Cathie.'

'I can't force myself on someone who doesn't want to see me. He hasn't answered my letters, so he can't want to see me.'

'How do you know? He may be acting the noble renunciation role.'

'If only I knew,' said Cathie despairingly. 'If only I knew.'

'Well, there's only one way to find out, but it wouldn't necessarily leave you any happier.'

'It would take away this dreadful feeling of facing a blank wall. If I knew for certain that he had lost interest, I would have to adapt myself to that knowledge. If I knew that our friendship still meant anything to him, I'd go on writing and at least have the satisfaction of some sort of contact with him and be content with that. But it's not knowing that's so horrible.'

'What do you think he feels about you, Cathie?'

'Our friendship was a very real and close one. That I know without a shadow of doubt. And I find it hard to believe that friendship can die so quickly just because two people are separated. New contacts, new interests, could push it more into the background, I know, but not kill it, not so quickly. Roger's not at all a casual sort of person.'

'Then why the silence?'

'I've either offended him in some way, and I can't think how, or else he thinks I want more than friendship and he hasn't any more to offer. But I should be so happy with just that,' said Cathie unhappily.

'Would you, dear?'

'Yes. Half a loaf is better than none, or even a few crumbs if that's all I can have. If we never saw each other at all, if our friendship rested only on letters, I could be content.'

'There might be somebody else one day, Cathie. Crumbs mean that you'll often be very hungry.'

'There will never be anybody else. I've known that for a long time.'

'I should have said that once. But not now.'

Cathie smiled gently.

'You go out to meet the world, Stella, and people who go out to life with open hands have full ones, too. There will always be many opportunities for you to find the right person. Not for me. I'm rather frightened of the world, outside my own home circle. I shrink from strangers. Oh, I know I don't show it, but inside me I'm always retreating from people. It's a miracle that I ever managed to meet one right person. There won't be a second chance. I know that.'

Stella made no reply. It was true, she thought. Cathie was so self-effacing that she would pass unnoticed in any assembly of people. She lived a very simple, quiet life, content with her family. If she didn't marry, she would become the mainstay of the family, and the prop of her parents in their old age. She would be taken for granted. She was the unassertive, selfless type which the kindest of families make use of without question. And opportunities to marry for a retiring person like Cathie were not abounding in Ashcombe. When Midge and the boys married, as they undoubtedly would, Cathie would be the perfect aunt to their children: the perfect daughter to her aging parents. Living, always at second hand, through other people's lives, never her own. And at this juncture in her thoughts, Stella decided that something must be done about Roger. Cathie must at least be given the opportunity of salvaging anything that was to be salvaged in that quarter.

'I'll see that you have an opportunity that weekend of seeing Roger and finding out where you stand.'

'No, Stella. I can't force myself on him. He knows where I am.'

'Listen, Cathie. I don't know Roger very well, but from what I saw of him, I judged him to be a very sensitive, conscientious man. The last person to be unkind without a good reason. He's ignored your letters. There must be a reason, and you've a right to know it. You're a modest type and so is he, but one of you will have to break the deadlock, and it looks as though it will have to be you.'

'It's not really a rôle I like. As though I'm hounding him.'

'Nonsense. If he makes it clear that he wishes to drop

whatever is between you, then you accept it. But you've a right to be told and not be left guessing, so you must just conquer that retiring disposition of yours and challenge him in the open.'

'You're so good at challenging, Stella. I'm not.'

'Tell me, Cathie. Is your friendship with Roger — we'll put it no stronger than that — worth fighting for?'

'Yes.'

'Then fight, even if you've got to fight yourself as well as Roger. Will you?'

'If I have the chance.'

'I'll see that you do,' said Stella grimly.

In Darrington's office the next morning, Stella broached the subject of Roger's visit cautiously.

'Rickie tells me that Roger Thornton is coming to spend a weekend with you,' she said casually as she collected the letters together.

'Yes. He's taking a week's holiday and spending a couple of days here before going on to Cornwall.'

'It will be nice to see him again. I suppose we couldn't have a little reunion here. Cathie and I, Roger and you.'

'I seem to remember proposing that quartet before.'

'Like the elephant, you never forget,' said Stella, smiling ruefully. 'You were angry about that, weren't you?'

'Yes.'

'You had a right to be. It was very discourteous of me. Did I ever apologise? No, I didn't. Well, I will now. I'm very sorry, Mr. Darrington.'

'You are forgiven. I have an idea you're hoping to wheedle me. Sorry, my dear. Nothing doing. I'm not going to embarrass Roger by digging up the past for him.'

'Would it embarrass him?' asked Stella guilelessly. 'Surely he'd be pleased to see us again?'

Darrington eyed her thoughtfully.

'Stella, my dear, by various ways, direct and devious, you have been trying to find out what Roger Thornton told me in confidence about Cathie. I can only advise you to mind your own business and stop wasting your time pumping me.'

Stella controlled her annoyance, since the last thing she

wanted to do was to put him on his guard over this matter. He was as sharp as a hawk, and as obstinate as a mule.

'It was only a friendly suggestion,' she said airily. 'No need to make such a thing of it. It's not at all important, and Cathie probably wouldn't be keen herself, anyway. Forget it.'

He was watching her narrowly and she tried not to appear hurried as she piled papers and files together and made for the door.

'Stella.'

She pressed her lips together as she stopped, but her mouth had resumed its normal shape when she turned to him.

'Yes, Mr. Darrington?'

'That weekend is a purely personal and private arrangement between Roger and myself. There will be no intrusions on that privacy while Roger is my guest. That is an order. You understand?'

'Of course. Would you like me to come in at the weekend so that you're not bothered with hotel matters? Saturday is a busy day with arrivals and departures. I could take that off your hands and leave you quite free for Roger.'

'Thank you, but I'll put Rickie on to reception to help Bob that afternoon. They'll be quite adequate, I think.'

'Right,' said Stella, and went.

The old devil, she thought. He wasn't taking any chances. She would have to pump Rickie to find out when Roger was coming and what their programme was. She wouldn't get a syllable out of Darrington, that was obvious.

During the next two weeks, she tried in vain to work out some plan to enable Cathie and Roger to meet alone that weekend. Rickie had evidently been told to hold his tongue, for he affected to know nothing of the weekend arrangements. Darrington and Roger would doubtless be together all the time, and an encounter with Cathie in public, even if it could be plotted, would achieve nothing but embarrassment to all, Darrington would stick to Roger like glue, and Cathie would run away, distressed and hurt. Somehow, Roger and Cathie had to be brought together for an hour at least, with the certainty of being alone and undisturbed. And two days before the weekend, she was no nearer to attaining this for Cathie.

160

Then a little help came her way in the shape of a conversation between Mrs. Dacres and the porter which took place in the kitchen while Stella was investigating the absence of coffee that morning.

'Everything's behind this morning. It's just on ready, Miss Verney. If you'll wait a moment, you can take the tray up with you. If the shooting brake's not back from the garage tomorrow, Bob, Chef will have to take Mr. Darrington's car. He's collecting a lot of poultry from Bankdown farm, and you know he won't let them send it without his inspecting it.'

'Well, the brake won't be back from the garage because they can't get the spare part until Monday. And Mr. Darrington wants the car to meet a friend at the station tomorrow afternoon at four o'clock, so Chef will either have to go in the morning or the poultry will have to be sent.'

'Chef can't go in the morning. You know that. And he'll never agree to having birds he hasn't chosen himself. If it's a choice between Mr. Darrington's friend and offending Chef, Mr. Darrington's friend will have to be unlucky, that's all.'

'You tell that to Mr. Darrington,' said Bob darkly.

Stella escaped with her tray of coffee, since the domestic side of the hotel was Mrs. Dacres' province and she never interfered unless appealed to.

Darrington was not in his office when Stella took his coffee in, but he appeared as she was putting the saucer on top of the cup to keep the contents hot.

'Good. I can do with that. A bit late this morning, isn't it?'

'Yes. It's one of those mornings in the kitchen.'

'And in the loft,' said Darrington, brushing his hands against each other. 'That confounded union near the cistern is leaking again. I've packed it up with soap, but Baynes will have to come and make a proper job of it. This is the third time.'

'Plumbing is my *bête noire*. "Send for Baynes" are the direst words I know, conjuring up cascades of water or no water at all, panic, fury, noise and damage. I'd sooner see the dentist.'

'The plumbing here is pretty archaic. It wants overhauling completely. I think we must tackle it before next summer. Anyway, get Baynes along as soon as possible, Stella, will you?

It's all right for the time being, but I think he'd better come in before the weekend.'

'Right.'

Back in her own room, Stella sipped her coffee while she brooded over the information she had gleaned about Roger's arrival. He would probably leave on Sunday afternoon or Monday morning, so that the only time that she would be on the hotel premises while Roger was there was from about quarter past four until five-thirty on Friday. If Darrington saw her around at any other time, he would smell a rat instantly. And during the whole of that hour, he would no doubt be with Roger. How could she separate them and conjure up Cathie? It was almost lunch-time before she had thought of a plan, and it was such a desperate one that she quailed at the thought of putting it into operation. All through the lunch hour her resolution wavered. Was she being unwise to meddle? She risked forfeiting Darrington's friendship, and she was only just beginning to realise what a lot that meant to her. She would be flagrantly defying him, and the strategy she planned to use was so outrageous that she felt hot every time she thought of it. But she could think of no alternative, and Cathie's despairing cry for the truth still rang in her ears. She was quite oblivious of the food she was eating as her mind hunted for an alternative solution as desperately as a rabbit for a hole, but she could find none. Perhaps the food gave her a little heart, however, for by the time she had finished her lunch, she had decided that she would have to do it, and heaven grant that the quality of mercy in Darrington would not dry up.

Once decided upon, the only consideration now was to make her plan work, she thought, as she walked across the lawn towards the cliff edge. Whatever price she paid, she must make sure that she was paying for something and not mess things up for everybody, Cathie included. If only, she thought crossly, Darrington hadn't been such a clam, she would not have been driven to these lengths. If he had told her that Thornton was not interested in Cathie, Stella could have broken it to Cathie as gently as possible and that would have finished it. If he had told her that Roger was fond of Cathie but could never marry her, then she could have told Cathie that and left it to her to write again to Roger. But no. A blank wall was presented to her as it had been to Cathie. And he would not even give Cathie the chance of appeal. Typical male arrogance, making its own decisions and not even bothering to explain them to those affected. By the time she got back to the hotel, she had whipped up her resolution to a fine pitch.

Before going back to her office, she went to the top floor of the hotel and inspected the loft. This led off from the top landing through a low door, and was a capacious place, being the largest of the hotel's three gables, and it housed, besides the cistern and tortured groups of pipes, some trunks and empty packing cases. There was an electric light bulb inside, and here it was that the darkest deeds of the plumber were performed. The only other room on that landing was a spare bedroom, not used except in emergencies since its low sloping ceiling and its close proximity to gurgling and groaning pipes rendered it neither attractive nor peaceful.

Stella moved a small chair from this bedroom into the loft, and then took a close look at the lock on the loft door. It was an old-fashioned type of lock and undoubtedly strong. After a few moments' cogitation, she returned to her office and telephoned the plumber.

That evening when she went round to Brierley, she was dragged into making up a set of tennis. R.J., on the spur of the moment, had decided that he would like a game. He seldom played, but the sight of a slight bulge in his waistline that morning had suggested to him that more violent exercise than golf was called for. He had roped in Mike, but Jimmy and Midge had eluded him. When Stella arrived, he was cajoling Cathie. In the end, he cajoled them both. Sweeping aside Stella's protests about being unsuitably dressed, he produced a pair of Midge's shoes and Jimmy's racquet, and led them off to the tennis court at the end of the garden, the grass on which was long enough for good grazing, and Mike, running round with the marker, was having some difficulty in following the faint tracks of the court.

'Some game this will be,' he said grimly, as Stellla came up. He was a good tennis player and took his game seriously.

'Spin for partners,' said R.J. happily.

'It's a bit much, burdening us with your waist-line, you know, R.J.,' said Mike.

'A lovely evening for a game of tennis. Do all of us good after being shut up indoors all day.' He peered down at the racquets. 'You and I, Cathie. And none of those cannon balls, Mike. There's not room behind this court to take them.'

'I doubt whether the ball will rise from this grass at all,' said Mike.

'Well, if you boys won't take your share in the mowing, what can you expect? I did it the week before last.'

'Mowing would be much better for your waist-line than playing tennis. You'll probably put something out. You haven't played for years and you're no chicken, you know.'

R.J. ignored his son's comment and said:

'The net looks high.'

'That won't matter if you're going to stand there and lean over for your volleys,' observed Mike caustically.

Stella's eyes danced as she faced R.J. and prepared to receive Cathie's service. He reminded her of a benevolent vulture as he bent his long body over his racquet, his bald dome shining from its fringe of hair, his long bony face expectant. With shoes too small for her, a racquet a good deal too heavy, and a summer frock not designed for sprinting, she felt herself at a disadvantage, but at least these antics would help to keep her mind off a grimmer performance tomorrow.

'I'll see that the old man gets his waist-line down,' murmured Mike as he passed her to fetch a ball. 'Leave this to me.'

And thereafter Mike, with diabolical skill, flighted almost every ball towards his father, placing it sufficiently near to tempt him and not near enough to enable him to get it without scrambling for it. Had it not been for the length of the grass and the absence of space round the court, Mike and Stella would have finished it off in record time; but R.J., making up in cunning for what he lacked in skill, put a peculiar spin on the ball whenever possible so that it showed a marked disinclination to rise from its luscious bed, and aimed as far as possible for the side line which was a bare yard from a ditch and hedge. As the hedge was mainly hawthorn, it was singularly inhospitable. It was therefore nearly dark and their shoes were wet with dew before Mike and Stella took the set at six-three.

'A good game,' said R.J., beaming. 'A pity the light's going. Thank you, Cathie. Thank you, Stella, my dear. That's a fine forehand drive of yours.'

Mike was winding down the net when the straining wire broke and it collapsed on the grass. Why it should break when it was being slackened, nobody knew, but it was the sort of thing that happened to the Elmores, and Mike bundled up the net, with Stella's help, and observed cheerfully as they walked down the garden:

'Well, that's the last game of tennis we shall have to endure with R.J. this season.'

And Stella, passing the half-finished structure which was more suggestive of a gibbet than a pergola, agreed that it was unlikely that the tennis court would be in use again that season.

It was not until she was repairing the ravages of the campaign in Cathie's bedroom that she was able to bring up the subject of Roger.

'Cathie, can you get away from the Museum half an hour earlier tomorrow?'

'I expect so. Why?'

'Roger arrives tomorrow afternoon. You know that dilapidated summer-house affair behind the garages at the Cormorant? Just inside the stone wall boundary.'

'Yes, I know.'

'Will you be there at five o'clock tomorrow? I'll see that Roger's there.'

'Can you, Stella?' asked Cathie eagerly.

'Yes. Don't come to the hotel. Approach it through the gate in the wall. You can have him for an hour. Take him for a walk or stay there. You won't be disturbed. I'll collect him again at the summer-house at six.'

'It all sounds very mysterious.'

'No, it isn't, but I had to think of a simple plan that would be easy for Roger to fall in with. He and Darrington have got a pretty full weekend planned, I believe. That will be the only opportunity, as far as I can see. O.K.?'

'Yes. It's nice of Nick to oblige.'

'Well, find out what's the matter, my dear. And I hope, I do hope, it's nothing that can't be mended. If there should by any chance be any hitch, I'll telephone before you leave work. If you don't hear, it's the summer-house, wet or fine, and . . . good luck. Now, where are my shoes? I can appreciate just how much Chinese women must have suffered when their feet were bound.'

*   *   *

Stella found it difficult to concentrate on work the next morning, and when Darrington came into her room, he found her wrestling with columns of figures in the Cash Book and looking rather worried.

'What's the trouble?' he asked.

'I'm thirty pounds out, and I can't find it. I've checked every item. It must be my addition somewhere. I've been nearly all the morning on it.'

'Leave it. I'll run through it when I've a few moments to spare. Have you drawn a cheque for Merton & Dalloway this morning? They've just sent in another statement.'

'Yes. It's among this lot, for your signature.'

'Good. By the way, what about Baynes?'

'He's coming after lunch.'

'Righto. I'll sign these now.'

Stella, watching his broad shoulders disappear through the door, was conscious of a slight sinking feeling.

The plumber and his mate arrived soon after half past three, as Stella had instructed, and ten minutes after their arrival, Darrington left in his car for the station. It was twenty minutes past four when Baynes and his mate left, and Stella watched them depart in an anguish lest Darrington should return and see them go, but her luck was in. The car drove up to the lodge at half past four. Roger's train must have been late. Stella hurried back to the hotel from her vantage point in the garden and sought out Miss Bromley.

'Would you telephone the lodge, Miss Bromley, and say that the plumber wants to see Mr. Darrington. It's urgent. We're in the loft, and having trouble up there. I must fly.'

Stella ran upstairs and hovered on the next landing until she saw Darrington striding up the drive. Then she ran to the top floor, put the Cash Book, a bank statement and a copy of *The Times* on a packing case inside the loft, and ran her eye over the note she had scribbled on the back of an envelope.

'Rickie will unlock the door in an hour. I'm terribly sorry but there was no other way. Perhaps you could spot my mistake in the C.B. while you are waiting. S.V.'

She doubted whether he would find that very consoling, but it might keep him quiet. She left the envelope on top of the Cash Book, slipped out, leaving the light on inside the loft and the door wide open. Then she slid into the spare bedroom, closed the door behind her, flew to a built-in wardrobe which backed on to the loft and proceeded to bang on the floor and back of the wardrobe with a walking stick in the hope that it would sound like the plumber in the loft. The cistern was in the farthest corner of the loft from the door and Darrington would have to be well inside the loft before he could see that no plumber was in fact there.

When she heard his footsteps running up the last flight of stairs, she felt that her pounding heart would choke her. However, her imitation of a plumber must have been sufficiently convincing to arouse no suspicions, for he walked straight in. Stella whipped out of the room like a streak of lightning, closed the loft door, locked it, pocketed the key and flew down the stairs as though pursued by devils.

It was terribly hot up there under the eaves, and she wished she'd left him a glass of water as well. She was pretty sure he couldn't force that lock, even if he had suitable tools, which he hadn't. It was a fine sunny day and no visitors were likely to be returning to their bedrooms before six-thirty, since dinner was not served until seven-thirty. It would not avail Darrington, therefore, to try to attract attention by banging on the floor. In any case, the plumber had been banging for the past hour and would be assumed to be still there.

She collected her hat and bag from her room and as she passed through the outer office, explained to Miss Bromley that she would not be back that afternoon, and she had a commission to execute for Mr. Darrington.

'What's happening up aloft?' asked Miss Bromley.

'Everything under control,' said Stella, hoping fervently that it was. 'If anybody complains of the noise, it's Mr. Darrington and the plumber taking it out of the pipes. Good night. Have a nice weekend.'

She glanced at her watch as she hurried down to the lodge. Rickie opened the door.

'Oh, Rickie, Mr. Darrington has got tied up with the plumber, and I'm going to look after Mr. Thornton until he's free. Hullo, Roger,' she added, as a tall, thin figure loomed up behind Rickie. 'How are you?'

She thought he looked a little startled as they shook hands. Greetings over, she said apologetically:

'Mr. Darrington's terribly sorry, but he's afraid he's stuck with the plumber for a bit. These things always happen just when you least want them.'

'Anything I can do?'

'No. They've got everything under control. I've been told off to take you round the grounds and bring you back by six, when Mr. Darrington will be free of hotel encumbrances.'

'Righto. It's certainly too lovely to stay indoors. It looks as though I'm going to be lucky with my holiday.'

Stella took him through her garden and beyond the garages. It was five minutes past five as she led him round the summerhouse. Cathie was sitting on the seat, a tense, huddled little figure, but her heart was in her face as she stood up and held out her hand, although she seemed unable to force any words through her trembling lips. Roger's eyes lit up as he saw her. For a moment he stood motionless, then he took her by the shoulders and said 'Cathie' as he drew her to him, and Stella saw and heard no more. As she walked back along the cliff, she consoled herself with the thought that, whatever barrier there was between Cathie and Roger, it was not a barrier of indifference. She had only heard Roger utter one word, but the tone of his voice was enough to tell her that.

The hour which doubtless seemed so short to Cathie seemed endless to Stella. At any moment, she expected to see a furious figure striding from the hotel in search of her. She wondered whether the hour was dragging as painfully for him as for her. It would be so hot up there and she doubted whether he would be in a frame of mind to settle to work, or to study *The Times*. Below her, the sea was calm and blue. She sat down on the cliff edge and watched a tramp steamer passing far out to sea, little more than a dark smudge. Then a sailing boat came round the headland, dipping playfully. She jumped as she heard footsteps behind her, but it was only an elderly couple from the hotel.

'Good evening,' said Stella, smiling, for they had recognised her.

They stopped and chatted for a few moments before moving on. Stella glanced at her watch. Half past five. Each second seemed a minute, each minute an hour. And then, a few minutes before six, she saw Cathie and Roger coming towards her from the golf course just beyond the hotel boundary. Cathie smiled at Stella as they came up, but all she said was:

'I've never heard so many larks before. It was as though the sun had inspired them.'

Roger looked pale and composed, but he took Cathie's arm as the three of them walked back towards the hotel talking of bird life, a subject which Stella felt was not really uppermost in any of their minds just then. For herself, she could not keep her eyes from dwelling, with a kind of fascinated horror, on the centre gable of the Cormorant, with its patch of new tiles standing out like a peony from the old weathered tiles surrounding it.

'I've just got to have a word with Rickie, Cathie. Will you walk on? I'll catch you up in a few minutes,' said Stella, as they reached the drive.

'All right. Goodbye, Roger. I hope you enjoy your holiday.'

'Goodbye, Cathie. Take care of yourself.'

Alone with Roger by the gate of the lodge, Stella found it rather difficult to say what she had to say, until she met his eyes and thought, as she had thought once before, that they were the kindest eyes she had ever seen. Then it wasn't difficult at all.

'Roger, I do hope you'll forgive me for what must seem unpardonable interference in your private affairs. I don't know

169

what is between you and Cathie. It's not my business, and please don't think I'm poking my nose in. I arranged this meeting for one reason only. Cathie was breaking her heart because she'd been left in the dark. She's got grit and she's not afraid of the truth, but not knowing the truth was tormenting her. I made this opportunity for her and practically forced her to take it for that one reason. So that she could learn the truth. I thought she was entitled to it. Beyond that is not my province. I hope you're not angry with me.'

'No. Why should I be? You've done me a great service, but whether you've done Cathie a service, I'm not sure.'

'Don't you think Cathie is the best judge of that? She's a very wise as well as a good person. Haven't you rather underrated her judgment and her maturity?'

'I underrated her feeling for me. Of my own for her, I was never in any doubt. Had I realised that her feelings were so deeply involved, I would never have cut away without giving her my reasons. As it was, I thought I was doing the kindest and fairest thing.'

His face looked even thinner than when she had last seen him and there were lines around his eyes and mouth which made him middle-aged, although Stella knew that he was still in his thirties. The mouth was too sensitive, the high forehead too intelligent. To be so fine-drawn was a handicap in this harsh world, thought Stella. He could do with some of Darrington's toughness. Austerity, patience and kindness marked Roger's face, but no happiness.

'Sacrifices which spring from love can be a privilege to those who make them, Roger, and bring their own kind of reward. Sacrifices which spring only from duty are not the same thing at all. But I won't trespass on your private ground. You and Cathie are both intelligent, good-hearted people and I'm sure that together you'll work out the best solution for you both. I was only concerned to see that it was worked out together. What I really want to say to you now is that Nick knows nothing of this. I don't want you to think for a moment that Nick has ever discussed you and Cathie with me, or has countenanced this meeting.'

'Well, I must admit I was a bit surprised at the idea that Nick had arranged it.'

'He most certainly hasn't. He refused to make any comment about you and Cathie, even when I tried to find out why you had walked out on her in the hope of being able to let her know the truth, and when I asked him to arrange a little party for the four of us, he flatly refused and forbade me to meddle or intrude on the privacy of your visit. I must make that quite clear, Roger. And Cathie knows nothing of Nick's objections, either. I don't want her to.'

'I see,' said Roger slowly.

'How much does Nick know? I don't imagine you had a heart-to-heart talk about Cathie. Men don't indulge in such unburdenings, particularly men as self-contained as you and Nick. But I know something was said about it when Nick spent that weekend with you.'

'As a matter of fact, the subject would never have been raised at all if Nick hadn't invited me to come here for a few days this summer. I hesitated to accept and felt forced to explain my hesitation. I didn't want to run any risk of running into Cathie. I knew she and Nick were friendly, and you were a link here, too. He assured me that I need have no fear. There was little chance of an accidental meeting and since I felt like that, he would certainly see that I didn't run into her at the hotel. He asked no questions. I told him that if circumstances had been different, I should have hoped to marry Cathie, but as I was not in a position to marry, and probably never would be, I had decided to make the break clean and final. Nick agreed that it was a very sensible decision, and the subject was dropped. That was all that passed between us. But as I know he always means what he says, I was a bit surprised when I saw Cathie today. Do you mean to say he knows nothing of Cathie's presence here today?'

'Nothing.'

'It was just chance that kept him out of the way?'

'No. I locked him in the loft.'

'Good God! You didn't!'

'Yes, I did. The plumbers had gone. It was the only way.'

Roger let out a long whistle.

171

'He's not going to like that.'

'No.'

'That was really going a bit far, Stella, wasn't it?'

'I was desperate. I had to put Cathie out of her misery of uncertainty, and this seemed the only opportunity we were ever likely to have.'

'He's the last chap in the world to tolerate interference of that sort.'

'Don't worry about it, Roger. It's my pigeon.'

'I'd better go and release him straight away.'

'No. I'll get Rickie to do it. I'm going to make myself scarce. Perhaps by Monday he'll have cooled off a little.'

'Stella, this can mean serious trouble for you, you know.'

He looked worried and she smiled up at him.

'How you do take everybody's worries on to your shoulders, Roger. Leave Nick and me to fight this out. I knew the risk and took it. I just wanted to absolve Nick from any part in my tactics. And I'm forgiven for tricking you?'

'Of course. I'll do my best to smooth things over for you.'

Rickie loomed up in the garden behind the lodge and Stella called him.

'Rickie, will you go up to the loft and unlock the door with this. Mr. Darrington's in there.'

'What's he in there for?'

'Because I put him there. Don't ask any questions, but go and let him out, there's a dear.'

'I wondered where he'd got to. He promised to let me have the wine for dinner. A special burgundy. Now I shan't have time to get it the right temperature. Oysters, fillet steak, fried onions, sauce diable; fruit salad and ice cream; and a really choice Stilton cheese. How does that appeal to you, sir?'

'It appeals very strongly. I think the sooner we get hold of the host, the better.'

Rickie's mind must have been too preoccupied with his preparations for dinner to have taken in the significance of Stella's information, but it now dawned on him for the first time that something ususal had been going on.

'In the loft?'

172

'Yes, Rickie, and if you don't go and release him soon, the roof will probably blow off.'

Rickie shook his head at her, still puzzled.

'You really ought not to have done that, Miss Verney. I don't know what he'll say, I'm sure.'

As Rickie hurried up the drive to the hotel, Stella said:

'I'm off. I hope I haven't spoiled the atmosphere for the weekend. When do you go to Cornwall?'

'First thing Monday morning. I'll do what I can for you. That dinner should have a mellowing effect, anyway.'

Cathie was sitting on the harbour wall, waiting for Stella.

'You've been a long time. Everything all right?'

'Yes. I'm going to be late home, and Nan's going to be cross if it's a hot dinner. What a heavenly evening! I'd like to go sailing across that sunny sea to the horizon.'

They were both quiet and preoccupied as they walked home, and they had reached Church Lane before Cathie referred to the events which filled their minds.

'Stella, we haven't time to talk now, but thank you so much for your help. I've got a lot to think about. Can we meet on Sunday. Then I can tell you about it. I haven't really got myself sorted out yet.'

'You don't have to tell me anything, Cathie, but one thing. Have I really helped by meddling?'

'You've let the daylight in, Stella. Without your help, I don't think I would ever have seen the daylight. I'm no good at forcing situations. I have you to thank for that, as for so much else, bless you.' Cathie stopped with her hand on the gate of Brierley. 'If it's hot on Sunday, shall we take our bathing things and some tea, and picnic in one of the coves?'

'Good idea. I'll be round about three.'

Cathie smiled and ran up the path. At least, thought Stella, she's come back to life again. That alone made it worth while. But her heart was full of foreboding as she walked on alone. Roger's disclosure of what had passed between Darrington and himself on the subject of Cathie and his visit made her situation seem even blacker with Darrington.

Chapter Fourteen

LYING in the shadow of a rock, with the murmur of the sea in their ears, Cathie told Stella something of what had passed between her and Roger.

'He thought that by going away like that and ignoring my letters, he would be making it easy for me to forget him. He didn't think that my feelings were too deeply involved to be able to free them. While his mother is alive, he says he can't and won't marry, and that may well mean that he will never marry.'

'Why won't he marry? I know his mother is a helpless cripple, but does that put a wife for Roger quite out of court?'

'Yes,' said Cathie sadly. 'I tried to argue against it, but I can see his point. He doesn't earn a lot of money, and he can't afford to keep two homes going. His mother needs constant attention. And unfortunately illness has affected Mrs. Thornton's nature, and Roger says she is terribly difficult to live with and would undoubtedly make hell for a daughter-in-law.'

'Are there no other members of the family to share the responsibility with him?'

'No. Roger was the only child, and his father died years ago. Mrs. Thornton is in her early sixties and has a good constitution apart from this frightful arthritis, so Roger's responsibility may well go on for twenty years.'

'But nobody could make things unpleasant for you, Cathie. You're so obviously kind and patient.'

'I learned from Roger on Friday that he was engaged to be married soon after his father died. Mrs. Thornton broke it up with her malicious tongue. He didn't go into the details. It was painful for him to tell me about it, but I'm afraid his mother is very possessive and terrified of losing her only prop. I said that, knowing what she was like, I could school myself to it and I refused to believe that anybody could come between us if we loved each other, but Roger was adamant. He would never ask any woman to submit to it, and he would never run the risk of seeing our marriage come to grief.'

'If he were a different type, of course, he would force his mother into some sort of tolerable behaviour. But not Roger. I can see that. It's a wretched situation. But what are you going to do?'

'Be satisfied with friendship, and wait. I managed to convince him that even that was manna from heaven after the starvation of the past months. The trouble is, he's so modest, Stella. He can't believe that he means so much to me, or could mean so much to anybody. Even now, he's made it quite clear that I'm in no way bound to him, and that I am free to marry someone else, and that he hopes for my sake that I do. Isn't that odd? He has no conception of the happiness he's given me just by loving me and being in my world again, even if it can only be letters that bind us. We shall try to see each other now and again, but Roger's terribly tied and he doesn't want me ever to come within range of his mother.'

'And you'll be content with that?'

'More than content. Wouldn't you be? If you loved someone with your heart and your mind. If you'd found somebody whose mind miraculously spoke the same language as yours when you thought that your rather odd language was destined never to be shared. Wouldn't you be happy just to be able to keep in touch?'

'Half a loaf, in fact.'

'I don't know that I've ever expected more. And to know that I can bring a little warmth into Roger's very bleak life makes me happy, too. Believe me, I'm right, Stella. It might not be right for others, but for Roger and for me, it is.'

'Yes, I think I agree,' said Stella slowly. 'You can't turn love off like a tap because circumstances are unfavourable. But I do wish that things had been different for you, Cathie. For both of you.'

'Yes. But we have so much. Don't look like a gravedigger, dear. You're as bad as Roger. I'm happy, and I can't convince either of you of that fact, it seems.'

'Yes, now you're happy, Cathie, because you've just learned that Roger loves you, but how are you going to feel in a year or

175

two? In ten years? Won't letters and an occasional meeting wear rather thin? Seem rather a poor exchange for marriage, a home, children.'

'Roger has left me free to choose that elsewhere if I wish. I shouldn't be surprised if he sends me a formal charter, setting it all out in writing and telling me to frame it and hang it on my bedroom wall.'

'Yes, you are still free to choose.'

Cathie smiled and did not reply, but seeing her expression, Stella said:

'You don't think you'll ever choose anything else?'

'I know I shan't. You see, I'm not free. And all the declarations of the world won't make me free. I lost my freedom from the moment I started loving Roger. It's as simple as that. And what is between us will never wear thin. It won't even have the shine rubbed off by the wear and tear of everyday life together, and if it's never more than a flower imprisoned in a glass, without roots or seed, it will still be lovely to me. So stop looking as though you're ordering a wreath for my coffin, and be happy about it. If it weren't for you, that flower might have been a withered thing pressed flat in a book like those sad specimens Midge hoards.'

And Stella knew that what she saw in Cathie's face then was happiness, unblinkered and unwavering, and she was satisfied.

'Right,' said Stella, briskly. 'Wreaths overboard. I shall worry about your fate no more, and rejoice in your conquest of your Curator. I like him very much. Life may hurt you, but he won't, ever, I fancy. What about a swim?'

As they ran through the breakers together and plunged, Stella reflected that she would be needing that wreath for herself very shortly . . .

Walking to the hotel on Monday morning as to the scaffold, she saw Darrington's car ahead of her. He must have just seen Roger off. The car turned off the main road for the climb up to the hotel and Stella continued on round the harbour towards the cliff path. She had been trying to comfort herself with the hope that the genuine friendliness which had underlain their relationship even in the early days and had seen them through stormy passages, strengthening to a very deep friendship dur-

176

ing the past months, would now temper Darrington's legitimate anger.

In the outer office, Miss Bromley greeted Stella with her usual jaunty air, and was expounding on the depressing quality of Monday morning when the telephone in Stella's room rang out.

'Starting early today,' said Miss Bromley darkly.

He was losing no time, thought Stella, as she lifted the receiver.

'Good morning, Miss Verney. Would you come across to the lodge at once, please.'

'Yes, Mr. Darrington.'

The Miss Verney was ominous. Lately he had taken to using her Christian name.

When she went into his study, he was standing with his back to her, looking out of the window. He turned for a moment and scrutinised her as though she were a doubtful specimen in a glass jar. The clock seemed to have an unusually slow tick. She had always found his habit of silent contemplation unnerving. He hadn't asked her to sit down, and she stood by his desk, clasping her hands to keep them from shaking. She knew from his face that she hadn't a chance.

'I shan't keep you long, Miss Verney. I don't intend to hold an inquest on Friday's events. Had it not been for Roger Thornton's intervention on your behalf, I should at this moment only need to hand you your insurance card and a month's money and tell you to go. However, Thornton did intervene and extracted a promise from me that I wouldn't dismiss you, a promise which I made most unwillingly and against my better judgment.'

'I had . . . ' broke in Stella, but Darrington interrupted her.

'I don't want to hear anything from you, Miss Verney. As far as I am concerned, there is nothing you can say to mitigate your disgraceful conduct towards me and your effrontery in encroaching on my private life. The hospitality I offer my friends has nothing at all to do with you. Whatever machinations you wished to carry out on Roger Thornton, you had no shadow of right to attempt them while he was a guest under my roof. Your interference was insolent and unpardonable. I don't think you would have dared to do it if I had kept you in your place here as an employee. I've made the mistake of letting a friendly element creep into a business relationship. I've taken you, up to a point, into my confidence, and I've discussed your own personal affairs with you and advised you as a friend. That was evidently a mistake. The result has been that you've abused our friendly relations and have forgotten that as your employer I am entitled to some respect, and as a private individual I have a right to entertain my friends without interference. It's a case of give certain people an inch and they take a mile.'

'Please, let me . . . '

'There is nothing you can say that I want to hear. In future, please keep in mind your position here. I shall do nothing to encourage you to forget it, and if you do, you will be dismissed. There will be no second chance. One more point. I understand that only Roger, Rickie and you know of the part I was given in Friday's capers. Is that so?'

'Yes.'

'Then I think it advisable not to spread the story further, amusing though it might be. Discipline, I feel, would be prejudiced if the staff heard of it, for I imagine they'd find it hard to understand why you were still here to tell the tale. It's to go no further.'

'I never intended that it should.'

'Very well. That's all. The subject is closed.'

As she opened her mouth to speak, he picked up the telephone and asked for a number. Feeling as though she had been dipped in boiling water and then put in a refrigerator, she turned and went. So much, she thought grimly, for friendship.

Somehow she got through the day. There was plenty of work to do, and, mechanically, she did it. She found that her error had been found in the Cash Book and the totals corrected. She presumed this had been spotted during that sun-baked hour in the loft, for he would have had no other time to spare for it during the weekend.

She felt unable to face lunch, and after a cup of coffee she took herself off to the cliffs. Although many times since Friday she had pictured the show-down with Darrington, her imagination had been far from the reality. She had expected to have to fight to put her explanation over, had worked out a humble apology and a full account of her motives. He liked Cathie, and she had thought that if she could convince him that her interference had borne fruit for Cathie he might forgive her. What she had never contemplated was not being allowed a hearing at all, and her worst anticipations had never approached the scorching quality of his observations on the liberties she had taken with him. She felt hot at the thought of them now, and the realisation that he had some justification for taking this view did nothing to cool her. He was the owner of this hotel, and one of his own staff had defied him and made a fool of him in the eyes of his servant and his friend. For the first time it occurred to her that she had acted too impulsively. That she might have been able to work out a less offensive plan to find out the truth from Roger. She sighed as she watched the breakers curling below into white foam. The sunshine and blue sky seemed to mock her. If she had any pride, she supposed she would resign after the things he had said that morning, but she clung to the hope that after a time he would soften and give her a chance of explaining her motives and saying she was sorry.

But it became apparent during the weeks that followed that this hope was not going to be fulfilled. She was treated with such rigid formality by Darrington that even mention of the weather seemed dangerously personal in his presence. In fact, she saw little of him. He left her to get on with her work and did not take any responsibility from her. She did her own correspondence, sending the carbon copies to him at the end of each day so that he was kept up to date. She entered up the books, gave Miss Bromley the accounts to type and went about the administrative duties behind the scenes just as she had done during the past months, but now there was no feeling of working together. He no longer discussed things with her. She was not consulted about staff matters. Decisions were taken and put into effect without her knowledge. She was told just what was necessary and no more. If he wanted to raise any queries with her, if she wanted his advice, their interviews were short and rigid. His personal correspondence he now dictated to Miss Bromley, much to that young woman's gratification.

They had a good season that summer. The hotel was full from May until the end of September, and there was little time to brood during working hours. As if the thorns of her own making were not enough, by the time July came round, it had become apparent that Phyllis Bromley had become yet another thorn. A thorn very difficult to deal with, thought Stella, watching her assistant at the filing cabinet one morning.

Phyllis Bromley was bright, ambitious and shrewd, and at twenty showed every sign of knowing from A to Z the technique of getting on. Just now she was demonstrating the cardinal point of cultivating those in power and discarding the sinking ship with all speed. It had not taken her long to sense that Stella was no longer a person of influence, and indeed was not in favour with Darrington. Once that realisation had dawned, she had ceased to be the willing, pleasant assistant and made it clear that she considered herself Stella's equal and under no obligation to take orders from anybody but Darrington, to whom she was all smiles and eager service. Sinking ship or not, however, Stella was not inclined to be abandoned in this manner by young Miss Bromley although she knew that her own position, lacking Darrington's support, was a tricky one.

Miss Bromley was looking through a file, frowning. She was a good-looking girl with a glowing pink complexion, blue eyes and bold, regular features. She would look even better, in Stella's opinion, if she would stop doing her black hair in that ugly horse-tail style which revealed ears that were too large. And those ears missed as little as those bright eyes, thought Stella, who had first refused to believe that a politician's head could sit on such young shoulders until the evidence proved overwhelming. Jaunty, sure of herself, adroit at changing her face, allying a diplomat's sense of what was expedient to a boxer's sense of timing, Phyllis Bromley was destined to go far in this world, and Stella had recently become aware that she was the first small hill in Miss Bromley's path.

'Will you slip down to the post office for some more stamps some time today, Miss Bromley?' asked Stella pleasantly.

'I'm afraid I shan't have time. I've a lot of letters for Mr. Darrington this morning.'

'Someone must fetch them, and I'm far too busy with

P.A.Y.E. to spare the time myself.'

'The porter had better go, then. I think we need an office boy here,' said Miss Bromley briskly as she collected her files and marched back to her own room, her hair bobbing behind her.

Stella sighed. She would have to make a stand, but she had no heart for a fight. She was too unhappy and shaken by Darrington's withdrawal to want to bother about this tiresome gnat. When she went into the outer office, her eye was caught by a pile of books on Miss Bromley's desk.

'Mr. Darrington's book,' she said brightly, catching Stella's eye. 'Have you seen it?'

'No. I didn't know it was published.'

'Oh, yes. At least, publication day is next Wednesday. These are Mr. Darrington's presentation copies. He's sending them to friends.'

Stella picked up a copy and looked through it. She could not have said why it hurt so much to learn from Miss Bromley that his book was published, but it did. Surely he could have mentioned it to her, knowing how interested she had been in the project.

'I shall buy a copy and ask Mr. Darrington to autograph it,' said Miss Bromley. 'You know, I think he's got something, don't you? Rugged type, and all that, but he's definitely got something. And he's jolly good to work for. No dithering, and makes everything so clear. I worked for a shocking fussy little man before I came here. He had a messy mind, like spaghetti; all ends and no definite conclusions. You've no idea what a treat it is to have somebody with a clear mind.'

'I agree. Mr. Darrington's mind is very clear and definite. He always knows exactly what he wants.'

Miss Bromley looked up at her from beneath long lashes.

'I'm awfully glad he's letting me do his correspondence. I didn't think at first that my shorthand would be up to it. I haven't been to classes very long. Mr. Darrington's very nice and doesn't rush me, and we get along famously.'

'Splendid,' said Stella, and just then the buzzer beside Miss Bromley's desk burred once, and she seized her shorthand notebook and flew off to Darrington's office.

Stella went on looking at the photographs in the book, most of which she had seen on that Boxing Night long ago when she had first been aware that there was some kind of bond between them. She stopped at the photograph of Darrington outside the tent in the valley, remembering how she had looked up from it to find him watching her. Deeply preoccupied with John as she had been that night, she could still remember the odd moment of significance which had followed her scrutiny of that photograph. What was it he had said? Something about wondering whether that was her Samarkand. The moment had passed, her troubles with John had obsessed her thoughts, but buried away beneath them that moment had reminded, crystallised, and it shone out now with a clarity which hurt her . . .

Darrington made one of his rare visits to her office that afternoon.

'Miss Bromley has her hands pretty full just now. In fact, we all have. She's been telling me that she really hasn't time to do the running about, and I think we can do with an office boy or girl. Will you get on to the Labour Exchange and see what the position is? I'd like to get hold of someone like young Bryant again.'

'Very well, Mr. Darrington.'

'And one other thing.' He looked round the room. 'I think Miss Bromley will have to come in here with you. There's plenty of space. Whoever we get will be in her room, and it will be a bit cramped in there for two.'

Stella looked down at the pay-slip she was typing. This was a blow. She had always enjoyed a room of her own to work in. To be told to share it now with Miss Bromley was a very unpleasant pill to swallow. Goodbye to privacy, and goodbye to peace, for Miss Bromley had a chattering tongue. On the surface it was a reasonable request, engineered by Miss Bromley with her customary skill. Stella had no valid reason for refusing, although she knew that this victory for her junior effectively removed what little authority Stella still had over the girl.

'I see,' said Stella quietly.

'You can arrange between you where to put the desks. Bob and I will see to the moving.'

182

'Very well. May I congratulate you on the appearance of your book, Mr. Darrington? It's a very nice production. I hope it will be successful.'

His pale eyes flickered over her for a second, then he said, 'Thank you,' and went.

The ship was not sinking, thought Stella. It had sunk, and was beyond salvage.

She went riding on the following Sunday, her twenty-sixth birthday, and when she returned to the stables she indulged in some spectacular jumping before dismounting, in the hope that this exercise would shift the pall of depression that had descended on her. The stables were attached to a riding school, the owner of which knew Stella very well. He came across to her as she was leading her horse to the yard.

'Nice work, Miss Verney. Will you ride Jamie in the August gymkhana for me?'

'I hadn't thought of entering,' she said doubtfully.

'Then it's time you did. I'll be surprised if you don't get a rosette. Jamie goes better for you than for anybody.'

'All right,' said Stella, without much enthusiasm.

Walking home, she tried to take stock of the situation. There were no birthday celebrations this year. The Elmores were away on holiday. They had left for North Wales the previous day, Cathie in a state of bliss because they were staying only five miles from Roger, and they would be able to see a lot of each other for the next two weeks.

Twenty-six, thought Stella, and what had she to show for it? Where was she going? The sensible thing would be to cut adrift from the stalemate at the Cormorant and make a fresh start elsewhere. There was nothing but pain and humiliation for her there, and in all conscience she had endured enough of both during the past two years. Her ego had been forced to accommodate itself so much that she felt she had no ego left, only a wincing pulp of jelly. Deeply conscious of a sense of failure and futility, she wondered why she stayed on at the hotel. But the answer came pat from that beaten ego: because she couldn't bear not to see Darrington again. Cathie was right. Half a loaf, or crumbs, she could not give them up. It was no use telling herself what was sensible, no use whipping her pride.

Love was not a thing of reason, nor had it any pride. John and Nick. She seemed to make a mess of personal relationships where men were concerned. Not that the wounds John had left were like the present wounds. Then there had been more anger in them, more bitterness, but the anger and bitterness had been like a purge and they had healed more quickly than she would have thought possible, leaving no scars. Now, there was no anger, no bitterness; only a kind of desolate weeping inside her which she felt would go on for ever, like the trickles down the walls of caves.

Somehow, she had to pull herself out of this trough of self-pity, a particularly futile form of self-indulgence. If she couldn't be ruthless enough with herself to leave the hotel, she must stay there on Nick's terms and stop whimpering. There was plenty to do, and there was always the problem of Miss Bromley to occupy her. Pulped as her ego might be, she was not going to allow that young woman to walk over it.

And that appeared to be the only positive conclusion to emerge from her efforts to take stock on her twenty-sixth birthday.

Chapter Fifteen

IT was at the gymkhana that Stella met Felicity again. The Craynes had been staying at the lodge for a week, but Stella had only seen them at a distance. They were accompanied by their son, a fair boy, tall for his fourteen years, and it was Peter who had persuaded his parents to come to the gymkhana. Stella did not know they were there until after her event, when Felicity broke away from the spectators, with Peter in tow, and met Stella as she was leading her horse away from the course.

'Congratulations, Miss Verney. My son is wide-eyed with admiration and pipping to meet you and the horse, although

184

which of you he wants to meet most, I wouldn't be sure.'

Felicity's warm smile as she held out her hand to Stella was most reassuring. Peter was introduced to Stella and Jamie, and talked about riding with a cheerful frankness which Stella found attractive. He had his father's looks and his mother's friendly personality.

'Nick was here,' said Felicity, 'but he left just now to get back to the hotel for the new arrivals, although why he couldn't leave them to Rickie, I don't know.'

'Have you enjoyed your week?'

'Immensely. It's gone too quickly. We have to go back on Monday. Hector has some conference or other to attend. We haven't seen you about much, Miss Verney. Don't tell me you've given up your garden.'

'No, but I don't have much time for it now, and often have to leave it to the gardener. We're having a very busy season this year, and the office work takes pretty well all my time.'

'Don't let Nick work you too hard.'

'We shall ease off in another month,' said Stella, 'but I really like to be busy, and I'm glad this season has made up for the awful one last year.'

And just then Jamie's owner came up and congratulated Stella on her success, and Felicity and her son faded away.

It became obvious to Stella during those weeks that Darrington was training Rickie to take over much of the hotel management in front of the scenes, and to her surprise Rickie took to his new duties like a duck to water. Although at first sight not an obvious candidate for the job, Rickie liked people and had a cheerful, confiding manner that disarmed even the most reserved. No greater contrast to both his predecessors could have been found. He possessed nothing of John's charm and presence, nothing of Darrington's quiet authority, and yet in his own way he was undoubtedly effective. Darrington now confined himself to an hour or two in his office each morning, and Stella wondered whether he meant to keep his hands on the reins to this extent or whether he would hand the whole of the office administration over to her in due course. Or to Miss Bromley. The latter took a somewhat dim view of Rickie's advance in the hierarchy, and thought he was getting above himself, a view which caused Stella some ironic amusement.

And so August came to its end, and on the last day of the month, Miss Bromley was able to produce another item of news for Stella's surprised ears.

'It will seem odd without Mr. Darrington for the next two months, won't it?' she observed, looking up from her typewriter. 'Didn't you know?' she added blandly, as she saw Stella's face.

'No. Is he going away?'

'Yes. To British Columbia. The Rocky Mountains. Isn't he lucky? Gosh, I'd love to see the Grand Canyon,' said Miss Bromley fervently, technicolor western films before her eyes.

Stella could not bear to point out that the Grand Canyon was in Arizona, U.S.A., more than a thousand miles away from British Columbia, whereat Miss Bromley tossed her hair, and Stella relented enough to add:

'Anyway, I dare say the country is similar, and I'm pretty foggy myself about distances in that continent. They're so vast compared with our pocket handkerchief of a country.'

The telephone rang out and Miss Bromley rushed to it before Stella, who had been at the filing cabinet, could reach it.

'Mr. Darrington's private secretary here,' she announced clearly.

Stella smiled a little wryly, wondering why she should relent when an opportunity to deflate Miss Bromley presented itself. It would be pleasant, she thought, to see a firm hand applied to the posterior now presented to her as Miss Bromley leaned across her desk. The caller, however, was the coal merchant with whom Stella had crossed swords earlier that morning, and he was asking for Miss Verney. Miss Bromley held the receiver out to her.

'Grenville's for you,' she said, and returned to her desk, the tail of her hair bobbing exuberantly.

Darrington sent for Stella just before lunch.

'I'm going away on Wednesday, Miss Verney, for a couple of months. I'm leaving Rickie in charge. You'll look after the office side, as usual. I think you should be able to manage, now that the season is coming to an end.'

'Yes, of course.'

'I'll have a discussion with you both before I go. I shall arrange with the bank for you and Rickie to sign cheques jointly if necessary, and I'll leave some blanks signed. Anyway, we'll go into all that next week. There's one point I'd like to raise now. Your holiday. You usually take it in October. Have you arranged anything?'

'No, not yet.'

'I expect to be back about the third week in October. If you could leave your holiday until the end of that month, I'd be glad.'

'Yes, I'll do that,' said Stella, picking up a small crumb of comfort from the fact that at least he conceded her fitness for responsibility in his absence.

'My brother-in-law will come down again at the end of September to see if all's well, and I've told Rickie to get in touch with him if anything out of the way crops up.'

'We shan't be able to get in touch with you?'

'No. I shall be away from civilisation for a bit.'

'I expect you'll be glad to get away from it.'

'Yes, I shall. I've told Miss Bromley, and explained the situation.'

'Yes,' said Stella gently. 'She had already given me the news.'

He looked up quickly and their eyes met.

'I've told her that you are in charge of the office in my absence,' he said.

Bless you for that second crumb, thought Stella, but she only smiled at him and said:

'I hope you have a very good trip.'

'Thank you.'

It was from Rickie that Stella learned more of Darrington's plans. He had been invited to join a party of Canadians who were undertaking a geological survey somewhere in the Rockies. The leader of the expedition was an old friend of Darrington's and his invitation had been accepted with enthusiasm. Rickie looked a little glum as he told Stella this.

'Poor old Rickie. Left at home.'

'Yep. I'm too much of a crock to be any use at that game

now. I'd give a lot to be flying out there with him next week, though.'

'Never mind. We need you to look after the Cormorant and comfort the rest of us,' said Stella. 'I'd like to be going myself. Away from the telephone and the typewriter, from P.A.Y.E., from people who cancel holidays at the last minute, from all duties and demands. With nothing but what God made around you, and all the complications of civilisation blotted out.'

'Well, of course, it's not all sunshine and honey, but it's a grand life if you're fit. You'd take to it very well, Miss Verney, I reckon. Not the right cup of tea for most females, but I think it would be to your taste.'

'I know it would. And, do you know, Rickie, I've never been abroad. I've never even been very far from Ashcombe. Sometimes I feel as though I'm caged for good.'

'Well, you never know your luck. Blessed if I thought I'd be managing a hotel.'

'Do you like the job?'

'Yes, as a matter of fact, I do. I like contact with people. Maybe that was in the chief's mind. A sort of consolation prize for me. Seeing people instead of places. And it does stretch the horizon a bit, I must say. That old Colonel Gentry's a card. Been in India most of his life. He told me some gaudy tales about it last night, I can tell you.'

'You'll still be able to travel, though, Rickie, even if you can't rough it any more.'

'A tourist in a party? Doesn't appeal to me after the kind of treks I've done. After all, cities are much of a muchness, and I don't see myself as a sightseer complete with camera and guide-book. That's a very different proposition from exploring unknown country, and I'm finished for that. Couldn't last a week. Still, I'm not grumbling. I've had my turn, and this is a nice little billet here at the Cormorant. Lucky for me that the chief picked me up after the hospital had finished with me.'

'You two get on well, don't you?'

'He's the right sort. You get to know people when you go on expeditions like ours together. The conventional world fades right out, and you're down to fundamentals. Then you see people without any trappings, and Darrington survives that well. In fact,' added Rickie thoughtfully, 'I think he's at his best, then. In his true element, maybe. Here, he's sometimes a bit raspy. As though his collar's chafing him. I've noticed it particularly lately. This break will do him good.'

'Yes. It's good to get away from everything now and again, if only because it helps you to get things into perspective. But we shall miss him.'

For Stella, too, it was easier to get things into perspective in Darrington's absence. When he was there, she was conscious of tension and conflict lying beneath the surface like a dangerous current, ready to engulf her and sweep her away if her rigid control slackened for a moment. Now she was able to relax her nerves, and give her mind to helping Rickie keep the wheels of the hotel turning smoothly. They worked well together, and since Rickie had quite won over Mrs. Dacres, who could be difficult, all fronts were in harmony. Only Miss Bromley seemed to find the situation unsatisfactory, for Rickie took a keen delight in teasing her and she did not hide from him the fact that she considered he was taking liberties, and said many times during those weeks that she would be glad when Mr. Darrington returned.

'Some people are fit for authority, and some are not,' she declared one morning. 'I consider Mr. Rickall an ill-bred man. I'm surprised that Mr. Darrington should make him manager. He'll regret it, I'm sure.'

'I doubt it.'

'Oh, you like Mr. Rickall taking over, I know. You and Mr. Darrington don't get on very well, do you?'

'Don't we?'

'It sticks out a mile. I don't think you understand him. You know, there's a way of handling men. Some girls have it, others haven't. I think it's important for a secretary to have it.'

'And you have it,' said Stella gently.

'Well, I think so. We hit it off, Mr. Darrington and I. With you he's as stiff as a poker.'

'I shall have to get you to give me a few hints,' said Stella gravely, and Miss Bromley looked at her suspiciously.

Stella hid a smile as Mrs. Dacres came in for her weekly

189

accounting session. During these weeks, too, her sense of humour had come to her rescue in her dealings with Miss Bromley, and apart from odd moments of exasperation, she was no longer troubled by her.

It was the weekend of the Craynes' visit, and Stella found Felicity beside her when she started for her usual after-lunch walk along the cliffs.

'Do you mind? Hector and Peter have gone off to fish, and if there's one thing that I find dull, it's fishing.'

'Yes, I'm with you there.'

'We had a talk with Rickie this morning. Everything seems to be going smoothly.'

'Yes. No trouble at all. I guess your brother will be happy to leave his mantle on Rickie's shoulders since it's proving such a good fit.'

'Yes. I think Nick's quite enjoyed running this hotel, though. A new experience for him. And it does provide him with roots of a kind. A background. Although he likes exploring, he's not really a rootless type.'

'Will he ever marry, do you think?'

'I don't know,' said Felicity slowly. 'I don't think anybody would call him a home-and-hearth man, but he's got a strong sense of family and tradition and all that. I wish he would, if he could find the right person. I think loneliness lies in wait for single people when middle-age comes along.'

'He's more self-sufficient than most people, and I'm sure he thinks that there are many more important things in life than women.'

'He's no monk, for all his poker face. A bit too well-regulated, that's all.'

'And can't that be infuriating!' said Stella.

'To badly regulated people like myself, yes.'

'He'd be furious if he knew we were discussing him like this. Undermines discipline to introduce the human element into business,' said Stella solemnly.

'Do him good to be upset by a few disorderly human elements sometimes.'

Stella thought it wiser not to observe that since he had come to the Cormorant, he had been beset by disorderly human elements, and she turned the subject to Peter, who occupied them until they got back to the hotel.

The halcyon calm of those weeks drew to a close, and on the day before Darrington's return, Stella found herself wondering whether she would have to buckle on her armour again or whether the interval would have softened his attitude to her at all. She had finished her work and locked up. Miss Bromley had gone, and so had Tom, the office boy, who was seldom to be found in the office but was usually performing some job for Rickie, causing another black mark to go against Rickie in Miss Bromley's record.

Surely, thought Stella, anger couldn't survive all those thousands of miles and all the interest and stimulus of his life these past weeks. It must have dwindled. Surely now he would be ready to accept her with a show of pleasantness, would fall in with the easy kind of working association that had existed before their quarrel over Cathie and Roger. She asked no more than that, and expected no more. He had warned her off any warmer ground in no uncertain terms and she was not likely ever to forget his warning.

She was idly flicking over the pages of the top magazine of a pile she was going to leave in the hall, scarcely taking in what she saw until her attention was caught by John Marbury's face. It was a glossy photograph of Mr. and Mrs. John Marbury after their victory in a Continental motoring rally. He was standing by the car, cigarette in hand, looking at the camera, and Eileen was shown in profile, talking to him. How odd, thought Stella, that once her bones had turned to jelly at the sight of that handsome face. Now she found it hard to believe that it had ever mattered to her whether that face frowned or smiled for her. How could she have been so blinded by physical attraction? She was glad that there was none of that madness of being in love in her feeling for Nick, or she would have felt suspicious of it. She had never been particularly conscious of him in a physical sense. It was the companionship of his mind and the friendship of his heart that she longed for more than anything in the world. The other was unimportant, a madness which she would rather be without. John had done that for her. She would never trust or welcome the shifting sands of the senses again, but what she felt for Darrington was something as enduring and certain as rock, and if he would allow her to live in the shadow of that rock, she would be content. Loving and being in love were two very different things, she had learned. The one was finite but there was no term to the other, and she knew that she was only now beginning to learn what loving was.

She put on her hat and coat. On Monday she would see him. He was flying back tomorrow. What armour would she need, she wondered, as she picked up the magazines, looked round the office and switched off the light. As she turned at the head of the stairs, she nearly bumped into somebody. He steadied her as the magazines slipped, and with no time to put on any armour at all, her face expressed all the radiant welcome of her heart as she said:

'Nick! You're back! Oh, it's good to see you again.'

And she let the magazines fall as she held out her hand to him, bereft of all power to act against the joy that had leaped up like a fountain at the sight of him.

'Hullo. How are you?'

He had taken her hand and his eyes looked kind. That much she recognised with relief.

'I'm fine. We didn't expect you back until tomorrow.'

'I know. I was able to catch an earlier plane, after all. I've only just arrived. Rickie told me you were still here.'

He looked brown and fit, and as he collected the magazines together, Stella said:

'Did you have a good trip?'

'Splendid, thanks. Where do you want these?'

'In the hall.'

They walked down the stairs together, Stella suddenly tongue-tied. She could not descend to small talk with a fountain bubbling and leaping inside her.

'Rickie tells me that you've all got on a lot better without me, and that I'm really quite redundant,' he observed lightly.

'I couldn't say that. But things have gone very smoothly.'

'I shall give a sop to my pride by telling myself it's because I've trained my staff so well. And I'm very grateful to them for letting me have a holiday without qualms.'

He had walked to the door with her. The porter was reading the evening paper. Stella smiled and said:

'Good night, then, Mr. Darrington. Unless you wanted me to stay for anything?'

'No, thanks. Rickie can bring me up to date, and I'll see you on Monday. Good night.'

His hand rested on her shoulder for a moment, then he turned and went back into the hotel and Stella plunged out into the wild October night ...

Chapter Sixteen

THE next day was a stormy one, with a south-west gale blowing, but it had blown itself out by Sunday afternoon when Stella, Cathie and Midge went walking along the coast. Midge was anxious to find some undamaged whelk shells, and she left Cathie and Stella on top of the cliffs while she scrambled down to the cove below. The tide was fairly low, and she was going to walk round the next two coves and rejoin them at the bay where the cliffs ran down to a cluster of cottages and an inn which could provide tea.

The heavy rains of the previous day and night had left the world clean and shining in the thin wintry sunshine. The sea had moderated and looked friendly and harmless as it curled happily on to the sand below. Only the litter cast up during the night reminded them that the sea had taken its toll. The lifeboat had been out during the night and had gone out again that morning to stand by a vessel in trouble.

'Air's like champagne today,' said Stella. 'I feel as though I'm drunk with it. Nick arrived back on Friday night. Just before I left.'

'How is he?'

'On top of the world, from the look of him, but I only saw him for a few minutes. It's nice to have him back. By the way, is R.J. all right? He told Dad that he wasn't feeling up to golf this morning.'

'He's pulled a muscle in his leg. Climbed a tree to rescue a kitten yesterday morning. The kitten jumped down and Dad had to be rescued by our window cleaner, who was luckily nearby. I hope that child keeps her eye on the tide,' added Cathie, looking down at the solitary figure pottering below. 'It's coming in.'

They watched Midge round the rocks which divided that cove from the next, and then walked on, not talking much, at ease with each other and the world. When they reached the inn, they sat on the seat outside and watched the sun sinking across the sea. It went behind a cloud, outlining it with a golden rim, then slowly spread like a dull red stain among the thin clouds brooding on the horizon. It was growing chilly and they went down to the beach to look for Midge. But the beach was deserted except for a woman and a spaniel.

Cathie looked at Stella.

'Do you think she went back to one of the coves again?'

'I should have thought the tide was too high, but I don't see where else she can be. We'd better walk back along the bay. We'll probably meet her. She may be hanging about in the caves at the end there.'

They walked back along the firm sand of the bay, but Midge did not appear. At the end of the bay they were cut off from the cove beyond by the sea, which now rolled across the rocks that were negotiable at low tide. They took the rough track up the cliff at the end of the bay, neither of them saying much but looking worried. They crossed the grassy peninsula at the top and had a clear view of the second of the two coves, but it was deserted.

'Where can the child have got to?' asked Cathie. 'Surely she wouldn't go back on her tracks to the first cove?'

'We'd better see. I hope not, because you can't climb the cliff there once the sea has got half-way up the rocks at the far end. Remember how you and Jimmy and I nearly got cut off when we were kids?'

'Yes, I do.'

They quickened their steps towards the next cove.

'She may have found herself cut off at this end and gone back the other way,' said Stella.

They heard Midge's voice before they saw her hunched against the cliff face on a narrow piece of sand which was even then being washed by the surf of the larger waves.

'Oh, Midge!' exclaimed Stella, in mingled alarm and exasperation. 'Now we're in a fix.'

Cathie had gone white. The cliff reared up vertically from the beach at that point, the first few feet worn bare and smooth by the wash of the tide and offering no foothold. And Midge was a timid swimmer.

Stella thought quickly. She knew every inch of these cliffs and she saw the only solution in a matter of moments.

'There's no way down to that strip, but I can get down to the rocks at this end and swim from there.'

'But then neither of you will get back. You can dive in from those rocks, but if you swim back to them, you'll never be able to climb up them.'

Stella looked at the steep, seaweed-covered sides and agreed.

'Too true, but I know what we can do. Swim out to Gannet Rock. That's got some nice flat ledges and it's clear of the sea by several feet even at high tide. Let me think. The hotel's the nearest place now. You nip back and telephone the harbourmaster or whoever you can get to come and take us off,' said Stella, waving to Midge, whose attention they had now attracted.

'Is that the only solution?'

'Yes. Midge will never tackle that swim on her own. Don't look so worried, my dear. It's not dangerous. Just darned uncomfortable on a chilly evening.'

'Can't I . . . ?'

Their eyes met as Stella said:

'I'm a better swimmer and I know this path down the cliffs as well as the one down from the Cormorant.'

'All right. Take care.'

'I don't see the point of ruining my only good suit,' said Stella in a matter-of-fact voice. 'Take it back with you, Cathie, with my bag, and get that boat round as soon as you can. It's going to be chilly playing mermaids on that rock this evening.'

Stella slid out of her skirt and jacket, and began scrambling down the track in jumper and slip with the agility of a monkey. Cathie turned and ran. The hotel was not much more than a mile away.

The only thing that really worried Stella was whether Midge would panic. She herself was a strong swimmer and the sea was moderate. Even if Midge couldn't swim all the way, Stella could tow her as long as the girl remained calm. Stella waved to her again as she paused to take a breather. Midge waved back, then lifted up her skirt and jumped as a wave curled round her legs. You're going to get a good deal wetter than that, my child, thought Stella as she slithered down again. The track petered out on the peninsula of rocks, and Stella negotiated these carefully until she found one from which she could dive safely into the sea. Then she discarded her woollen jumper, wishing she could somehow waft it across to Gannet Rock, and plunged in.

Midge managed a smile as Stella waded through the waves to her.

'Gosh, I'm glad to see someone,' said Midge. 'I've been calling and calling. But what are we going to do?'

'Go for a swim to Gannet Rock, ducky. What on earth made you come back here with the tide running so high?'

'I couldn't find any whelk shells in the next cove, and I remembered I hadn't looked round the other end of this one, so I came back. I thought I'd have time to climb over the rocks, but I didn't notice how high it was until it was too late. Still, I found one shell. Not a hole or chip in it,' said Midge triumphantly, patting the pocket of her coat.

No, thought Stella. She needn't worry about Midge panicking. She had the true Elmore temperament: no sense of proportion where her enthusiasms were concerned, and a blithe carelessness in pursuing them.

'Well, you'd better take that coat off and we'll get started. You'll have to shed your skirt, too. It's a heavy one.'

'Mother will be annoyed. That's my new winter coat,' said Midge.

'Too bad. How far do you think you can swim?'

'I've never been out of my depth, but I think I could manage about half-way. What happens when we get there?'

'A boat comes and takes us off. Cathie is seeing to that end of the expedition.'

'Well, I'm not taking anything else off,' said Midge, whose sense of propriety was very strong. 'If I tie my shell in my handkerchief, I can tie the handkerchief through the buttonhole of my blouse.'

With this operation performed, Midge looked at Gannet Rock and the swell of the waves intervening. For the first time, she looked a little daunted.

'I suppose we couldn't wait here?'

'It'll take about an hour before a boat can reasonably get round. I don't fancy being a cork against these cliffs for that time, do you?' asked Stella, as a wave sent Midge staggering against the cliff.

'No. I thought perhaps someone could lower a rope.'

'The chance of anybody being handy with a rope that long, my poppet, is a bit too remote to consider. At least on Gannet Rock we'll be on dry land. There's nothing to worry about. I've done this dozens of times with Jimmy and Cathie. Take it easily and sing out when you're tired.'

And Midge did as she was told and swam like an anxious dog for about ten minutes, when her breast stroke became rather wild and she made little progress.

'I'll tow you now, Midge. Over on your back and I'll take your head. O.K.?'

'M'm,' gasped Midge.

She kept still and Stella had no difficulty in getting her to the rock. They both hung on to the ledge for a breather, then Stella hauled herself out and dragged Midge up beside her. The flat top of the rock was white with bird droppings, and looked singularly inhospitable.

'I hope that boat won't be long,' said Stella, as she began rubbing Midge's legs. The girl looked blue with cold and was shivering like a jelly.

'Will the lifeboat come?' asked Midge.

'No. It's out already. There are plenty of boats in the harbour, though.'

'I should think that we m-m-might be in the local paper,' chattered Midge.

'Very possibly,' said Stella, smiling. 'You'll be able to give the reporter an interview.'

'Would you l-l-like me to rub your legs now?' asked Midge politely.

'No, poppet, it's all right. This keeps me warm.'

'I think the sea looks horrible when it's nearly dark,' observed Midge, rubbing her hands together.

They had been on the rock for about twenty minutes when Ben Watson's boat came up, with Cathie, Nick and Ben's son, Joe, in it. The rock rose sheer and they were able to get along-side and take them off without much trouble. Huddled in blankets drinking hot sweet tea from a thermos flask, Midge sat by Cathie and said little, the presence of the men acting as a restraint.

'All right?' asked Nick, as he filled Stella's cup again.

'Yes, thanks. Quite an afternoon. You must have run like a hare, Cathie. I expected to be on that rock for quite a time.'

'It was some moments before she had breath enough to say a word,' said Nick. 'Fortunately I had the car out and we were able to nip down and catch Ben before they got away.'

'We're prepared for this sort of job in the summer,' said Ben, 'but not in the winter. That must have been a tidy pull for you, Miss Verney.'

'Not too bad. Midge helped by keeping her head. Have you still got your whelk shell, Midge?'

'Yes.'

'You'd better put it in a glass case. Did you telephone your mother, Cathie?'

'Mrs. Dacres was going to. And we asked her to telephone your father, too.'

'There won't be anybody at home. Dad's gone to see an old pupil. He won't be back until late. And it's Nan's day out. Just as well. No need to put them in a flap for nothing.'

'My new winter coat and my best skirt have gone, Cathie,' said Midge tragically. 'I bet Mother will be cross.'

'She'll be too glad to see you safe and sound to be cross, pet.'

'Oh, there was never any danger, but perhaps I'd better not tell her that,' said Midge thoughtfully, and they all laughed.

Mr. and Mrs. Elmore were at the harbour and bundled Midge into the car. Mrs. Elmore took Stella in her arms.

'My dear, are you all right? We were so anxious.'

'Quite. It was nothing more than a chilly dip. Midge played her part very well.'

'Bless you! What a family I have for getting into scrapes. Come along, dear. Hot baths straight away.'

'I'll look after Stella, Mrs. Elmore,' broke in Nick. 'We've got her clothes at the hotel and Mrs. Dacres has a hot bath laid on.'

The Elmores shot off and Stella, feeling like a squaw in her blanket, climbed into Nick's car. They were back at the hotel in a minute or two and Mrs. Dacres was waiting for them at the hotel entrance.

Soaking in a hot bath, Stella felt none the worse for her exploits. Mrs. Dacres had produced some underclothes and a shrimp-pink jumper, all of which were far too voluminous for Stella. However, dressed in these and her suit, she slipped her feet into a pair of shoes which she kept in her office for use on wet days, and rubbed her hair as dry as she could, regretting the fact that she had no make-up in her bag. A few minutes later, she descended to the hall feeling extraordinarily hungry. Nick was standing by the door glancing at the *Sunday Times*. He smiled as she came down the stairs.

'Feel like tea at the lodge, or would you prefer bed at home?'

'Tea at the lodge every time,' said Stella firmly. 'I'm starving, and never felt less like bed.'

'Tough,' observed Nick solemnly, adding, as they walked down to the lodge together, 'Any damage?'

'Grazed my leg getting down the cliff. That's all.'

She was installed in an armchair in front of a blazing fire while Nick supervised the boiling of eggs. Tea was already laid on a low table in front of the fire.

'Rickie informs me that his new duties now preclude him from looking after me, and he suggests that I get a house-keeper,' said Nick, as he brought in the eggs.

'You're very snug here. I expect you'd sooner keep it an all-male establishment.'

'It depends. Done all right?'

'Perfectly. I've got a very unladylike appetite. Don't expect me to refuse anything.'

'I'm quite peckish myself. I'm not used to all this excitement. I get home from a nice peaceful expedition and find trouble as soon as I'm back. A good thing for young Midge Elmore that you're a good swimmer, otherwise the situation wouldn't have been at all funny.'

'No. But I don't think it occurred to her for one moment that she might have been drowned. She's like her father. They're both convinced that they have charmed lives and are not liable to the risks other people run. She didn't turn a hair. Her chief concern was to keep possession of her whelk shell.'

Nick laughed.

'She'll be a handful for some man one day.'

'Tell me about your trip. I'm longing to hear about it.'

They cleared everything eatable from the table except one forlorn slice of fruit cake, and talked on happily. Stella, listening to Nick's description of the Rocky Mountain country, was conscious of a sublime state of ease. How completely at home they were together, she thought. They might have been married for years. Their quarrels seemed unreal and as distant as childhood. It was hard to believe that there had ever been a time when they didn't belong as easily as this: two pairs of feet on the same hearthrug, a feeling of perfect relaxation, both as unselfconscious as any cat blinking by its own fireside. She started as the telephone rang out. The outside world had seemed so far away. She wanted no contact with it just then. It was Cathie asking after Stella. Stella took the receiver from Nick.

'Hullo, Cathie.'

'How are you feeling, dear?'

'Never better. How's Midge?'

'Sitting up in bed dramatising everything for R.J.'s benefit.'

Stella laughed.

'They're as bad as each other . . . No, dear, nothing but a graze or two. I've just eaten an enormous tea and I'm hoping

Nick doesn't turn me out just yet because I feel I can't move...'

When she returned to the fire, she was conscious of a more purposeful look on Nick's face, which was a pity. She sank into her armchair again and said:

'I feel as contented and comfortable as a cat full of cream, Nick. Can I stay a little longer?'

'What do you expect me to say to that?' he asked, smiling.

'Blackmail, isn't it?'

'That jumper's not your colour.'

'I know. Shocking.'

Her damp hair had curled chaotically round her face, and without lipstick she knew that she looked anaemic, but she didn't care. She only knew that friendliness and affection looked out of Nick's eyes, and that during the last hour something as irrevocable as time itself had been stated without any words.

'You're very fond of Cathie, aren't you?'

'Yes. We've grown up together. Even after all these years, I still think she's a rare person.'

'I agree. Is she happy, do you think?'

Her eyes met his. He was not going to let that issue drop without words.

'Yes, I think she is. You still blame me for what I did?'

'For the way you did it, yes. For the result . . . well, I'll tell you in ten years' time.'

'I didn't interfere, Nick. I only gave Cathie the chance to make her own decision in the light of the facts.'

'And you think her decision will turn out to be happier for her than Roger's?'

'Who can judge what is best for a person? Only the person herself. I have sufficient confidence in Cathie's wisdom to believe that she is capable of making the right decision for herself.'

'I wonder.'

'The mere act of loving, Nick, divorced from everything else, can be its own source of joy. Even if you loved a man who hadn't love to offer you, I still think no woman would want to be without that love for him. And Cathie has Roger's love. Whatever happens, she hasn't had to dam up what she aches to give. It's the damming up that can be dangerous. If you can

201

express it only in letters, or in friendship or service of any kind, I think it's better than not being able to give expression to it at all. I wish it could have been somebody else for Cathie. But hearts can't be directed to suitable berths like ships. For better or worse, they insist on taking their own course.'

'You may be right. We'll see, in ten years' time. But the way you treated me over that affair, Stella, was disgraceful,' said Nick firmly.

'Yes, it was.'

'Disgraceful on two counts. I gave my word to Roger that he wouldn't run up against Cathie while he was staying with me. You made that promise worth precisely nothing.'

'I did make it clear to Roger that it was my fault.'

'I know, but my promise was broken. I didn't like that, Stella. For all you knew, Roger may have been trying to free himself from a girl whose attentions were embarrassing him.'

'Then I can only say that if a man hasn't enough spunk to tell a girl outright when he's through, he deserves to be made to. It's cruel to leave people dangling in doubt.'

'It was a rotten thing to do on a second count. You made a fool of me, but that wasn't important. I was furious, of course, but I could have recovered from that. But you put me in an absolutely impossible position with regard to you. How on earth could I, your employer, allow you to bundle me out of the way when it pleased you, in defiance of my explicit order that you were not to interfere, and still allow you to stay on in my employment? Imagine if you were employed in any business concern and did that to your chief. How could you expect not to be sacked?'

'I'm afraid I've never been able to think of our relationship as a strictly business one, in spite of your drilling, Nick.'

'Well, in that respect,' he said dryly, 'you showed yourself more of a realist, perhaps, than I. But couldn't you see what an impossible position your hare-brained scheme put me in?'

'It was foolish of me, Nick. I realised it afterwards. And I was truly sorry to have to do it.'

He threw up his hands in despair.

'There you are. You were sorry to have to do it. Have to do it. So you'd do it again if the circumstances arose?'

'But what else could I do? It was the last chance, and Cathie was so terribly unhappy. Her mother and I were desperately worried about her. I honestly couldn't think of a single alternative.'

'Of course there were alternatives. You could have written to Roger yourself, or dragged Cathie by the hair of her head up to North Wales, which I'm sure you were quite capable of doing if you'd made up your mind to get them together. Why did it have to be over my body?'

'Dear Nick, because it was the handiest and most obvious one. But I've done penance for an awfully long time, and I know you've forgiven me now.'

He shook his head at her.

'You could melt a High Court Judge, my dear, let alone a poor defenceless man like me. I can't imagine not being able to forgive you anything, which is only another way of saying that I love you. And I know your heart is so big that my own imperfections will be dealt with far more gently than I deserve. I'm not good at speeches,' he added, and stopped.

'Except when you're angry. Then you make marvellous ones,' said Stella, smiling at him with fond eyes.

'Well, I'm short of rehearsal time for this. I wasn't expecting the sea to wash you up in my arms today. What I'm trying to say is that I think we'd make a good team. Will you marry me, Stella?'

'Yes, dear. You'll be a grand husband.'

'I'll do my best, but I can't guarantee not to beat you if you ever treat me like a bundle of washing again. If I couldn't gain any respect as your employer, I'll jolly well exact respect as your husband. I only wished I'd been in a position to take a stick to you when I came out half-roasted from that loft. If you commit your person to my care for the rest of your life, you take the consequences. You are warned, so you can back out if you wish.'

'I have no wish to back out. And Nick . . .'

Her face was serious, for behind his half-joking words she had sensed a real hurt.

'Yes, my dear?'

'I have always, ever since I first met you, respected you, no matter what our relations were. Always, I think above all people. What I did may have made it seem as though I had no respect for you, but it would be as far from the truth as we are from the stars. Please believe that.'

He smiled.

'All right. Maybe my sense of humour was a bit lacking. I'll assume that to be treated like a bundle of washing was your way of reminding me of my own advice that egos have to learn to accommodate themselves.'

'Well, mine has done quite a bit of accommodating during the past year.'

'It has. And done it with a remarkably good grace, I might say. You know, I didn't think you'd stay on after I'd had my say that morning.'

'You must have rehearsed it. Hardly a word less than three syllables, and all dipped in acid.'

'I was not feeling exactly like sugar. I'd been congratulating myself on building up a warm friendship between us, wondering a bit where we were going but enjoying the journey very much, and not disposed to force anything, when you blew it all sky high by showing every sign of not giving a fig for my opinion, or my position here, by treating me neither as friend nor employer but as a confounded nuisance to be tricked and pushed out of your way.'

'But, Nick darling, you were so unaccommodating about Cathie. And I did leave you a chair and *The Times*,' she added wickedly.

'That was a delicate touch, I admit. Unfortunately I was not in the right frame of mind to appreciate the fourth leader just then. However, we won't go into all that again. But it had dawned on me by the time I went away that you would never have stuck it out after what I said to you if you hadn't been in some way rather attached to me.'

'I couldn't leave. If I'd had any pride, I would have resigned. But I couldn't bear to cut myself off from you.'

'Well, that's nice to hear, anyhow. By the time I went away, I knew, too, that we couldn't go on as we were. At least, I couldn't. Your endurance is superb.'

'I didn't believe you could hold on to your anger indefinitely.'

'Ye-es. Yes. I think I am,' said Stella slowly. The quizzical expression on his face prompted her to add:

'Nick. Did you purposely keep that other version in the background?'

'I thought he should be produced later rather than sooner. Somehow, I gathered you'd had enough of that sort of man for a time and that he might scare you off if he came on the scene too soon. I hope I've been right and haven't worn a hair shirt for nothing.'

'You were right. Dead right.' She smiled suddenly and held him by the ears. 'Clever, aren't you?'

His eyes teased her.

'Not particularly. Only, just occasionally, I do manage to be half a jump in front of you.'

'Too well-regulated by half. I don't feel a bit tired now.'

'Well, I'm going to take you home all the same. It's getting late and your father and Nan will be wondering what's happened to you. Shall we tell them tonight?'

'I certainly can't hide it. I feel as though I'm carrying a searchlight round with me. How relieved Nan will be to learn that I'm marrying a sober, respectable man!'

'I'm not feeling specially sober or respectable just now. However, we will try to present a reassuring front. Your face has a beautiful transparency about it without any make-up.'

He kissed her again, taking a long time over it. Then, arm-in-arm, they went out into a calm, dark night. The sky was black velvet pricked with stars, and the sound of the sea which reached them as they walked to the car was as soft as a woman sighing.